The King of Evil

The King of Evil

By

Josh Stricklin

HOLLISTON, MASSACHUSETTS

THE KING OF EVIL
Copyright © 2016 by Josh Stricklin

This book is a work of fiction. Names, characters, places and incidents are products of the author's imagination or are used fictitiously. Any resemblance to actual events, locations or persons, living or deceased, is entirely coincidental.

Printed and bound in the United States. All rights reserved. No part of this book may be reproduced or transmitted in any form or by any means, electronic or mechanical, including photocopying, recording, or by an information storage and retrieval system—except by a reviewer who may quote brief passages in a review to be printed in a magazine, newspaper, or on the Web—without the express written consent of Silver Leaf Books, LLC.

The Silver Leaf Books logo is a registered trademarks of Silver Leaf Books, LLC.

All Silver Leaf Books characters, character names, and the distinctive likeness thereof are trademarks of Silver Leaf Books, LLC.

Cover Art by Paul Tynes.

First printing September 2016
10 9 8 7 6 5 4 3 2 1

ISBN # 1-60975-175-2
ISBN-13 # 978-1-60975-175-3
LCCN # 2016946755

Silver Leaf Books, LLC
P.O. Box 6460
Holliston, MA 01746
+1-888-823-6450

Visit our web site at www.SilverLeafBooks.com

The King of Evil

Fatigue makes cowards of us all.
                        - Vince Lombardi

Prologue

In the 1940s there was a hospital on the back way out of town where the poor people had their children. It was far enough out of the way that the city was only a murmur, and the trees surrounding the building threatened to break in through the windows. The red brick building was small, and there were only a few rooms. At the edge of the tall grass where the trees stopped, a chipmunk stared in wonder at the marvelous brick structure built by man. She had spent a long day trudging through the swampy Louisiana woods, which was much harder now that she was carrying a litter. The far away sky bruised with the arrival of an oncoming storm.

Bars guarded the glass, but the chipmunk had no problem watching the commotion inside. She didn't see the brownish-orange, diamond-shaped head easing through the tall grass. She watched as the big people picked up the small people from tiny beds and walked out of view. Then a big person would return and lay the small one back in the bed. No one but the chipmunk seemed to notice when the black smoke rose from the center of the room. None of the people reacted whatsoever, because only the chipmunk saw the ashy gray person materialize in the center of the nursery. The head crept closer. The life inside the chipmunk's belly stirred. They were hungry, too.

The gray person stood above the tiny bed with wide eyes fixed on the small person. He looked back and forth between the one in front of him and the one just to his right. Then he turned to the one on his right as if suddenly more intrigued with that one. The chipmunk had no idea what to make of this. She just wanted food, and there was the feint smell of something sweet coming from that building. The chipmunk stood on her hind legs. She stopped, tilting her head. The new person, the one no one else seemed to notice, lifted an arm above his head. The copperhead sprung forward, sinking its teeth and venom into her back. The arm descended. As life drained from the chipmunk, the ashy gray person vanished, and the other people in the building seemed to panic.

1

The First Night

"Shh," Jack said, glaring through the space between the drapes and window next to the back door. "There's someone in the yard. Get your phone."

"Cut it out," Cindy said, playfully. "Come back to bed."

The room was pitch black, but she knew he stared out one of the tall narrow windows flanking the back door. His moonlit face shined from beside the drapes. The cold night invaded the house, and Cindy shivered. She could almost see his breath in the glow reaching through the glass like a phantom. Not sure what to believe—Jack wasn't one to make jokes like this—she reached for the light switch. Her finger came upon the cold metal barrel of Jack's shotgun. There was no time to consider what she felt before her foot grazed a moving box at the bottom of the stairs between the kitchen and the family room. She thought certainly there would be a full-fledged family to fill that room by now. She caught the teetering stack and stabled the tower of boxes before a loud crash sounded through the open ground floor. She turned back to Jack. She could see the look of anger and concern twisting his face.

"Shh," he whispered again. He didn't want to alarm her. "Don't move."

The initial thought that Jack was kidding her morphed into something just outside of sheer panic. The change was instantaneous. She went as cold as the barrel of the gun. "Jack," her voice trembled. "Jack, what do we do?"

"Where's your phone?" he whispered.

"By the bed."

"Go upstairs and call the police. Don't make a lot of noise. Everything is going to be fine. Nothing is going to happen. Let's just be quiet. We don't want anything to happen, and if we stay quiet nothing will." His voice was soft and confident. He did his best not to send her into a panic. That wasn't something she usually did, but they had never gone through this sort of thing before. Jack kept his attention on the back yard.

In the far corner of the privacy fence stood a dilapidated shack that housed old paint cans, the lawnmower, and little else. Jack had mounted a floodlight above the door that illuminated the yard every night at eight until six the next morning. Between the house and the shack there was a small garden where they grew tomatoes together, but since the move began they hadn't done more than water the dying leaves.

Jack watched the figure standing next to the shed. Not

quite in the light, but Jack could see the silhouette of a person standing, waiting. Whoever it was stood tall enough to bump his head on the roof of the shed. His build was lanky, reminding Jack of the slender man videos he had seen in college. He had to shove that thought away before he really started to fall apart. Jack kept his eyes fixed on the black outline encroaching on their property and interrupting their feeling of safety.

Cindy's voice came from the bedroom upstairs. Jack nearly called back to her when he realized that she was on the phone. She was using her headphones because he could see a feint glow from the cellphone's screen lighting up the stairway. Jack listened to Cindy give the police their address and ask them to please hurry. There was enough fear in her voice to warrant an emergency, but she managed to keep composed.

"What are you doing out there?" Jack whispered to himself. He glared at the black shape through the windows. It didn't move. It seemed to be staring right back at him. "Nobody's bothering you."

"They're on their way," Cindy called down the stairs, making an effort not to be too loud. "They said someone is already in the area."

"Okay, honey," Jack said, feeling awkward after calling his wife of nearly five years "honey" for the first time in their lives. The words tasted like medicine he didn't need. He grimaced. "Just stay up there, alright? Do you remember where we put the other gun?"

"Behind the suitcases?"

Jack had actually forgotten. The tedious work of packing up the house caused the location of many things to lose their place in his mind. "Grab it and don't put it down until the police come, okay?"

"Okay," Cindy was crying. "I love you, Jack."

He knew what she was doing. After this long he could probably spell out with the exact words what she was thinking. "Don't go thinking anything is going to happen, Cin. It's just a guy in the yard. Probably just a wonderer. Just wait for me in bed." He felt a little guilty and told her he loved her, too. "I'm serious. Nothing's going to happen."

"Can he hear us?" She asked.

"He isn't moving. If I had to guess I'd say he doesn't."

"What does he look like?"

"I can't tell. He's standing in the shadows by the shed."

"I knew we should've gotten rid of that thing." Cindy said, more to herself than Jack. "I can't believe this is happening. Thank God we're getting the hell out of this shitty city."

"It's okay, Cin," Jack said, going over a mental list of reasons the city had been shitty for them. There was one big reason, and a ton of little ones that made it seem so much bigger. He had to make a conscious effort to slow down before his thoughts spiraled out of control. He focused on the person outside until the feeling was out of his system. He could only think of one thing to say that might keep Cindy calm. He said it without knowing anything of its validity. "The police will be here in no time. They'll be here before this guy has time to do anything crazy in the first place."

The shadow moved. It remained in the same spot but it's arms flailed eccentrically. There was a little hint of red where the person's head was. Too bright to be hair. The movement was familiar to Jack. *Almost like a pitcher's wind up,* Jack had enough time to think. In front of his eyes, the window cracked, dead center in the pane. The break speared out in all directions like ice. Cindy screamed. Her voice rang in his ears.

"What's happening, Jack?"

"The son of a bitch threw something." Jack was taken aback, offended. Not only did this asshole have the nerve to step onto his property, but he was also destroying it, literally right in front of Jack's eyes. Jack had to focus on keeping his voice calm. He didn't want to stir her into a frenzy, because when Cindy felt something, it spilled over to the people around her. That's the kind of person she was. What she felt, everyone felt.

Jack pulled the handle on the door, tightening the grip on the shotgun. The knob was locked, and the door didn't budge. He supposed that wasn't a bad thing. His heart pounded as Jack realized he had never even shot the gun in his hand. His mouth quivered. His eyes watered.

From across the house, he heard knocking on the door, shaking Jack back to reality.

"Don't let him come in!" Cindy shouted, hearing someone outside fumble with a knob.

"It's the cops, Cin," Jack walked through the house. He heard thumping overhead, and Cindy raced behind him to the front door. Jack confirmed the policemen on the front porch through the peephole and ushered them inside.

"Is everyone alright, sir?" The officer in charge asked.

"Come on," Jack rushed back through the house. "He's out by the shed. He threw something at the house."

A second police officer stayed behind, talking to Cindy.

Jack unlocked the handle and threw open the door.

The policeman behind him charged forward with a handgun loaded behind the beam of a Maglite. "Nobody move," he shouted in the direction of the shed. "Come out here, right now. You're under arrest."

Jack followed for a few steps, but he knew the shadows would be empty. That's how these things worked after all. They could scan every inch of the back yard, but it would be a waste of time. The intruder was gone. Just like that. Fast as the pitch that destroyed the kitchen window.

"Shit," Jack said under his breath.

He's gone, he thought. *Thank God we're leaving this shithole town.*

"Mr. Simmons, did you get a good look at him?"

The blue and red lights from the police car chased each other across the walls of Jack and Cindy's living room in the dull shine of the end table lamp. Jack and Cindy both wanted the lights to be turned off. In a small neighborhood like this, all it took to become a spectacle was the dancing red and blues of a police car.

"I don't really know," Jack explained. "He was tall. His

head nearly touched the roof of the shed. But that's really all I could tell you. I'm not even one hundred percent sure it was a man if I'm being totally honest. I didn't go outside, but he looked pretty scrawny from here. I just watched him from the window and made sure he didn't try to come inside. I probably wouldn't even be able to pick him out of a line up."

"What'd you see?" The officer asked. Jack felt a tinge of impatience in his voice. "What was he doing, I mean?"

"He was just standing there."

"Okay," the policeman said. "How did you discover him?"

"I woke up about an hour ago, and I couldn't go back to sleep. I had a weird dream so I was already on edge. Maybe I was looking for something to jump at. Eventually I came down for some water, and I noticed something moving in the flood light on the shed. The shadow passed over the window. I peeked through the glass on the side of the door and saw someone, so I ran and got the gun. I was about to go outside and see what was happening when Cindy came down. I didn't want anything happening to her, so I stayed where I was. That's when she called you guys, and I guess in the time it took to answer the door he jumped the fence."

"Notice any damage to the property?"

"He threw something at the window. It's busted." Jack pulled the curtain to the side, revealing a shattered panel of glass. Part of him was beginning to worry that the man was never there at all. But seeing the fractured glass put that thought out of his mind.

"You see what he threw?"

"No idea. I was keeping an eye on him. I didn't even see anything move. He didn't pick anything up. He must have already had it on him."

"Anything else you can tell us? What he was wearing, which way he went, did he say anything? Anything like that that could help?"

"No." Then something came to him. Wasn't he wearing something on his head? Wasn't something red up there? He didn't know for sure, but it wouldn't hurt to tell the police what he saw. "He might have been wearing a hat I think."

"What kind of hat?"

"Like a baseball cap. Maybe a bandana, or something. I just know it was red. Again I couldn't really see much."

The other officer returned from a perimeter check. He noticed the boxes throughout the house. It was difficult not to see them. "Y'all moving?"

"Yeah," Cindy said. She pushed the hair out of her eyes and locked her arms together at the front of her robe. "Within the week."

"I hope this isn't why," the officer chuckled.

"No, it's more than just this," Cindy interrupted. Her tone froze the room and everything in it. She told herself to calm down. *Nothing good will come from you snapping at someone. It's not his fault. Whoever or whatever it was is gone now.* She took a breath and said, "We're moving to Metairie."

"Louisiana?"

"You've heard of it then?" Cindy said. She was being sarcastic, but that went right over the policeman's head.

"Oh, yeah," the cop said. "Why so far away?"

"It's only a couple hours," Cindy said. "We'll come visit if you start to miss us."

"She got a better job in New Orleans," Jack told the officer, glad to see Cindy was melting back to normal.

"What do you do?"

"I'm a physical therapist," she answered

"So I shouldn't assume anyone would want to…you know…exact their revenge on you?"

That's not an appropriate way to say that, Jack thought but didn't say.

"No," Cindy answered. "I can't imagine anyone would. I only help people get better. No one ever gets mad at someone for that, right? Besides, ninety percent of the people I work with are retirees."

"Never know. We'll go ahead and assume not. If you think of someone, let us know." The officer pointed the end of his pen at Jack. "What about you? Anyone wanting to get back at you for anything?"

"I'm an artist," Jack said.

"So were John Lennon, Phil Hartman, and Tupac Shakur."

"I'm more or a graphic designer."

"And he's better than he acts," Cindy said.

"I'm not 'Phil Hartman' good."

"Hmm…" the officer said. "And do you have any reason to believe someone was breaking in to harm either of you?"

"No," Jack said. "We always keep our appointments. Keep our yard clean. Recycle."

"We used to recycle," Cindy added.

"Anything like this happen before on the property?"

"No," Cindy said. "I think this is a first for both of us."

"Okay," the officer closed his notepad and put the pen in his uniform pocket. "We'll keep a car around the neighborhood just in case. A neighborhood like this, if you jump out of one yard, you jump into someone else's. We'll come by in the morning and see if anyone else saw anything. Lock the doors. Close the windows. If anything happens again, just give us a call." The officer handed Jack a card with no more information than he could get by dialing 911. The officer's signature was scribbled on a line in the middle, but Jack couldn't read it.

"Sure thing," Jack said, leading the policemen out of the house. He closed the door behind them and locked both the knob and the deadbolt. He turned to Cindy who stood in the hall between the living room and kitchen. He felt the air change. Now it was just the two of them again. She could be honest.

"I'm so ready to get out of this place, Jack." Cindy said. She leaned back against the wall and slowly slid down to the floor. He joined her.

"I am, too," Jack pulled Cindy to him. He kissed her forehead.

"Every shitty thing that ever happened to us happened here."

"It's almost over. We start the move tomorrow. Louisiana is just around the corner. Look on the bright side. At least it didn't happen when we first got here. We'd be a nervous wreck from day one. Now we can know we made the right decision to move."

"I already knew that, Mr. Simmons." Cindy said, talking like the police officers.

"Let's go back to bed," Jack said. He pretended to put her in a headlock. "You have to be up in two hours."

They walked up the stairs together, in one another's arms.

The next morning Jack rose as Cindy showered in the adjacent bathroom. He heard the water slap onto the floor of the tub as she wrung out her hair. He rarely woke early enough to catch her before she was ready for work, but today was a big day for him. Not only was it the first official moving day, but he was also turning in the final draft of the cover for *The Homerun Killer*, a thriller by Steven Bell.

Jack spent weeks bringing the little dickhead's concept to life, and a week editing it, and a second week re-editing it. He almost didn't give Bell the painted version of his cover, but he did it for every client. No matter how difficult a client was to work with, he always did it. Bell was by far the worst, but Jack didn't think being petty would help move his career forward. He had to keep every client regardless of their never-ending inflexibility. Plus the money he made from *The Homerun Killer* paid for the move and the first month on the house note. *Might as well chew the bullshit and smile,* he told himself when he applied the first coat of varnish. He didn't even bother painting the edges or using black duct tape to cover the sides like he usually did. This was just a small gift for a client. Strictly for fun. Unless Bell decided to show some form of last minute appreciation for putting up with the pompous attitude and condescension toward Jack's work, then Jack didn't take anything away from this endeavor aside from the debt free move across state lines. If Bell had anything to say other than "Thank you, Mr. Simmons," Jack would break the canvas over his tiny head. Tom, Jack's agent, could pitch a fit if he wanted. To be honest the little dickhead was getting on Tom's bad side as well.

Jack poured himself a mug of coffee and walked into the garage. He looked at the painting lying across the smallest of his four easels. He didn't love this cover and deliberately left his name off the list of credits on the book jacket so no one would see it. Although he would never say it out right, Jack had much better ideas than the writer, every time. After all he went to college to know more about the visual aspects of a book than a writer would. Steven Bell was no exception to that rule. That's why he insisted on the consultation before he even put the pen to paper. He understood an author's intent on being more involved in his process, after all it was their show, their livelihood, their art, but they hired him to do a job. He just wanted them to step aside and let him do it. Most authors were more than happy to honor the tacit agreement to let Jack work his magic. Steven Bell was not one of them. It wasn't that Jack didn't get to use his ideas, but that his ideas weren't even listened to. That's what dug at him. If Bell knew exactly what he wanted, he could've gone to anyone. That didn't stop Jack from cashing the checks though.

Jack sipped his coffee, inwardly swearing at the painting. Staring at it like this, he thought of the way the shadow moved last night. *It winded up and threw that rock.* He felt the corner of the canvas for wetness as he walked it into the kitchen. *It's actually not that bad.*

"Great job, baby," Cindy said, pulling her almost-black hair back in a ponytail. She never asked to see his work while it was still in progress. She was only there to hear his euphoric rants—and in the case of Steve Bell, talk him off the ledge—as he worked his magic on the computer. She preferred to look at the final painting so the magic wouldn't be ruined. To have it come to her all at once, the way it came to the customers in the bookstores, made it more special. Something about the texture and the weight of the canvas felt more real to her than a print out. More complete. And when she held the canvas, she could feel her husband's passion in what he had done. "The brooding guy in the corner's pretty creepy." She sipped her chocolate milk, grinning behind her freckles at Jack over the glass.

The painting displayed a vivacious crowd of baseball fans, some of their faces red from screaming, others painted maroon and yellow in support of the fictional team, many of the fans were dressed in Vikings shirts. One burly, hairy man dressed in a dark red Viking costume pumped his fists and stoked the flames of their enthusiasm. At the top of the frame, the title of the book shown brightly on the scoreboard under the line *next at bat*—something Jack passively fought until finally giving up after soothing a minor tantrum from his employer—and the bottom of the page was an advertising-style board leaning against the fence, which read *a thriller by Steven Bell*, which was also not among Jack's favorite ideas. The arms of the fans were raised in a cheer that pointed up and to the right of the frame. Even the hairy Viking pointed to the corner of the frame. The simultaneous raised arms subtly directed the viewer's eye to the top right side of the cover where a shadowy man stood, leering down onto the field. He wore a maroon baseball cap with a yellow "V" sewn onto the front. Everything else about the Homerun Killer was hidden in shadows. The bottom corner of his face was all that could be seen. Just a small triangle of a stubbled jawline.

"What's his story?" Cindy asked. Another thing she waited to hear about until the end was the story behind the artwork. She wanted to be like everyone who stumbled across Jack's covers in the bookstores, totally clueless. And that's how she thought of them. Not as the author's books, but as Jack's covers.

"Well, that's the Homerun Killer," Jack told her. "Don't get too close. He's a *maniac*."

"Oh, save me," Cindy feigned terror. "Why do they call him the Homerun Killer?"

"Because every time someone comes close to breaking his homerun record, boom." Jack ran a finger across his throat. "He 'homerun kills' them."

"Ew, gross," Cindy laughed.

"It's pretty corny." Jack examined his work. "But it's

published, so it must offer something."

Cindy walked across the kitchen to Jack and put her arms around his neck. She ran her fingers over the back of his head and brushed the dark hair out of his eyes. *I'll have to cut that for him before we leave,* she thought. Her scrubs were the same color as her big blue eyes. Her bangs twitched when her eyelashes rebounded from a blink. Her cheekbones were showing a little more than they used to lately. They had both lost a little weight. It wasn't from a total lack of money, but partly from not knowing where Jack's next check would come from, and they both cut back without thinking about it. Little things here and there. Less eating out, only one popcorn at the movies on the sporadic nights they went, Cindy finally quit the gym she was too busy to go to anymore. The other part of their weight loss, the more obvious part, came from a simple lack of time. Between her dozens of clients a week keeping her after hours, and his constant travel and self-promotion, searching for the next project, they rarely had a night to eat together. That typically made for multiple meals a week consisting of a TV dinner tray or a can of ravioli, followed by a book for an hour before bed for both of them. That was another reason Cindy was thankful for her new job. The money and the hours would be much better, and moving closer to a bigger city would give Jack higher potential for more local clientele. Cindy couldn't wait to get out of this nowheresville town. The last few years had taken a considerable toll on her, but now she and Jack were finally in a place where they were both happy again, together. That was something Cindy had truly missed. She rubbed Jack's back, helping him examine the painting. "Well at least you don't have to worry with the little dickhead anymore."

"That's very true," Jack said. "Some people never learn how to murder their darlings."

Cindy looked at him with an expression somewhere between confused and genuinely frightened.

"It's just an expression." Jack sipped his coffee. His face sagged a little.

"What's wrong?" She asked. She saw something sad in his eyes. Just a flicker. His face was red from mowing the lawn the day before and would be tan by the end of the day. She was secretly jealous of how dark he could get without even trying. "You usually have a lot more pep when you finish a cover. Did he really torment you that badly?"

"Nah, I just slept weird last night."

"Because of what happened?"

"I didn't sleep at all after the police left. My cage was rattled. The reason I woke up in the first place is what got me. I had this weird dream that the Homerun Killer was real, and he homerun killed me."

"That's silly," Cindy chuckled. "You don't even like baseball."

"I hate baseball. Still, it woke me up." Jack squeezed his arms around her waist so that she wouldn't be able to get free. "He just came at me with his bat and..." he pretended to bite her neck, snarling and growling like a monster. Chills rose all over her skin, and she giggled the way she had when they started dating.

"Walk me through your day." Cindy kissed him on the neck and laid her head on his shoulder. She swayed with him in her arms. They danced without music.

"Well, I'm going to take this piece of shit in to my agent."

"Wonderful." Cindy's voice was muffled against him.

"Then I'm going to call ahead to confirm the appointment for the cable guy in Metairie."

"Very important."

"Make sure he knows to bring the Internet too, so I can go back to emailing people instead of making them CDs like a caveman."

"Of course."

"And then come back here to let the movers in."

"Yay!" She quietly cheered.

"Then finally, I will wait tirelessly for my loving wife to come home from her last day of work before we blow this pop stand."

Cindy backed away from him, smiling ear to ear. She wasn't crying but her eyes were ready to. "I love you, Jack."

"I love you too," he answered.

She kissed him again, and angled the painting toward her. She put both hands on the corners the way a parent does to a child to really explain why what they did was wrong. Cindy gazed at the painting.

"Careful, it's still a little wet. Don't get it on you."

She looked at it the way she looked at all of his paintings. The way a connoisseur would take in a classic by Rembrandt or Michelangelo. Sometimes he thought she cared more about the paintings than he did.

"You know, it really is good." Cindy stepped back and really looked at the painting. She may as well have been in a museum. Her eyes shined with wonder. "It's amazing to me that you can do that. Paint it exactly like the covers. It's a shame it has to go to such a *tool*." She hadn't seen this cover but all the ones before it looked exactly like the paintings. "I wouldn't have done it if I was you, honestly."

"Well, I definitely didn't want to," Jack said. "I kind of think they expect it now. Plus, he paid more than anyone else has. I felt like he earned it."

"You're a good man, Charlie Brown. I got to go. I don't want to be fired for being late." Cindy kissed him again, tousled his hair, and left the house for her final day of work.

It is a pretty cool cover, he thought. *God, what a dickhead though.*

"I just heard that today was your last day, Mrs. S." Mark said. He had quickly become Cindy's favorite patient. He was the only one she actually looked forward to seeing. A few months ago he was in a horrible accident, and Cindy understood why the doctors told him he would never walk again. His tibia plateau had been broken so badly that at a glance she honestly mistook the x-ray for a mishapened hand. The plate in his leg made the images look like a slasher movie prop. His file said he was six feet, five inches tall, and he hung off both ends of the plinth table. That gave

Cindy reason to think maybe six-five was undercutting him a little. He was a tiny bit over weight but Cindy could tell by his slightly drooping figure that he had lost a lot of his size recently. Mark was her ideal patient. He was sweet and charming, and always did his exercises at home. Cindy hated to think about what happened to him. That sort of thing was just a testament to how horrible this town was. "What gives? I still got a couple weeks before I'm out."

Mark was winding down his appointment with ankle stretches. He doubled up two of the thickest bands the complex carried. His drive to recover was admirable, and at the rate he progressed, he'd prove everyone wrong and continue with his life as if nothing happened to him at all. *What kind of doctor could tell a patient to give up before the bone even mended?* Cindy thought for the umpteenth time.

"This is Mark," Cindy told Dana, her trainee and replacement. Dana was new to the field just like Cindy was three years ago and fresh out of college. She was small—maybe five feet tall, a big maybe—and Cindy was a little let down that she wouldn't be able to watch her work on Mark's huge structure. She imaged a squirrel trying to climb a tree. "Now even if you somehow manage to kill everyone else, you must work very diligently to keep this one alive."

"That's right," Mark added. "I have to be alive, so that when her husband strikes it rich as an artist, she can leave him and we'll run away together with half of his money. Perfect crime. Plus, if the world ends, don't you want someone tall to reach the high stuff?"

"Exactly," Cindy told Dana. "And as you can tell, his

oxycodone kicks in right before we have to bend his knee."

"Why do you always hurt me when all I've ever done," Mark paused, looking down at the floor, then continued, "is love you. Actually now is a better time than any. I can't feel my face, and that is the typical indication that I am sedated. Also, no one ever says 'behold' anymore. They just start talking about whatever the hell their thing is. Just—, it's—, there's no flare with the language anymore."

Dana did her best to hold back a laugh. She held out her hand to him. "I'm Dana. I'll be taking over with you when Cindy leaves."

"It's great to meet you, Dana," Mark let go of the rubber bands, launching them into the nearby hamper with the rest of the used bands waiting to be washed. Mark shook Dana's hand. Then he slapped the thigh of his injured leg. "Watch that left leg. It's a stubborn one."

"See," Cindy said, grinning. "This one's a good one to keep alive. Ready, Mark?"

He slapped both hands on the plinth and hopped over onto his stomach. "Let's do this."

Cindy took her place at the side of the table and grabbed the ankle of Mark's injured leg.

"So, Mark," Dana asked. "What happened to your leg?"

"Well," Mark began. "Actually could you hand me that gray ball in the corner?"

Dana tossed mark the dense rubber ball, and he caught it with one hand.

"Here we go," Cindy said.

Mark groaned in pain as Cindy bent his knee, pulling on

the scar tissue that had built up around the bone. "That's not all you got, is it Mrs. S? This is our last time together. At least give me something to remember you by."

Cindy laughed. "Just getting warmed up." She shook his leg by the ankle to loosen up the joint. She bent his knee once more. Mark's face turned red, and he squeezed the ball so hard Dana thought it was on the verge of popping.

"I'm sorry to interrupt your questioning. I was hit by a car while riding my bike home from work two days before Christmas. Ooo! Oo! Uffta! That's what I'm talking about, Mrs. S. Right now, I'm sure you can tell by my chart thing there that I have a metric shitload of scar tissue in my knee right now, and it's now your job to break it up."

"Well that's not all," Cindy said. "We have to get you back on your bike, right?"

"Exa-*a*-actly," Mark said, grimacing in pain. He dropped the ball and Dana scrambled to pick it up for him.

"We've been getting a one hundred-degree bend in the knee," Cindy told Dana. "We've hit a bit of a wall with the tissue, but we're not giving up, are we?"

"Absolutely *not!*" Mark laughed once the piercing bolt of pain shooting up his left side abated. "You only do that when I'm talking so you can hear me scream, don't you?"

"Awe, does baby need a nap?"

"No-*oh!*" Mark said.

Cindy shook his leg, loosening the knee a little more. "One more time and we're going to measure, you ready?"

"Give it to me. I can take it."

Cindy bent the leg until Mark groaned and bounced the

bend causing the groan to crescendo loudly. Just then Estelle, the seventy-five year-old woman responsible for teaching the Norwegian exclamation "uffta" to Mark and the therapists, walked into the building. Cindy couldn't really tell how she felt about the woman. She was mean, but she made up for it with her eccentric sense of humor. She and Mark got along very well from across the room.

"That must be Mark." Estelle called through the gym.

"Hello, Estelle," Mark said, catching his breath. "You're up next."

"That's horrible," Dana said. "Did he go to jail?"

"I like to think he just went home and drowned in the tub," Mark joked. "I doubt it, but he must have been in a hurry to do something. He didn't have time to stop apparently."

"Are you kidding?" Dana said. "What did the police say?"

"He said 'What do you want me to do about it?' as if helping wasn't an option. Of course he probably couldn't remember what happened anyway. He took a week-long vacation and locked the case in his office so no one else could help me either."

"That's horrible," Dana said.

Cindy agreed. She'd heard the story a few times, but it still managed to stir her into a minor frenzy. That made bending Mark's leg a little bit easier.

"Yeah," Mark said. "But I got these cool scars, and a badass story to tell. It could be worse. I could've gotten hit by the car and died. Then I wouldn't have anything to show for it. That would have fucked everything up. Sorry for swearing."

Cindy laughed. That was a new addition to the story. "Always the optimist. Got your breath?"

"I guess," Mark rolled over onto his back.

"Ready for the goniometer?" Dana asked.

"Oh yeah," Mark said. "It's protractor time." He lifted his leg in the air slowly.

"You want to measure or bend?" Cindy asked. "Dealers choice."

"I can bend," Dana said. "I may as well get used to it."

"Okay," Cindy said. She lined the goniometer even with Mark's leg, placing the pivot point on his knee. "On three." Cindy counted down and the three of them strained to bend Mark's knee farther than they had before. After a minute of groaning and heavy breathing they stopped. Cindy checked the measurement. "One oh six."

"Yeah!" Mark shouted, exalted. "I knew we weren't done with this. Well, Dana you are clearly my good luck charm. You have successfully been passed the torch, and for the remaining two weeks of my time here we're going to have a lot of fun."

Cindy used a towel to wipe the sweat from the plinth table. "Worked hard today, I see."

"Had to see you off in style." Mark winked.

"Cute," Cindy laughed. "You want the electricity or just the ice today?"

"Give me both," Mark said. "Feeling good about myself. The painkillers are also starting to wear off, and I don't want to feel any of that when they do."

"Okay, I'll be right back. Dana, do you mind getting the electricity?"

"Sure thing."

Cindy walked to her office and returned with the electrolysis pads. She affixed them around Mark's knee. *I wish they'd just make these easier*, she thought. *Can they not figure out how to combine these machines so one does ice and electricity? There are too many wires.*

"So why are you moving?" Mark asked.

"You want the real reason?"

"Obviously," Mark said.

"I'm just not happy here. The hours are stressful. The pay isn't as good, and it's hard for Jack to keep up momentum when he's always on the run. New Orleans will give him a bigger pond to fish in. Besides, there's no moving through the ranks here. We're a mom-and-pop organization. I'm as high as I can go here. At least there I'll be at a great facility and can move up. There are hundreds of employees there to take up the slack. It's a better place for me."

"I get it," Mark said, massaging the side of his leg where the plate was drilled into the bone. "Although you could've stopped after the first thing you said. Who cares why you're moving if the place you're moving from makes you unhappy, right? Are you happy to be moving there? And by that I mean are you just as happy to be moving there as you are moving away from here. I'd hate to find out that you got out of the frying pan and into a different frying pan."

"Oh, of course. A lot of my friends are there, I love the

city, and Metairie is far enough away for quiet, and close enough to watch a good basketball game."

"I hear that," Mark tipped his sweat-stained Dolphins cap. "Go Pelicans."

"Let me know when you can feel it." Cindy slowly dialed up the intensity of the electrolysis machine.

"Well, I'm happy for you, Mrs. S. I've always wanted to go to Phoenix."

"Not Miami?"

"No, talk about a gross city. That's good, I can feel it." Mark rubbed the ice pack on his leg. "Phoenix is clean, and there's no beach. Almost no reason at all to go there. It's everything Florida isn't. What are you, twenty-six? Twenty-seven?"

"Thirty," Cindy said, giving him a "yeah right" grin.

"You're six years older than I am? You look like you could be my baby sister."

"Come on," Cindy added.

"Well I hope in six years I'll be as happy as you. You have officially set the benchmark for me. I get to thirty and I'm getting out of here. Goodbye, hometown." He flicked his hand toward the ceiling as if sending out a preemptive wave. "Maybe I'll stop by on my way out West. I'm going to miss you, Mrs. S."

"Well, good luck, Mark." She hugged him. Her heart fluttered. Mark had become her friend, and it was actually difficult to tell him goodbye. She was going to miss him, but the only thing that let her leave with a clear conscience is that she knew in two weeks he would have his last visit to the institute. He'd be on his own again. Never coming back to the University Blvd. Physical Therapy Institute. "You stop screwing around on that bike," she said. "I will come back here."

"Because you'd miss me." Mark laughed.

Cindy continued her rounds and helped Miss Estelle onto the stationary bike. She finished her day like every other normal day. And at the end, there was no party, no sentimental moment with her co-workers. Just a wave across the parking lot. That was enough for her, because in the morning she would be on her way out for good. That thought made her smile. *Goodbye, hometown,* she thought.

Jack picked up the cordless phone and held it between his shoulder and ear as he continued making dinner. The movers had pulled out about fifteen minutes ago, and he wanted to surprise Cindy with dinner as well as an almost completely empty house. He answered the phone, wiping his still sweating face dry with his shirtsleeve.

"Jackie boy!" his agent, Tom Dwyer, yelled into the receiver. He was never "Jackie boy" unless Tom had a job lined up.

"Hey," Jack said. His obvious preoccupation with dinner had seeped through the phone.

"Whoa," Tom said. "Cindy must be gone. You sound so boring."

"Thank you." Jack said in a robotic monotone voice.

"She's coming home now. I'm just getting dinner ready. Got something new for me?"

"So domesticated. Why yes I do, my friend. And holy shit, are you going to love me."

"Well, I hope so," Jack answered. He perked up a little. Tom usually started the good deals this way. *Why aren't you as excited about this as me?* he would usually say. *Because you haven't told me anything yet, Tom*, would typically be Jack's answer. "I'll need a backup plan if Cindy ever wises up and realizes she married a bum."

"Ha!" Jack flinched at the sound of Tom's voice peaking the speakers in the phone. "Are you on the toilet, Jack? I just don't want you to shit yourself."

"What's the job, Tom?" He allowed a little excitement to creep into his voice. The truth was, Tom Dwyer never got this excited about just anything. Jack was wondering the last time he was ever *this* excited. Tom had blown right by "Are you sitting down, well don't because you'll just stand right back up when you hear this," and skipped directly to toilet humor.

"Ever hear of Joe McDermott?"

"Which one?"

"The writer, Jackie boy! *The writer*."

"I actually think I have."

He hadn't.

"Of course, you have," Tom's voice was coaxing, like a snake charmer. *Come with me, Jackie boy. I have great news. Right this way. I'll lead you to the truth.* "Everything he does turns to diamonds lately. International bestseller. Two of his books have already been made into movies, and another is in pre-production as we speak. Fox picked it up as a summer series. He released a book of poetry a few years back and won the National Critics Butthole Award or something like that. I never read the shit."

"Good for him." Jack repositioned the phone to stir the pasta. He was losing interest. "His mother must be very proud to know her son won the Butthole award. I bet she's polishing that gold-plated anus trophy right now. She probably calls the neighbors."

"Well," Tom said, matter-of-fact. "This guy McDermott has decided to branch out into even newer forms of literary prowess."

"Right?" Jack stopped stirring the various pots and skillets of food. He turned all the eyes on the stovetop to simmer. He was starting to believe this wasn't just another cover.

"Ah ha, I see I have the wiseass's attention. Well you will be happy to know that your boy Tommy here is working for ya. I caught wind of his new project accidentally. That's bullshit. Son of a Bitch Jennings at the firm left his laptop open when he went out to take a piss. Jennings was his agent until he got too big and Jennings didn't have enough time for him. I guess they keep in touch still. I saw an email from McDermott pop up on his computer, talking about a serial graphic novel that has already been picked up with an advance by IDW. Said he *thinks* he found an artist. Said he likes his work, but he's not totally committed to him yet."

"No shit?"

"Yes shit, Jackie boy. I took a picture of the email with my phone and bippidy boppidy mother-fuckin boo! Twenty minutes later I had him in the palm of my hand. I sent him your entire published portfolio."

"Whoa, what? Tom—"

"Now, I know you don't like when I do that without permission, but trust me. This time is worth it. He didn't want to wait. He wanted to see something right then. Plus, I didn't send him anything you hadn't sold or copywritten already. I'm telling ya, I got your back."

"Well what'd he say?"

"*What'd he say?*" Tom sounded disgusted. "Why would I be calling you if it was no? Come on. Actually, what he said was, he had a guy in mind already, but he hadn't committed to anything yet. He told me he loved what you do. The cover of *Bone Dry* was the exact kind of creepy he is after. Believe it or not, *Homerun Killer* is what won him over."

"Bullshit," Jack said. "I hate that one."

"You take that back," Tom joked. "He loved it. He thought your work was brilliant. And if all goes well, I'll call it even. You had to work for the little dickhead but it may have gotten you a much better deal. See what I'm saying. It's all about paying dues, my friend."

"I see what you're saying," Jack said. "What's the new project?"

"Well, that's the only thing. Like I said, he already had a guy in mind. He's going to float the idea to him, but it's going to be sort of an audition process. You haven't gotten the job yet, but you can get it. All he wants is the cover first. 'Oh, Tom, are you kidding?' No, I'm not. I know this is all you ever do. Which is why I have the utmost confidence that you are going to hit this one out of the park. Nail it to the wall."

"That's it? Just a cover?"

"That's all he wants. Basically all you and this Trevor something has to do is wow him with the front. 'If it makes me want to work with them, it'll make the readers want to pick it up and read it.' His words, not mine."

"Well, what's the story about?"

"It's called *The King of Evil*." Tom brimmed with excitement. "And this is the part where you need to get to a toilet. I'll wait."

"Not necessary."

"It's about the legendary King of Voodoo."

"You're kidding me."

"I am not kidding you, sir."

"That's where I live now. Right in the heart of Voodoo country."

"Exactly," Tom said. Jack knew he had a lit cigarette and he was jabbing in the air to emphasize his words. Jack could almost smell the smoke from the Pall Malls through the phone. "And don't think I didn't bring that up to Mr. McDermott. Apparently years and years ago, before our time, the Voodoo King lived on an island where people would go as a rite of passage. If you can stare down the Voodoo King and not show fear, you win kind of thing. Something happened along the line that caused him to leave the island and go after people. Then after stealing her baby, a witch locked the King in a magic box and our protagonist stumbled upon it and let the Voodoo King out. Our protagonist..." Tom trailed off, scrolling through the email. "Robert Taylor is pitted against this wily King, who *will not stop* until he takes the heart of another, trapping *them* in the weird magic box. That's all he's giving either of you to work with. He just wants the cover."

"And?"

"And what?"

"Did he say anything about adding our own little flares and individuality that my last client had such a tizzy over?"

"Actually I just replied to his email with that same question. I'm waiting for the answer now. This is big though. Not only will you be getting to work with a great pre-established author, but they're giving you a lump up front to complete the work."

"If I get the job, obviously," Jack added.

"Well yeah, but you're going to get it."

"What's the lump?"

"Still on the toilet?"

"Haven't moved."

"A hundred and fifty thousand per volume."

Jack nearly dropped the phone into the bubbling marinara. "You're fucking with me."

"I have never, and will never," Tom said with pride. "And that doesn't include a split royalty deal with you and McDermott. You're going to get paid, and you'll see profit if the series does well for once. I can't imagine his agent knows he's telling people that. He's probably going to be pissed if he finds out, so don't say anything. Let me do the negotiating. Now did your boy show up for you, or did he show up for you?"

"He showed up big fucking time," Jack said, remembering to stir the sauce and noodles before the house filled with smoke. "I'm totally blown away right now. I don't even know what to say. This is huge."

"Goddamn it," Tom shouted with excitement. "Pop some champagne! Scream and shout! Fuck your wife, this is a game changer, buddy."

"You better believe it is." Jacks voice had gone back down to where it was when the conversation began.

After a few moments of silence, Tom said. "Alright, calm down. I'm going to let you sit for the night."

"Wait, wait. What's the deadline?"

"I told him you were currently in the process of moving so he agreed to wait and let everything settle before asking for anything. He has another book he's working on so he's got time. He wants it by the fifth. That's three weeks away. I figured that would give you enough time to walk around the city and get some ideas first. I'll call you when he gets back to me. Oh, I got an email from a guy with an indie film. He wants you to do the poster. He's still editing it, so it doesn't have to be done for another month. I figure that could be a quick buck while you get unpacked. They've already sent the pictures and credits. Just wants you to put it together."

"I'll swing by in the morning before we leave town."

"CD or flash?"

"I'll bring my flash."

"I'll see you in the morning, Jackie boy."

"Thank you, Tom."

"Don't thank me yet. You got work to do first."

"See you in the morning, Tom."

Jack placed the phone back in its charging cradle. Jack stared down into the sauce bubbling in the pot. He didn't know what to do. He touched his face to make sure he was awake.

Cindy opened the front door then. Jack picked her up and laid her onto the air mattress on the living room floor without saying a word. It was the only thing left in the house. Jack kissed his wife, hoping to make her blush. He slid the scrubs off of her and tossed them on the floor. When they finished, and the house smelled like burnt Italian food, he told her about the conversation with Tom. They threw the pots and skillets into the garbage outside and ordered a pizza. When the delivery kid knocked on the door, Jack hurried off his wife and to the door, fumbling his clothes back in place. Jack gave the kid a thirteen-dollar tip, hoping he hadn't noticed the teepee Jack was sporting. He slammed the door and went back to his wife on the deflating air mattress. When they finished, Jack apologized for burning the food. "I really wanted to cook for you tonight," he told her.

"That's fine, babe," she said. "I would rather have this anyway."

❖ ❖ ❖

The next morning Jack and Cindy walked into Tom's office in the center of town. The room was small and the mounted fish and small animals along the walls made it seem even smaller. Jack never asked him about his hunting career. Mostly out of a strong desire to never have a conversation about hunting. The closest Jack ever came to starting something was when he jumped at the one enormous moose head above Tom's desk. Tom must be good. There seemed to be a new animal every time Jack walked into his office. The smell of Tom's Pall Malls wafted up to him.

Tom's wet-looking hair pointed up in the front as usual, and he was swimming in his oversized suit behind his desk. *Must be going around*, Jack thought. Usually Jack thought he looked much younger, but now something had aged him to match reality.

"The couple of the hour!" Tom stood up and hugged Jack, nearly spilling the coffee in Jack's hands on his suit, then Cindy.

"Wow," Cindy said. "You seem to have gotten good news recently. What happened?"

"Did you not tell her?" Tom asked Jack. "Why didn't you tell her?"

"I'm just messing with you," Cindy said.

"Oh," Tom laughed awkwardly.

"Do you have it saved anywhere special?" Jack asked.

"Right there on the desktop," Tom said. "*Coda's End*, I think it's called."

"Lame," Cindy added.

"No shit," Tom agreed

"Found it," Jack inserted the flash drive and worked through the process of uploading the files onto it. Jack saw a folder marked "YearEndTaxes" and wondered briefly if that's what he would find in his agent's work computer. He managed to avoid opening the folder, wondering how many people on the planet had a folder that actually kept their yearend taxes. "Mind if I see what they sent?"

"Go ahead," Tom told him. "You still don't seem very excited. Everything alright?"

"I just want to wait before I do," Jack told him. Cindy slid her hand across her husband's shoulders. "Not because it may not happen, but so I can let it all out at once when it does. That way I can be fully excited when we get the job."

"He's the sensible one," Cindy told Tom. "When it comes through, he'll be wetting his britches just like the rest of us."

"That's true," he affirmed, dully.

"Well that's good." Tom adjusted his jacket. "I wouldn't want to be embarrassed."

Unimpressed with the shots from the indie film producer, Jack turned his attention back to the graphic novel. "Do you mind if I read the email from Joe?"

"Oh, no," Tom made to walk back around the desk. "Let me log—"

"Don't bother. The password is written on the back of your name plate."

"You see," Tom said to Cindy. "This why I can't have people sitting there."

"Cin, can you take out your phone and text me this information." Jack said. He was clicking through the emails in Tom's account looking for the thread from Joe.

"Sure, sweetie," Cindy said.

"First National Bank dot com. Username T Dwyer eight six seven," Jack said, reading off the sticky note on the back of nameplate at the end of the desk.

Tom snatched the nameplate off the desk and stuffed it into his pocket. "Funny."

"Play nice," Cindy laughed.

"And he says I'm weird about my paintings," Jack said, still scrolling through emails. "Where is the thread, Tommy?"

"It should just be his name and some numbers behind it," Tom said.

"I'm still in today's emails? Jesus, how many do you get a day?"

"Like three, I don't know. You're not my only client." Tom leaned beside him. Jack handed him the mouse, and within seconds Tom found the thread. "There it is."

"Okay," Jack said and started reading. Cindy came up on the other side of him and leaned on the armrest. "Well he didn't give much. Are you cc'd from the other agent, too?"

"Yeah, I think I got a couple he sent back before he realized what he was doing. Why?"

"Just want to see where the other guy is from. Did he say his name yet?"

"Yeah, it's somewhere in there."

Jack found a name, Googled it, and came up with his competition. Trevor something was in fact very good, but there was a glaring advantage Jack held over him. Unless he was mistaken, there wasn't a very active Voodoo scene in Montana, and that meant good news for Jack. He was certain that Trevor Jones had the same access to a computer and therefore the Internet, but he was probably nowhere near a place that knew the history of Voodoo the way Jack was.

"I think we got this one in the bag," Cindy announced.

"This is a big deal, babe," Jack said, suddenly realizing that everyone in this room counted on Jack to get this job. The pressure set in, creating a nice cushion of anxiety in the pit of his stomach. Jack sipped the coffee he brought with him, and the feeling faded.

"You're going to kill it."

"From what I can tell," Tom began. "It seems like neither of you are overly familiar with the genre. Luckily you can get that way."

"He just sent a new email," Cindy said.

Jack clicked the boldfaced font in the new message box. Two sentences were typed on the white box of the message. One complete. One fragment. "Absolutely not," Jack read. "That's what they're here for."

"What did you ask?" Cindy turned to Tom.

"I actually don't remember," he answered.

Jack scrolled down. "Do you have a problem with the artists adding their own ideas in the cover or do you want only what you've given me?"

"Oh, thank God," Cindy said. "I hadn't even thought of that. I couldn't deal with another stubborn little dickhead."

"We couldn't either," Tom said. He wasn't married yet so he didn't understand all the "we" talk Cindy and Jack made. They were cute, but it was a little off to him. Numerous times he wondered if Jack ever said "we" had this patient the other day with his leg turned all the way around backwards. There were times when they'd lose a bid for a job, and she start in with the "we" talk. Tom always wanted to ask what she had actually done to move the project along. He never did, of course. Cindy was his favorite artist's spouse. She was smarter than all of them combined. She was smarter than most people combined.

Most of Tom's clients were women, and more times than he would like he got a visit or a call from a jealous husband wanting to know where his wife was—often times in the backyard tanning—or when the check was going to be deposited into their account. Cindy was a rare spouse that didn't really care until everything was over, and she could cheer on her husband's triumphs. "Reply back, 'Great, we'll see you on the fifth.' And, I don't know, XOXO, hugs and kisses, whatever seems appropriate."

"Wait, we're going to meet him?" Jack asked.

"Yeah."

"Where?"

"He wants to meet the two of you in Seattle, so you can talk through your cover concepts in person."

Jack stared up at him, eyebrows at the top of his forehead.

"He's paying for it," Tom said.

"Okay, good." Jack said. "I think I've committed this

whole thing to memory now."

"Want me to forward it to you?"

"Please."

"Hopefully, you won't have to meet him with Trevor there, too," Cindy said. "That would be incredibly awkward. 'Hello I'm the man who's going to take money out of your pocket and food out of your family's mouth.' That's psychotic."

"I would never actually say that, though," Jack added.

"No," Tom said. "I'm pretty sure it's just him and his agent with you and your agent. It happens all the time. I've just never been a part of it."

"Awe, that's sad," Cindy rubbed Tom's arm.

Jack ejected the flash drive and dropped it into his pocket. "I now have everything. Send me an email if you need anything from me. I'll have the Internet at home soon. Or around then."

Tom awkwardly shook Jack's hand too hard and escorted him and Cindy out of the office. "Send me your address so I can pick you up on the way to the airport."

"See you in three weeks."

2

Two Weeks Later

The house in Metairie was three stories tall, and it sat on a river in the woods. The driveway was a quarter-mile long path through a tall trail of evergreens so thick it was like driving in the late afternoon. No one would ever come down this way but the mailman, and that made them feel safe in the light of their last few nights at their old home. The first floor was a carport and nothing more. There was thick post all around and separating the space so that two cars, even large trucks, would fit comfortably between the rows the posts made. The house was wooden and the inside was open and felt like a cabin. Cindy's Soul and Jack's Xterra had enough room to back out of their respective cubbyholes with the doors open. There was even a space in between for a third car. At the end opposite the house, a staircase on both sides rose up half a floor and met in the middle to make one staircase up to the house. The covered porch reached from one end of the house to the other, there were wide doors leading to the kitchen on one side and another set lead into the living room on the other. Between the two sets of doors there was a tall window that offered a view into an office, or maybe even a bedroom for one of their future children. They had unpacked everything in the previous two weeks, making multiple trips back and forth to sell or bring their old things. The cable and Internet had been set up to perfection. The furniture, all of it they decided to keep, fit exactly how they imagined it would. Back behind the house, a steel shed protected a lawnmower, a gas can, and nothing else from the elements. They talked about getting rid of it, but it was much more sturdy than the one they had left behind, and Jack thought he would be able to use it more. They agreed to make one of the three bedrooms a guest room in case one of their parents or friends wanted to make the three-hour drive down to visit them, or had to fly out the next day. There were only two rooms to decide on: Jack's office, and their bedroom. Jack's computer was the last thing to come out of a box. The folding table he used as a desk leaned against the stairs to the studio attic.

"You know what I just realized?" Cindy asked. She was wearing jean shorts and a tank top. Her hair stuck through the back of a Pelicans cap. She didn't sweat, but she did have a shine coming from her face.

"What's that?" Jack asked, sweating through his V-neck, and shorts.

"The stove is one of those flame ones. It goes *woof* when you turn it on."

"We've been here like two weeks. You just now turned the stove on?"

"You've cooked all the meals. Stop spoiling me and I'll turn the stove on more." She grinned at him. "You need help moving that?"

"Actually," Jack said. "I was thinking about something. What if you and I both took the upstairs room as a gym and office?"

"Will that work?" She asked. Her nose wrinkled slightly.

"Well, I only work when you're not here. You always do your yoga when I'm on the phone and getting dinner made. We'll be out of each other's way. We can get a new couch up there if you want, and watch the sun on the river through the windows. It'll free up a room down here for the future. Plus I'll have an excuse to come in and watch you stretching." He struck the warrior pose and she tapped him on the chest.

"Shut up," she grinned.

"Besides," Jack continued. "After seven years of doing this, I would kind of like your help occasionally. Not so much in the area of doing anything artistic, just 'do you like this' and 'yes' or 'no' is all I'd need. Maybe the occasional explanation."

"Really?" She blushed a little. "I'm no good at that."

"Yeah, but you know what you like."

"Okay," she smiled wide enough to show her back teeth. "Let's do it."

They set up the studio room within twenty minutes. The table came up in no time. Cindy's plug-in stereo sat on an end table in the corner. The majority of the work consisted of finding the surge protector for the computer, and once that was found in a discarded box, they were all set. The next order of business was picking their bedroom. Jack offered a room in the corner with windows that wrapped around the wall, which turned out to be the dining room. That left the next biggest room where they had been sleeping on the mattress for two weeks already, and once they assembled the bed frame, their house became a home. They climbed into bed and Cindy laid her head on Jack's chest.

"You want me to call the cable guy and have him put a box in this room, too?"

"Sure," her voice was tired. "Babe?"

"Yeah?"

"When you said future, did you mean kids?"

"Of course."

"I know we talked about it before, but then things came up."

"Yeah, I know," Jack said. "Moving here definitely opened the door for that."

"I want a baby," she snuggled closer to him.

"Me too," Jack said.

"Just one." Cindy started to snore. It was a tiny, cute sound and Jack started to laugh. The movement of his chest woke her up. "Jack?"

"Yeah?"

"Walk me through your day tomorrow," she was already going back under.

"Okay," Jack started. "First, I'm going to cook us breakfast."

"We're out of sausage and eggs."

"First, I'm going to get us Dunkin Donuts. Then I'm going to call the cable guy. And I was thinking that since your first day at your new job is Monday, I would take you to the city and we could spend the day walking around."

"Yay," she whispered.

"Maybe I'll get some ideas for the cover due in a week."

"Big day."

"Have lunch in the city."

"Mmm…" Her voice vibrated against his ribs.

"We could go to the Pelicans game in the afternoon, if you want to do that. Starts at two. Then on our way home we will get groceries, and I will make you your favorite. Parmesan Chicken with Penne noodles."

"Mmm…" Her voice was deeper this time. It made him laugh. "I love you, Jack."

"I love you too, Cin."

As she fell asleep Jack ran through a number of ideas for his cover. He had an image of a man with a painted face, dreadlocks, and a top hat. That wasn't enough to win him the job though. He needed something to put him in a distant first place. He was the underdog. This would be his road to the top. The pressure he suddenly felt was unyielding. Luckily he was dosing too fast for his worries to keep up. He fell asleep to images of voodoo symbols and the man with the painted face and top hat.

❖ ❖ ❖

Bourbon Street was not their scene. Maybe five or ten years ago they would have enjoyed it, but they had crossed the age where the street's vulgarity outweighed its charm. They parked in a garage on Canal Street and got out. The garage was connected to a mall, which at this early time of day seemed relatively empty. They were on their way out when Cindy pointed out a navy and gray crop top with "Go Pels!" scrawled across the front in swooping cursive letters. Jack convinced her to try it on as they stood outside the store looking at the mannequin. She gave in and tried on the one small the store still had. Even though he was responsible for Cindy's interest in the team, when he saw her in that shirt his love for basketball spiked. He loved that he finally lived in a city with a professional team he could visit.

Once they left the mall they made their way down the street hand in hand, Jack carrying the bag with Cindy's new shirt. Places to eat sprung up on every block. The streets were lined with so many novelty shops and hole-in-the-wall food joints that Jack didn't know when to pull off the sidewalk and go into one. They walked for nearly an hour until finally settling on a place between streets.

"Oo, let's go in here," Cindy said, pulling Jack behind her.

After the colorful beads at the entrance, the shop was a dingy, narrow space with myriad voodoo trinkets, posters, and smoking paraphernalia. The store was a labyrinth of dark clothing with skulls and weird symbols. On the walls hung shelves of sculptures and carvings of fake shrunken heads and mythical creatures made up of parts of multiple animals.

"Look at this place," Cindy said. "You could definitely get something out of here."

Their hands slid apart and Jack set out to explore the shelves. He came across a number of strange things. He imagined most of the things he saw covering the walls of some angst-filled teenager's bedroom. Pentagrams seemed to be the logo of choice. There was at least one on nearly everything in the store. There was a skull made to look like the grim reaper with a bat around his head in place of the hooded cloak. The eyes and nose were painted with a cheap black paint and peeled off in some places, giving it an interesting and creepy look. There were dead figures with their skin stretched tightly across their cheeks and ribs. There were voodoo dolls, and multiple pictures of an old man hunched over with a cane.

"Can I help you?" A voice hovering somewhere along the border between Southern and French boomed from behind a tall counter in the center of the store.

"I'm actually here doing research for a project," Jack told him. "Could you tell me who this older person is in the pictures?"

The lumbering black man stepped from behind the counter. "Ah, yes. That is Papa Legba. He is the gatekeeper to the Lwa spirit world."

"He's the gatekeeper?" Jack asked. "He's a little old isn't he?"

The storekeeper laughed. "He is not older than St. Peter. In fact, many people consider him to be the same person."

"Really?" Jack said, genuinely fascinated.

"Yes, voodoo and Catholicism are very similar. Papa Legba is just like St. Peter. The Lwa are the same as the Saints. The pope even recognizes voodoo as a valid religion. Although, real voodoo is nothing like what you see in the movies. Things rarely are the way they are portrayed in the movies."

"I'm actually here for inspiration to make something just like that for the sake of art," Jack explained. The man laughed. "I do want to keep it authentic though. If nothing else, I could bring a little truth to the Hollywood representation."

"You're a good man, mister…"

"I'm Jack. No mister."

"Well, Jack," the man said. He spoke to him as if telling him a secret. "Maybe you could take a look at this, if Papa Legba is where your interests lie."

The storekeeper led Jack to where Cindy stood on the opposite end of the counter. He opened the glass case and brought out a pewter figurine. Light reflected off its smooth surface. It had a base on which two carved men stood. On the left was Papa Legba, an old man wearing a wide brimmed straw hat and smoking a corncob pipe. He was slightly hunched over on a cane. At his feet was a small insignia that looked like a decorated crosshair. The other figure was an emaciated-looking man in a tuxedo and with a top hat covering a full head of dreadlocks. He held a staff in one hand and a bottle of rum in the other. There was something stuffed up both nostrils and a cigar coming out of his mouth. At this one's feet was a different insignia. It looked like an altar with a cross and on either side were two small caskets.

"Hey, do you have a bathroom in here?" A skater asked from the front door.

"Je comprend pas."

"What?"

"Désolé, Je ne parle Anglais."

"Whatever, bro." The kid stomped away with confusion painted on his face.

Cindy laughed. "C'est une façon de se débarrasser d'eux."

"Merci," the man grinned at them.

"So, what is this?" Jack asked.

"This is Papa Legba," the man gestured to the old man on the left. "He will be waiting to usher you into the Kingdom of heaven. He stands for good and can communicate in all languages. That way he can welcome people from all over the world into his Kingdom." The man gestured to the other figure. "This is Baron Samedi. He is one hundred and eighty the opposite. You have no doubt seen something like him in the movies. Some even give him the name Papa Legba by mistake. He is tricky, debaucherous, and evil. He is also of the Lwa, but the Lwa of the dead. Baron Samedi lives at the crossroad between the worlds of the living and the dead. That is why dresses like a corpse at a funeral. He can go unnoticed in either world, living or dead. He is the master of the dead and uses them to do his bidding. Where Papa Legba ushers a soul past the gates into the spirit world,

Baron takes your soul from its living body into the underworld. Those symbols in front of them are called veves. They are the marks of each spirit."

Jack and Cindy stared at the pewter sculpture. Jack immediately recognized Baron Samedi from his own imagination. *This is going to help me get the* edge, Jack thought. Cindy nudged him with her elbow.

"How much?" Jack asked.

"Forty," the man said.

Jack laid two twenties on the counter as the man wrapped it up. Jack dropped the heavy stone into Cindy's bag, and the two of them walked to the first place to eat that they saw, which was on the corner of the street.

The sign on the outside of the building was old and broken. There was a picture of a shrimp wearing a chef outfit stirring a large pot. The word "cajun" came up in the middle of the weathered sign, giving them confidence that this place would be worth their time. They were seated and ordered drinks. Jack opened his menu while Cindy took the pewter statue from the thick plastic shopping bag. The light from outside reflected off the smooth stone. She laid it on the table and examined it closely.

"So what do you see with this?" She asked.

"I don't know yet," Jack said, laying his menu on the table. "It's called *The King of Evil*. I don't think that describes either of these guys. One is definitely easier than the other though. Maybe one guy saves the protagonist from the other. What do you think?"

"That could work," she told him staring down at the

rock. "Although if you do that, the old guy would need a thing. Something that makes him stronger than the feeble looking guy there. Like super non-fibromyalgia powers or something to make sense of his being old yet superhero-esque. Has Joe Whatever written the story yet?"

"No clue," Jack angled the tiny statue so they both could see. "I've never heard of him, and I can't imagine them giving someone a contract just for an idea if he isn't that famous."

"He could've given you something else to work with."

"I'm starting to think that's why he didn't. He needs ideas too."

"That's a scary thought." Cindy wondered briefly if this would really be better for them. This whole project could just as easily flop as it fell into Jack's lap. *No*, she thought. *This is his big break. This is what he is meant to do.*

"I know," Jack said. He was looking around for something else that may be able to help him with ideas for the King.

"It'll happen though," She said with finality. There was no other way it could work. "The detail on this is outstanding. Can you imagine getting in there with a tiny chisel to make their faces? If nothing else, we got a really cool decoration."

Just then Jack noticed the box holding the sugar packets. It was made from stained black wood with metal latches. On the lid there was a carved out triangle with three spiral shapes inside. Jack picked it up. The box was very light despite its appearance and the fact that it was full. "That's pretty cool."

"Yeah," Cindy agreed. "Think it has anything to do with voodoo?"

"I don't know," Jack said, taking out his phone. "We can make it work though."

The waiter returned to the table with two glasses of water just as Jack's flash went and lit up the table. Jack scrambled to cover his phone's flash, hoping it was enough to not draw any more attention to the table.

"I'm sorry," Cindy told the waiter. "He's never been to America before."

"This…is…" Jack said in a Slavic accent. "Cocaine?"

"No," the nervous kid said. "It's sugar."

"Ah," Jack said, nodding his head vigorously. "Yes. America!"

"Do y'all know what you want?" The kid asked Cindy.

"I'm going to have the jambalaya chicken," Cindy handed him the menu.

"I am having sh-shreem…"

"Sound it out," Cindy encouraged.

"Shreemp pah-bowee," Jack grinned like a fool and looked up to the waiter.

"Good job," Cindy said enthusiastically and applauded his effort.

The waiter started to clap, but looked around and simply jotted their order down.

"I am talk English," Jack said.

"You did," Cindy said. Tears were forming in her eyes, and she was barely able to stop from falling out of her chair.

"Okay," the waiter said to Cindy. "I'll bring that right out. Just let me know if I can get you a refill or anything else." He walked away from the table and into the kitchen. Cindy bet he was already spreading the word about the woman and her strange foreign friend to the other waiters and cooks.

"When he comes back you be foreign and see what he does," Jack said between fits of laughter.

"I didn't expect you to go along like that." Cindy wiped the tears from her cheeks. Jack always managed to surprise her.

All the eyes at all the tables in earshot were on them. But Jack and Cindy laughed, and they didn't try to stop. Cindy wanted every moment to be this great. She loved this city. She could feel her roots seeping deeper into its soil. Part of her didn't want to go to work tomorrow, and in that moment, she thought that if Jack could support both of them by himself she would never go back to work. She would stay home and be with him all day. She put her hand over his, and they waited for their food together. Their eyes met for probably the billionth time. Jack didn't think billion was enough, because he knew it was somewhere close to infinity. There was something about his wife that changed him. She was funny, and being around her made him funny. She had that way. That way of spreading herself into other people's personalities. However she felt, which these days Jack was elated to say was mostly happy, spilled over as if it was too powerful to be contained by just her.

"You make me better, you know?" Jack told her.

"No," Cindy said, playing coy.

"I mean it," he said, kissing her hand. "You make me and everyone else around you just as happy and funny as you are. It's like your personal bubble takes over everyone else's."

"I think you're trying to get lucky," she said, grinning sideways at him.

"I think you're right."

"Do you *have* to go to work?" Jack groaned, following Cindy through the dining room to the kitchen. His bare feet slapped on the wooden floor. He still wore his pajamas and he tugged at the waistline of Cindy's Khakis.

She giggled and pulled away from him. Jack caught a glimpse of the top of her underwear as it peeked above the waist of her pants. "Quit it, you."

"I don't wanna," he whined.

"Besides, you have to work, too," she reminded him.

"I know." He straightened immediately. "You sure I can't cook you anything before you take off? You've got time."

"I'm just going to pick something up on the way," she said, gathering her purse and other things and headed for the door. Jack followed her to her car. "They want me to come in early to fill out the new hire crap."

"Ah, the workforce," Jack said, putting her purse in the passenger seat. "I don't miss it." He walked around the car and wrapped his arms around her. She put the tips of her fingers down the back of his waistband like she always did. "Have fun, and make a shitload of money, because you've been off for two weeks and I am hemorrhaging money."

She playfully tapped his cheek with her palm. "I love you," she said, and kissed him.

"I love you, too."

Jack watched her back out from under the house and drive off to work. Then work began.

He bounded up the steps as if in a hurry. He started the stove and took six strips of bacon from the refrigerator. He removed two pieces of bread from the bag and laid them beside the bacon on a Styrofoam plate.

"Okay," Jack said. "Let that stuff warm up, and I'm going to start on the project." He skipped upstairs to the computer. The flash drive jutted out the back like a knife. He felt for the power button, and waited for the chime and white screen to feel the attic. He ran back down stairs while the computer warmed up.

For the next five minutes Jack fried bacon and toasted the bread until both were nearly burnt. He squirted a little ketchup on one piece of bread, put the other on top and separated them. He dropped the bacon on the bread and made a glass of orange juice and carried his breakfast to the computer. The user password screen displayed on the monitor. He typed Simpsonsdidit1st and moved on to the desktop. Jack bit into the sandwich, before he could chew he said, "Ah, shit." He had completely forgotten about the busy work of *Coda's End*. He pulled up Photoshop and imported all the pictures from the flash drive. He finally laid the sandwich back on the plate and didn't pick it up for twenty minutes when he was finished with the poster. At this point it was almost robbery to have a client submit all the artwork and information and still make them pay, but a man's got to eat. He emailed the first draft to Tom and asked to get back if they wanted something different. They rarely did.

Now the fun can begin.

The pewter statue sat next to the monitor and faced Jack. It didn't seem as white as it had been in the store. Probably just the lighting in the attic. "Okay," he said to the empty room. "What are we going to do with you?" He opened the picture folder on his desktop and loaded the one of the sugar container. He looked back and forth between the two. Nothing came to him immediately. Jack leaned back in the folding chair. *I really should have put more thought into this before now. Cindy's going to be home and I'll have nothing to show for my day.* He stood at the window gazing through the tree branches at the river behind the house.

I wish we had a bigger yard, Jack thought. *I'm a better thinker when I'm on the lawn mower. Did I call the cable guy about our bedroom? Yes, I talked to a machine. They said they'd call today during office hours. Should I call them instead? Nah, the system works, just be patient. I wonder if I should get a better lock for the shed out back. Nah, no one's going to come all the way down our driveway to break into our shed. What if that guy from back home finds us all the way out here? No, that's just dumb. That was just a fluke. What if we have a kid and he needs a bigger space for school projects? We don't even have a kid though. What if she's having a girl? God, I wouldn't know what to do with a girl. Cindy isn't even pregnant. Although she could be pregnant. We have been having sex a lot lately. I don't remember the last time we did it the safe way. Does she still take the pill? I don't think so. I wonder what panties she's wearing today. I saw blue. Maybe those nice ones that are between the flossy kind and a normal pair of panties. The kind that doesn't cover her all the way.*

"Alright," he interrupted his train of thought, sitting back down at the computer. "What does this 'King of Evil' need? What's his motive? His purpose for being evil. Well, he needs a heart. Why does he need a heart? Because he doesn't want to be trapped in the box." *There we go. That's a good place to start.* He stared at the picture of the box with the triangle and spirals carved into it. He zoomed in on the screen. *Well I know one thing. I want that to be on the King's coat pocket.*

Jack highlighted the triangle in the picture and cropped the rest of the photo out. Then he highlighted the triangle and the swirls and cut everything else out of the picture. He changed the background to black and made the selected triangle design totally white. Then scaled it back, showing the grainy wood so it would have texture. *Almost perfect.* He turned the design upside down. It stood on its point. *That's weirder for sure. Progress has been made.*

Now for the box. *But what if he wasn't stuck* in *the box, but with the box. Sure he can live or be trapped in a box, but that's not the one he needs to worry about. That's just a Red Herring. Even though that's what the legend says. Legends are wrong all the time. Should I call the cable guy?*

"No, fuck no." Jack stood from the desk. "Stop thinking about the cable guy. Hang on…"

The cable guy had a belt. A utility belt. Like Batman. What if the King of Evil also had a belt? And what if he kept his heart in a box on the belt. That way it's always near him. Always where he can protect it. What if it's not his *heart, but the heart of the last victim, and he has to keep getting hearts or he dies* "and shrivels into nothing. Goddamn! We got a story going!"

From then on Jack was mad with creativity. His hands couldn't move fast enough. His computer, despite the thousands of dollars he spent on the significant machine, just couldn't process his thoughts fast enough. He wanted to see it as soon as he thought it, but everything was too slow. His cursor flew across the screen. His chin rested on the opposite palm, the fingers drumming on his lips. His left leg bounced up and down as if anxious to see the final product of the hands and mind.

Jack used stock photos he had taken while moonlighting as a photographer. That way he didn't have to pay to use someone else's. He used one picture before of a thin man with a grimace. The picture was actually of his old boss from the radio station. A pretty candid shot of a belligerent man on the brink of firing Jack wound up paying the rent multiple times. Jack could remember Howie Mercer's back-to-work rant bouncing around in his mind even now. His wide angry eyes look sinister enough for an evil villain. He had to doctor the photo each time he used it so it wouldn't be obvious that it was the same one. That was as easy as flipping the picture and adjusting the colors. He would often crop different parts of Howie out of the picture all together. Howie was also the kind of thin that bordered on sickness. That was something else Jack wanted for the King.

Jack didn't want to assign a race to the King. Instead he placed a fire around the King, and added creepy shadows to his face, making the sinister look appear even more evil. He added a tuxedo from another photo he took from a wedding assignment he had in college. It was the only picture he could find of a man wearing a jacket that had coattails. He changed the pocket square from Easter blue to dark purple, and added the tux to his old managers disembodied head. The hat came next. If he was going to use Baron Samedi as a template, he couldn't possibly stop at the top hat. He revisited the wedding folder. There was one person wearing a top hat and it wasn't a good match. He took the picture anyway and severed the hat from the rest of the picture. He stared at what he had so far. Jack tried adding the triangle to the front, but he didn't like that. He made a purple and black band and didn't like that either.

Jack moved away from the hat for a moment. He picked up the pewter statue and examined Baron Samedi closely.

"What else can you tell me?" Jack asked the stone.

Cindy arrived at the Bone and Joint Specialists of Louisiana almost an hour before the building opened. The parking garage connected to the building with an overhead footpath that crossed the street. Samantha, her lab partner in college, waited for her at the front door with the key in hand and a smile on her face. She hugged Cindy tightly around the neck. She still had her softball body from college and nearly squeezed the breath out of Cindy's lungs.

"Oh, my god, I'm so happy you're here now!"

"I know," Cindy said, almost matching her excitement. She handed Samantha a bag from Dunkin Donuts. "I brought you breakfast. You're still a vegetarian, right?"

"I am," Samantha said. "Wow, that's sweet of you, Cindy. Thank you. Somehow I skipped breakfast this morning. I don't know. Sometimes I just get to thinking, and I zone out completely, you know? Come on in. I can walk you through the computer set up and show you where everything is. By the time we finish, Dr. Douglass will be here to fill out the rest of the paper work."

Samantha bounced with glee toward the front door, and Cindy did her best to follow with an equal excitement. Cindy was thrilled to be at her new job, but she wasn't a morning person. Not to this level anyway.

"So you will probably work with people who have patients today," Samantha said, leading her into the building. The doors made a loud clacking noise as the locks disengaged. "You'll get anyone new who comes in and you'll cover when people are on break or if something comes up. It's pretty easy for the first couple days. Don't worry though, that's just until you have patients of your own. It'll give you time to learn the machines and figure out how to read Dr. Douglass's handwriting, which by the way is terrible." Samantha laughed, and Cindy weakly joined her. All the nervous energy she had managed to avoid had finally snuck up on her.

It pounced on her.

"This place is a lot bigger than my last job." Cindy stared around at the building in fascination. She could hear the footsteps echoing on through the corridor. There was only one room at her last job.

"Well, it's a hospital. We do everything from consultations to recovery here. The only thing we don't have is an emergency room. People come here when they need something done. Mostly knee and hip replacements, but we get plenty of everything."

"How many patients do you see a week?" Cindy was taking in everything around her. The size of the place alone amazed her.

"About twenty," Samantha told her.

"Are you serious?" Cindy asked.

"Mhmm." Samantha's short ponytail bobbed with her nodding head.

"That's only three days worth of patients where I come from."

"Well they don't like for us to get more than that. Usually they keep us at nineteen in case someone calls out or needs to be covered. It's so you can focus more on each patient instead of spreading yourself too thin. It's also so you don't go crazy or get over worked."

"What do you do for the rest of the time?" The lights were off in most of the offices they passed. Cindy took note of the bathrooms and waiting rooms as she passed. The building was large enough that the idea of getting lost was becoming a genuine concern of hers.

"Paperwork mostly. It's all electronic though. Each patient takes about ten minutes. But you'll figure out how to time everything so there's not much downtime. A lot of patients expect a good bedside manner because it's a private institution, so they talk and talk. And this is where we'll be working."

Samantha pushed open the double doors and turned on the lights to the room. The gym was far and away the best one Cindy had ever seen. A semi-circular desk greeted them with a glossy black surface that reflected her distorted image. The exercise stations were new and sleek. The bands and straps were organized in a large plastic chest of drawers. Cindy saw places every twenty feet or so to dispose of used towels or bands. Each plinth table had its own ice and electrolysis machine. The free weights went up fifteen pounds and were filled with sand instead of big metal dumbbells. The carpet was cushioned so even if she would be walking around all day it wouldn't be hard on her feet. There were computers mounted onto the wall instead of filing cabinets. Behind the reception desk there was a dock station where ten tablets rested, their screens all displaying a full battery icon.

"Samantha, I—I don't know what to say. This place is amazing." Cindy hugged her old college friend. Her nerves had settled. Cindy was happy. "Thank you so much for getting this job for me."

❖ ❖ ❖

There we have it.

Everything was complete except for the top hat. He wasn't sure what to do with it. At the moment it rested straight on the King's head but there was a gash torn out of the middle, causing it to droop to one side. He didn't love it, but Cindy would be home any minute and he could get her opinion. The King was alive. The King stood lanky with the staff in one hand and a jug of whiskey in the other. His skin gray and eyelids purple, giving him the look of a dead man. The tuxedo was dirty with tattered coattails, but the triangle could still be seen, as could the spiraling shapes inside, which Jack had, through the power of the Internet, learned was called a triskele. Another triskele was carved in a knot on the end of the staff, feathers dangling from the center of each circle. At the opposite end was a heavy weighted block that served as a mallet for the King. To top everything off there was a black box dangling from the belt around his waist. It was small but decorated like an armoire with the altar and casket insignia burned into it. The black-stained wood was splintered and streaks of red colored parts of the box. At the bottom corner, there was a single drop of blood leaking out of the box. It unnerved Jack a little to look closely at what he had done. It was *exactly* what he imagined. The box wasn't perfect but he would make another trip to the city for inspiration later. It worked for now though.

I just can't figure out the fucking hat.

He heard Cindy's car under the house and went downstairs to talk about her new job. She was inside before he made it down the steps. She walked to him and hugged him tightly. He wasn't sure if it was good news or bad news.

"I love my job so much," she said.

"So do I," he met her excitement. "Tell me about it."

"It's incredible. I have half as many patients. The facility is a huge upgrade. Everything is new. Ah! I'm just so happy we came here. There's also virtually no paperwork. It's all on tablets and they have them synced to the computers. Didn't I say that about the other place?"

"You have," Jack agreed with enthusiasm, although having absolutely no idea if she had told him that or not.

"They have escorts. Security guards. I never have to leave the gym. And I can't leave with a patient. It's against the rules."

"That's something we can both be happy about."

"It's perfect. Do you want to go out tonight?"

"Well, of course. Tom told me about a hole in the wall place that apparently serves the best pizza in the universe."

"Perfect," Cindy said. She pulled him to her again and squeezed.

"Come on, I want to show you something."

Cindy followed him to his computer and looked on as he pulled up the Photoshopped picture. "Oh, my god," she said. "Is that one Howie, too?"

"Yep."

"It doesn't look anything like him. You did all this today?"

"Yep, worked all day. Finished right before you came in."

"It's great, Jack."

"Well, thank you, baby," he kissed her head.

"I like that he's a drinker," she laughed. She stared at the computer screen studying everything she saw. "So what do you hate about it?"

"What do you mean?"

"Well, I know you wanted me to be involved now, but I still don't think you would show it to me unless you wanted me to tell you that I don't like the same thing you don't like."

Jack exhaled. "I don't like that hat."

"Yeah," she said. "It does look a little Mad Hatter-y. I saw a lot of bones in the store yesterday. Maybe you could do something with that."

"Okay," Jack made a note of it on his computer. "What was your problem with it?"

She hesitated. "You're not going to get mad at me?"

"No," Jack said. "Both of us are going to be affected by it. You can have your say, too."

"Okay," she thought for the gentlest way to say it. "He's the King of Evil, right?"

"Should be, yeah."

"Well, from the picture, he is definitely a bad guy. He's menacing. He looks dead. He just isn't quite *evil* yet. This guy seems like he has a weakness somewhere deep down. Like you could reason with him. I'm not saying it'd be easy by any means, but eventually he would get tired of being mean all the time. But *evil*. Evil is bad for the sake of being bad. It's perpetual. There's no talking out of it. It's, like, breathing. You can't just stop."

"Hmm," Jack said. "That's a great point."

"You're not mad?"

"Of course not. My favorite thing to hear is keep going." Jack made a note underneath the first one. "I'm glad you said something."

"Are you going to be able to eat with this on your mind?" She asked.

"Yeah," he said, saving his work. "I still have until the end of the week before it's due. Plenty of time. Today's just the first day."

"Did you ever think of a way to bring this other guy into the mix?" Cindy asked, holding up the pewter statue.

"I couldn't," Jack said, a little defeated. He stood from the computer. "I just didn't know how to do anything with him on the cover. I want to though. I feel like it's more interesting to see them both. They are so different. Maybe if I get the job, I'll think of a way to use him."

"What if they're the same person?" Cindy said, thinking of the story the shopkeeper told them about both of the figures. "One ushers the soul out of the body and into the afterlife, and one ushers you into heaven. One smokes a pipe, the other a blunt, or whatever that thing is. That sounds similar enough to me. Maybe that was why they were joined together into one sculpture instead of two separate statues."

"Holy shit," Jack said, the connections were being made in his head. Pistons fired off, but his voice remained neutral. "What if that's something that makes him evil. His disguise is Papa Legba, and he uses it to trick people into letting their guard down, but Baron Samedi is who he really is. Just when the story gets good he changes, and Robert Taylor has to fight off a demon. We got a story here!"

"That's pretty evil," Cindy agreed. "If the devil showed up as St. Peter and all of a sudden I was in hell, I would be pretty pissed off, wouldn't you?"

"Damn right, I would."

"Who's Robert?"

"He's the main character."

"Ah," she said. "Poor guy."

Jack made a third note beneath the other two, saved the document to his desktop, and turned off the computer.

"You sure you don't want to stay?"

"No," Jack said. "Gotta know when to put down the pen."

"Okay, I'm going to get changed."

"I'll watch," Jack said allowing a childlike excitement to change his voice.

Cindy giggled as he chased her downstairs, friskily poking and pinching.

When they left the room, a dull shine emanated like heat off embers from the place on the table where the pewter statue rested.

They never made it to the hole in the wall that serves the best pizza in the universe. They fell asleep without any clothes. Just after midnight Jack stirred awake. He tried to go back to sleep but something wouldn't let him, so he slid on his pajama pants and went upstairs. The gong of his computer was much louder than he expected, and he had a tiny panic attack, hoping that he didn't wake Cindy. Waiting for the desktop to load, he looked out the window. He thought of that night a few weeks earlier when the man was in his back yard. Luckily there was no one else down this stretch of the road for miles. He saw something floating in the river behind the house, a log or an animal. It got caught on something and stopped. It stayed there for a few second. Jack watched it carefully. Then it moved forward with the current, out of site.

The computer screen darkened to the user screen. Jack typed Simpsonsdidit1st and pulled up the file labeled KingOfEvil. He wanted to work on the hat some more, so he searched the Internet for "Voodoo hats" and scrolled through. Nothing struck a chord with him so he checked his notes. He added the word "bones" to his search, and again nothing came as an inspiration. He scrolled and previewed, scrolled and previewed. It was all the same. Most of the pictures showed some version of the top hat with chicken bones and a tiny human skull, or cartoonish Halloween costumes on ample-breasted women showing off their painted faces and cleavage. One constant throughout was that there was always some sort of skeletal visual. *Well bones are definitely the way to go it seems.* Then a picture of a Lego version of Baron came up as he scrolled and he nearly missed it. He stopped and enlarged the photo. *He's even got the white hands. Nice touch Lego.*

He wondered what would be under the tuxedo in a real

life situation. All of these pictures had people who painted their faces and hands to look like skeletons. *Would that make their bodies skeletons too? Would they have organs? Like a heart? Where is the heart located? In the chest. Protected all kinds of bones. So what if the hat was wrapped in a ribcage.*

Jack pulled up pictures of skeletons and ribcages until he found one with which he was comfortable manipulating. Then he deleted all the unnecessary bones—the spine, sternum, etc.—and added a brown shade to the cream-colored picture.

"It's not enough to look dirty," he whispered. "They need to be cracked."

So he added fractures to the bones. He edited one of the ribs in the middle to look like it had broken and dangled from the rest of the bone. He made his cursor a small circular eraser and used it to take out parts of the ribs. This gave the bones a serrated edge, like a steak knife.

That's the stuff.

Jack added the fiery shading to the ribs and wrapped the image around the hat on his cover. He used a red color tool to add a few bloodstains. He added a dangling drop on one of the bottom ribs over the brim. After a few size and erasing adjustments, Jack was finally happy with the top hat.

"That's what it needed."

He leaned back, proud of his work.

Still not evil enough though.

He caught a glimpse of the pewter sculpture in the light of the computer screen. He referred back to the notes where he typed simply, "they are the same person."

Jack opened the wedding photos again. He searched for old man, any would do. Finally he found one that wasn't wearing a tuxedo. It didn't really matter because he would be putting overalls and a yellow plaid shirt on the man. *Good thing he's bald.* Jack didn't think it would matter but he didn't want the old man to appear to be of any definite race either, and hair would obviously make that more difficult.

Once the clothing and corncob pipe were layered over the man, he found a picture of a cane. He added the triskele at the top and darkened its color to match the pipe. He added the feathers, then took them away, then added the feathers back and left them. He added the cane to the old man, and added the old man to the background of the King.

"This is what it needed," Jack whispered.

Jack wanted to add an effect that made it obvious that Papa was changing into Baron. He didn't want to join them together, their faces each taking up one side of a head, because that had been done to death. He noticed that the old man was too close to the fire. *Or maybe that's just how big the fire is. Either way that would be really fucking hot. Like the night we spent in Vegas a few summers ago. Jesus, that city is the dog breath of America. It was so hot and muggy, you could literally see the heat boiling up off the road.*

"Probably like that fire would be doing to Papa Legba."

He scrolled through the effects toolbar and chose one that he often used to distort background images. It made whatever he clicked on become a little bit wavy, including Papa. While he had the effect toolbar pulled down, he highlighted the layer with Papa, and added a black windblown affect and angled it so that it looked like a violent blast of air vaporized Papa, blowing his remains in the direction of Baron Samedi. It created the exact visual that Jack needed. The picture looked as if while Papa Legba walked away from the surrounding fire, he changed into Baron Samedi. The effect gave motion to the cover. The eye naturally started at the center with Papa Legba, and the windblown particles drew the eye frontward and to the left where Baron Samedi menacingly stood, glaring into the eyes of the audience. Jack imagined how he would paint this cover when the time inevitably came to that. He'd let the paint dry then outline Papa Legba in thick charcoal. He'd get the effect by smearing the black dust with his hand toward Baron. Simple as that.

"This is the one," Jack whispered.

Jack noticed the pewter statue again. It wasn't as white as he remembered. It was darker now. That could easily have been the light in the attic. The sun pouring through tree branches and the windows was all he ever used aside from the monitor's glow. At the moment the statue just looked dirty in the blue-white shine from the screen. He blew on it, hoping to loosen the dust that settled in Papa and Baron's features. Nothing changed. He laid the statue back down.

The clock in the top right-hand corner of the monitor said it was four fifteen. Despite Jack's racing heart, he was exhausted. He heard a noise like a piece of rock chipping off the whole. Jack picked the statue back up and saw nothing out of the ordinary with the figures holding their stony positions. Only now, a thin, shallow crack divided the two. It was almost perfectly straight and dead center of the base. Thinking it was a hair, Jack swiped at it with his finger. The crack remained, almost spiteful, between the two carvings. It was as if Papa Legba and Baron Samedi were having a silent argument, and they had created a line of demarcation like juveniles.

Jack crept back downstairs, trying not to wake Cindy. The floorboards creaked, but Jack managed to get out of his pants and back into bed without waking her.

This is the one that's going to change our lives.

"Well hey there, sleepy head," Cindy called from the kitchen. She wore one of Jack's football jerseys, a large number twelve stood boldly with tribal texture over her bare legs. The name on the back was FAN, and if she wore it that way to a game, the twelfth man wouldn't be the loudest in the league anymore. Maybe they would, but they'd have to pick their collective jaw off the floor first. "I'm starving, I cooked everything we have. We can't miss dinner again. Not if we're going to be doing that all night."

"Noted," he smiled and kissed her.

"Could you make us something to drink? I'm almost ready."

"Thank you for cooking." Jack did as she asked, orange juice for him, chocolate milk for her. "And thank you for wearing that. I'm positive when Seahawks made them, that's exactly what they envisioned."

"Whatever I can do to help out the team." Cindy did a cute curtsey.

They walked to the living room once everything was prepared, and Jack turned on the television.

"Do you remember eating at the dinner table when you were little?" Cindy asked.

"Yeah, we all hated it."

"We did too," she said, and swallowed the eggs. "I bet that's the next thing to go. First it was landlines, next is the dining room."

"Everyone we know just goes out on the back porch when there's an occasion. That's where the big tables are. I bet you're right. Say goodbye to bulky tables, folks. It's patio furniture and living room floors from here on out."

Cindy laughed. "Do you love it here?"

"I'm surprised at how much I do."

"I do too. I don't ever want to leave." She put down the fork and grabbed his hand.

Jack was glad that she was happy. After everything she went through over the last two years, he was genuinely scared that she wouldn't be able to recover. He was relieved that she was able to make it out without growing bitter. He still saw the scar on her stomach every time they made love, and when he did another fragment of his heart chipped off and fell into a void.

Two years ago, the company Cindy worked for—the University Blvd. Physical Therapy Institute—experienced an overwhelming amount of employee turnover in the span of two months. Everyone she had started the job with was suddenly gone. The people who were left grew bitter toward management. The hours became erratic and long. The therapists grew tired and constantly more irritable with each other.

Through it all, Cindy managed to keep a strong composure. Even while training new hires and maintaining patients of her own. Even while working fourteen-hour days. Even while pregnant. She couldn't even bask in the joy of being a mother, because the job took all it could from her. Her time. Her energy. But when she was home, Jack and the baby were all hers. She hadn't told anyone at work yet. She was only a few weeks into the game. Jack and their parents were the only people who knew. Maybe Tom, but she wasn't completely certain about that. She thought it would be fun to see how long her co-workers would wait before someone asked. No one ever did though. They never got the chance.

The patient's name was Tiffany Maxey. A knife fight with her boyfriend's wife severed her medial collateral ligament. Only Tiffany fancied it up by calling it a head-on collision when she appeared in the lobby area of the University Blvd. Institute. Eventually Cindy understood that lie. No one wants her garbage strewn out into the street for everyone to gawk at and pick through. Every dog wants to be a good boy and every person wanted to get the trophy and a gold star. Cindy never truly forgave her though. Not because of the lie. The lie she could sympathize with. What Cindy couldn't get past was everything else that happened.

One day Tiffany's ride came to the Institute, blaring the

horn and yelling at the outside of the building. Tiffany's leg was still under an ice pack when the receptionist walked outside to calm the driver down as best she could. The man in the pickup truck told the receptionist to pull Tiffany out to the parking lot and put her in the car. Apparently, he had shit to do. He continued honking even when the receptionist walked back into the building.

Cindy asked who he was there to pick up. When Tiffany found out it was her, the screaming, honking lunatic was there to see, her only reply was, "He can wait," as she folded her arms between her weighty breasts and her gut.

The noise became too much. Cindy stopped the electrolysis machine and, with help from one of the trainees, walked Tiffany to the car. The honking continued over the shouts of, "About fucking time," and "Are they serving food today," and, of course, "I've got shit to do." Even as Cindy and the trainee carried the patient across the sidewalk the horn and screams continued.

Cindy pulled the door handle. It was locked. *If only during his sophomoric bullshit he had just unlocked the goddamn door,* Cindy thought thousands of times afterward. She and the trainee helped Tiffany into the beat-up truck just as an equally beat-up sedan slammed into the tailgate. Cindy tried to back away from the truck, but because he was parked in a handicap space at the corner of the parking lot, there was a curb behind her. Cindy fell onto the grass. A pain grew low in her stomach. She clutched it, breathing heavily hoping to abate the pain. Trailer park screaming filled the parking lot, as the sedans driver left her place behind the wheel, screaming. Cindy saw that therapists were coming out of the building. A cacophony of ignorant swears and attempts at calming the riled up hick berated her ears. A tire on the opposite side of the pickup popped, hissing as it deflated. The back end of the truck dropped a few inches. The back glass of the pickup shattered.

"And you got that bitch with you, too, don't cha?" the violent woman screamed.

Cindy heard the woman making her way around the car. The other therapists tried to stop the woman. *If they had only let her go she would have avoided me altogether.* But they grabbed her shirtsleeve. She yanked away from them and tripped over the sidewalk.

The knife went deep into Cindy's stomach. She looked down as the blood rushed out of her around the blade. The screaming woman got off the ground and kicked the handle of the knife as she made her way into the passenger side of the truck.

Cindy woke in the hospital. Jack was holding her hand. It was the last time he would for nearly a year. Jack's and her parents came to visit her. No one from work, but they never knew about the baby. When she came back to work a week later, nothing happened. No "welcome back." No "we all pitched in and bought you a cake." No "let me get the door for you, Cindy." Nothing. She was shoved right back into her fourteen-hour a day schedule. It was the same bitter people working the same bitter, dead end jobs.

Cindy's hatred grew, compounding over and over after that. Jack did his best to make things better, but it never worked. He bought her flowers, made her dinner, made sure the house was always clean. None of it mattered to her. He stopped trying when she slapped him one night at his computer over an argument he can never remember. She had never done that before. He wanted to leave. Somehow he felt responsible. That's not why he stayed. He stayed because more than anything, he loved her.

The two of them rarely spoke in that year between the accident and the decision to move. Nothing seemed to be right. After months of sleeping on the couch Jack finally stopped her at the kitchen sink and asked what she wanted to do. She just stared through the back window, washing her hands at the sink. He walked up to her and lightly held her by the arms. She shrugged him off, crying, and left the house. She did that a lot those days. She'd find herself driving around the city, or on the interstate, not knowing where she was going. Eventually she would find herself in bed, alone and crying.

Jack stopped showing her the paintings. He took pictures of them though. Deep down he knew that this would eventually be over, and she would want to see what he'd been doing.

The Thursday before Easter the year before they moved, Jack picked her up from work. Her car was being repaired and the idea of being in a car with anyone else for that long literally made her want to vomit. She cried the entire way. Instead of stopping at the dealership, Jack kept driving right through Gulfport until he hit the beach. He turned off the headlights. The sky was the color of fire. Neither of them said a word as the seconds spun out into ten full, excruciating minutes.

"What are—"

"Goddamn it, Cin." He didn't scream. He just said it. "I can't stand this. I hate that you're so unhappy, Cindy. I hate seeing you cry. I'm so sorry this happened, and I'm sorry I was so utterly powerless to help. I need you to help me now. I can't keep this up. You have to move on with me. I can't see you for three hours in a car and all you do is cry. You don't talk to me anymore. We haven't so much as touched in over a month, and even longer than that if you don't count the time I brushed into you when you were doing the laundry. I shouldn't have to remember what happened at six twenty-five one random night thirty-three days ago. I hate telling you I love you, and you say nothing back. You just look at me with cold...nothing. I'd rather you hate me for not being there. I'd rather you tell me you hated me for not having a 'real job' where I have to deal with strangers like that every day. I'd rather you blame it all on me. I would gladly welcome it over this cruel silence. If you want out, then let's get out. You can have whatever you want. We'll end it tomorrow. If you want to fix it, then goddamn it, help me fix it. I know it hurts. I know it was the worst thing that ever happened. But we have to do something. I'm tired of it. I'm sick of being nothinged to death. You don't even wear your ring anymore." The cab of the Xterra was brutally quiet. The silence took up every available inch of space in the cab, threatening to suffocate them. "Do you want out of this city?"

"Yes." She was crying, but not tears brought on by what happened or the crippling depression that followed. She was crying because of what she was doing to her husband, for the year she wasted as he stuck by her like no one else could. She was crying because she missed him. She missed who they were together. He never hurt her. He only stood, agonizingly helpful, watching as the city in which she studied, worked, and prospered slowly killed everything she loved. Her job. The baby. Her husband.

"Then let's leave," Jack pleaded. "Let's never come back. We're going to get you a new car today, and we're going to start over in a new house, with a new job. And we're never coming back."

They did exactly that. Jack paid for the repair to Cindy's clutch, and traded in the old car for the Kia Soul now parked under their house. Jack paid for the difference with the money he had made over the past year. The car was a vibrant yellow. That was a happy color. It radiated life. Cindy imagined herself as a black tree with blue leaves. She needed the yellow to make herself green and brown. Yellow became her favorite color.

Jack was her yellow.

That morning on the couch as the two of them ate breakfast together, all Cindy saw was perfectly endless yellow.

"I don't want to leave either," Jack told her. He squeezed her hand back, not lifting it from the couch cushion. He was so happy things were different now. "Guess what."

"What?"

"I think I finished the cover."

"What? When?"

"Last night."

"No," Cindy said, dropping her head. Her ponytail swooped around her onto her shoulder. "I know what you were doing last night. You weren't working."

"I woke up in the middle of the night. I had a weird dream about the King."

"You dreamed about your own bad guy?"

"Yeah," he says. "I always do with ones like that. It means it's a good one."

"So you woke up and finished?"

"I tried to go back to sleep first. I certainly was in no hurry to leave the naked lady."

"Well, can I see it?"

"Sure," Jack said, adding another forkful of eggs to the sausage in his mouth. "Want to eat first?"

She thought about it. "I think so."

Jack laughed quietly. No one made him laugh like she did.

"So were you naked up there?"

"I had pants on."

"So you put pants on to go upstairs," she said, chewing her food at the same time. "Then before you came back to bed, you took your pants off."

"Is there a problem, madam?"

"It just seems weird that you put them on to begin with, then weird that you took them back off. Together it's just chaos."

"Well, I don't want to get used to working naked. What

if your parents come over? And I didn't want to get back in bed clothed and be overdressed. I didn't want you to look silly when you got up as the only one naked. Just looking out for you."

"You're such a damn gentleman." She bit off another piece of bacon. "I love you, Jack."

"I love you too, Cin."

Jack loaded the picture on his computer. When the image of the King flashed onto the screen Cindy inadvertently rose on her tiptoes and stepped back.

"Wow, Jack," she breathed. "This is the best thing you've ever done."

"That may be so, but is he evil enough for you?"

"Oh yeah," Cindy said. "Nice job with the ribs. That's fucking terrifying."

"That's what I wanted."

"They look like they came out of a little kid."

"I didn't even notice that." Jack leaned in to look closer.

"He looks so sinister. That is a person who is evil. Bad for bad's sake. I can't wait for you to finish. I want to see how you paint this one."

"I've already been thinking about it. Not much. I don't want to get my hopes up."

"No one is going to beat this," Cindy assured him. "I think it's okay to expect something good this time."

"Well I still have to figure out a way to put the words on

there. I guess that's what I'll do today while you're having a blast at work."

"That feels good." She wrapped her arms around his neck and fell against him. "I'm going to have *fun* at work."

"I'm just glad you still love doing it. You're great at it."

"We're both great at what we do." She kissed him. "I have to get ready for work."

Jack scoffed. "You always say that."

Cindy laughed. "Gotta pay the bills."

"You know, if you want, I can get you a jersey when I go there this week."

"Nah," she said, walking down the stairs to the bedroom. She took the jersey off just as she left the view of the door. "That's more of a man's game. I never played it so I don't know the rules. Unless it's cute, then you can get one. And if it has plenty of cup holders."

Jack pulled his archived fonts and let them load while he went downstairs to clean up after breakfast. He felt good about today. He always felt good when the picture was finished and there was nothing left but the words.

Cindy entered the building using her brand new card key. She was already used to the day-to-day of the new job. She introduced herself to every new face she passed walking down the corridor to the gym. Today was extra special, because she would be getting her first patient. Her name was Beth Rosenburg, and given the woman's age, Cindy assumed it was short for Bethel, not Bethany. She would be there at nine, right when the facility opened. That was thirty minutes away. The lights took a moment to hitch before filling the gym with life. Samantha was so close behind her that Cindy couldn't believe she hadn't heard her footsteps.

Cindy flinched when the door swung open behind her. "Whoa, you scared me."

"You're not nervous, are you?" Samantha asked. "First new patient. Big day."

"I'm actually very excited."

"She's actually been here before. This is her third hip."

"What does she do?"

"I think she's an FBI agent."

They laughed.

Jennifer, the receptionist, walked through the door then in a hint of a hurry. She had been there to help Cindy with both of her interviews and as Cindy waited in the lobby to meet Dr. Douglass, Jennifer had struck up a lengthy conversation about her last job. "Sorry I'm late. I got you guys a donut."

"Thank you," Cindy said. Her stomach was full from breakfast, so she took the paper bag Jennifer handed her and dropped it in her purse. "That's sweet."

"We just got here, too," Samantha told her. "I'll get the sign-in sheet ready for you."

"Do we need to clock in or anything?" Cindy asked.

"No," Samantha said. "We're paid by the year. They sort of assume we show up when we're scheduled. They're really strict about it though. The guy you replaced was fired for missing three days without an excuse."

"And he was an ass," Jennifer added.

"If that's the worst thing about the job," Cindy said. "Then I'll just show up when I'm scheduled."

"I forgot yesterday was day one for you," Jennifer said. "How was it?"

"It was so great," Cindy said, taking two tablets from the charging cradle. She handed one to Samantha. "I love it here already. Is the user login for the tablets the one with the W in front or the one that's just a number?"

Samantha looked up, clearly having to think about the answer. "Hang on, I've done it so many times I can't remember which." She opened her tablet and logged into the database. "It's the W. Weird how that happens."

Cindy logged in and where yesterday there was a white page with "*no current patient activity*" typed across the center, there was now the bold typed "Rosenburg, Beth – hip repl."

"There she is," Cindy announced with pride. "My first patient." She tapped the name. The tablet loaded Beth's information and on the right hand side of the screen, there was a link to a calendar that had every day's exercise regime listed in order for her. Ninety percent of the paperwork she would have had to do three weeks earlier had already been finished. There was even a blue link for each day for adjustments to the schedule if Mrs. Rosenburg wasn't progressing at a normal rate. "I love this job."

"Any questions before the day begins?" Samantha asked, laying a sign-in sheet on the counter between them.

"Could you walk me through the steps of using the electrolysis? I know it's really easy, but I'm used to a complicated rig and I don't want to screw it up."

"Why, certainly," Samantha said, doing her best Curly impression.

Samantha walked her through the simplified steps. Cindy had been taught to use two separate machines. One applied the ice or coolant and the other added electricity. This machine had one simple, nylon band with four electrodes on the inside to adjust around the patient's afflicted area. The machine could then add heat or coolant depending on what the patient needed.

"Now there are interchangeable bands depending on what the injury requires," Samantha explained. "Some of them like the shoulder and hip attachments don't have the electrodes. That's just because it'd be gross. For now, that's okay, because Mrs. Rosenburg doesn't like the electricity anyway."

"Does she come in here a lot?"

"She's kind of a regular. She spends a few months a year in here. She fell asleep at the wheel and hit a tree. Since then she falls down a lot. Tries to do more than she should. She's a sweet lady though. Everyone here loves her."

"Good," Cindy said. "I've had troublesome patients before."

"We all have. Luckily we have plenty of security."

"Your patients are on their way in," Jennifer told them from the front desk.

"That's so cool," Cindy said. "This is like the Cadillac of PT jobs."

"That is what they listed it as online," Samantha laughed.

The doors to the gym opened and a security guard ushered in an old woman using a walker, and a young black boy wearing a Dolphins tee shirt with a wrist brace on one hand and his mother on the other. Cindy thought of her old patient, Mark, with that dirty black cap. She smiled, glad that she wasn't homesick. The old woman had salt and pepper color hair that was once black as night. Her skin was the color of desert sand.

"You must be Mrs. Rosenburg," Cindy said.

"*Miss* Rosenburg, darlin'," the older woman said. It was only a few notches below yelling. "No man could ever rope this cattle." She cackled like a madwoman. Her voice carried an accent that Cindy had never heard before. Mrs. Rosenburg leaned to one side and caught herself on her walker. "I'm only messin' with yaw, darlin'. They told me yaw is the new girl. That right?"

"I'm new to this place, yes ma'am," Cindy said, moving closer to catch Mrs. Rosenburg when she inevitably fell. "My name is Cindy."

"Well, Cindy, I hope yaw not mindin' a little fun at work."

"Of course not," Cindy assured her. The woman's laughter was infectious and Cindy couldn't stop grinning from ear to ear as the woman led her to the plinth tables.

"Where we wantin' to start now, sweetie?"

"Let's start out with some stretches first." Cindy helped Mrs. Rosenburg onto the plinth. She turned to Samantha with wide eyes, trying to hold in the laughter.

Have fun, Samantha mouthed.

Jack worked for twenty minutes trying to match fonts with his picture before he decided that the only way he would be happy is if he drew the text himself. It was a much more tedious affair, but part of being a perfectionist was doing the work perfectly. He managed to weave the title into the oranges and yellows from the flames. It stood out perfectly without taking too much attention away from the King himself. The letters were simultaneously flaming and melting on the screen. He etched the words, "written by Joe McDermott" into the ground between Papa and Baron. *I'm finished,* Jack thought. *I think she's right. This is the best thing I've ever done.*

"I'm going to paint this one," he told the empty attic. "Even if he doesn't choose it."

Jack searched the house for his supplies and found that he was out of black paint and only had an eleven by seventeen canvas. *Well, I'll have to go to a craft store it seems.*

Just then his phone rang.

"Hey baby," Cindy said jubilantly from the other end of the line.

"How's work today? Everything you dreamed of?"

"It's better than that. Why don't you come to town? We'll meet up for dinner since we didn't get to last night."

"That sounds good to me. Want to meet in a couple

hours?"

"Okay, but don't be too late. I'm starving."

"What time is it?"

"Five thirty."

"Oh, damn," Jack shook his head to take away the shock. "Okay, yeah I'll leave now."

"Why? What's wrong?"

"I spent all day working. It feels like noon. I didn't even eat lunch. Now that I'm aware of that, all I want to do is pump myself full of pizza."

"Okay," she laughed. "I'll meet you there in a half hour?"

"I'll be there."

"Hey baby," Cindy kissed him good morning and continued brushing her teeth. She left her embroidered polo shirt on the bed to avoid getting toothpaste on it. "Your hair's pretty crazy. How'd you sleep?"

"Good, I think," he said, wiping the sleep out of his eyes.

"Are you alright? You haven't been sleeping well since we moved in."

"I think I'm just worried about the presentation tomorrow." Jack stepped behind Cindy and wrapped his arms around her waist. "I have to work on it today. If I make you dinner will you go over it with me when you get home."

"Of course."

He kissed her between her neck and shoulder, and as always, chills ran all over her. "Do we need anything other than breakfast food from the store?"

"Mustard," Cindy answered. "Mouthwash, and I'm expecting a visit soon so I'll need some tampons. Remember which ones?"

"Pink and orange sport kind," he called from the bedroom. He put on jeans instead of pajama pants for the first time all week.

"Atta boy."

"It's on the list."

"What else do you have?"

"Mustard, mouthwash, pink and orange sport kind, breakfast, black paint, canvases, and Cherry Coke Zero."

"You running out of paint stuff?"

"Yeah, I've been doing a lot of nudes lately."

"With black?" She giggled.

"That's why I'm out of the large canvases."

"Shut up," she playfully punched his arm. "Oh, can you get some sandwich meat? I think I ran out of everything making food today."

"They don't have fancy high class cafeteria food at that place?"

"No, can you believe that shit?" She spat and rinsed.

"It's like they don't even know who you are."

"I should quit."

Jack kissed her goodbye, and walked down the wooden steps to his car. He saw the river running behind the house and pulled out his phone to add a fishing pole to the list. He was looking down at his phone when he saw someone standing in front of him wearing all black. He jumped backwards, his breath escaping him completely. The corner post under the house was all that stood before him. "Shit," he whispered. "Working too hard this week."

He put his phone back in his pocket without adding anything to his list. When he returned home an hour and a half later he kept his eye out for anything or anyone that shouldn't be in their driveway, there was one thing he brought back that wasn't on the list. He came inside and put the bottle of liquid melatonin on the bathroom sink.

Jack packed his duffle bag and the bottle was the last thing inside. He wanted it on top before he boarded the plane early the next morning. He hated flying, and with this past week of barely sleeping, he didn't think the medicine would be necessary, but he wanted it there just in case. Jack spent the rest of the day ironing the lumps out of his presentation. He ran it forward and backwards, and when Cindy got home from work, they ate and he walked her through his presentation, because if he could do it over dinner, he could do it over lunch.

"It's great, baby," Cindy said, genuinely impressed with her husband's work. She looked back and forth at the printouts of the cover in her hands. "We're going to get this. And this will mark the project that allowed you to never work with stubborn little dickheads ever again. Let's go to bed. I'll clean all this up in the morning after you leave."

When he was finished, Jack took his wife by the hand and led her to their bedroom.

❖ ❖ ❖

Jack woke in the middle of the night again. The drapes were separated, and the trees waved shadows into the bedroom. Cindy was face down, snoring into a pillow. The small of her back was exposed, so he covered her up. After ten minutes of unsuccessfully getting back to sleep he stood from the bed, put on his pants, and walked to the attic. He opened his computer and opened the KingOfEvil file. In the light of the computer monitor, he sketched a rough outline of the King in pencil. For five minutes the lead never left the canvas. He had drawn a thousand sketches just like it but never so easily, so quickly.

He wanted to start etching the outline of Papa Legba in the background, but he somehow couldn't get the pencil to move in that direction. It was like he was holding onto a piece of metal near a magnet. He had the idea in his head and on the computer screen but every time he motioned toward the right side of the page, his hand moved right back.

When he was finished he put the pencil down. *That's a good place to pick up Sunday.* He thought, groggily. He put the easel back in the corner and the canvas facing the wall under his computer table. Jack felt like he had completed a marathon. His breaths were deep and loud. He nearly fell down the stairs when the computer powered down. He stopped in the bathroom. He didn't flush so he wouldn't wake Cindy. *I'll do it in the morning. It's yellow anyway. If it's yellow, let it mellow.* His pants slid off with no effort. He was out before his head hit the pillow.

❖ ❖ ❖

Tom called him an hour later. "You up?"

"I don't want to go to school," Jack's scratchy voice mumbled into the phone.

"Rise and shine, Teddy Bear. I'm only five minutes away. We gotta be at the airport before sunrise."

Jack snorted and cleared his throat. "Okay, I'll meet you outside."

Jack stumbled back into his pajama pants and hefted his duffle bag into the living room. He poured mouthwash into his mouth and almost immediately spit it into the sink. "Too early," he groaned and flushed the toilet.

"You up, baby," Cindy mumbled from her side of the bed.

"Yeah, I gotta go," he whispered, kneeling beside her.

"Don't go," she said.

"I have to. For the good of the land."

"Weirdo," she groaned. "Come here." She pulled him closer and kissed him. "I love you, Jack."

"I love you too, Cin."

"Do you want me to walk you out?" She held onto him, refusing to let go.

"No," Jack whispered. "I don't want my agent seeing my hot wife naked."

"Shut up."

"Besides, I think you're already back to sleep." He waited for a reply. None came, so he picked up his wallet, keys, and duffle bag. He made sure to lock the door. He was too tired to do anything else. He didn't notice the noise of the dead leaves breaking behind him. He only heard the wind in the trees. The noise stopped once Tom's headlights crept up the driveway.

Everything from driving to the airport, waiting in all the lines, and actually boarding the plane happened in a haze. He did remember to take a dropper full of melatonin before leaving his bag at the front desk. He sat in the window seat near the wing. He could barely keep his eyes open. He didn't want to miss the take off. That was the best part. It was the maintaining altitude that freaked him out. That's where the turbulence waited for unimportant planes to knock around. Tom must have known he was fading fast, because he wasn't talking. Jack rested his forehead on the cool window. The melatonin was starting to kick in.

I must be losing it. He thought.

Thin gray lines, like marks from charcoal, formed on the runway below his window.

That's my drawing.

The heathered lines formed a crude sketch of the King on the runway. The lines maneuvered not around on the paved street, but up off the ground. Standing on the runway was the ashy gray outline of Jack's greatest work. It stepped toward him. Jack saw the distant trees through the drawing. It stared at Jack. Its head tilted forward, the weight of the ribcage tilted the hat on his head. The drawing's wild eyes honed in on Jack, staring though him.

Jack could see every detail he had put on the canvas. The symbol on the coat pocket. The ribcage wrapped around the top hat. The eerie grimace on the King's face. It was all there, somehow alive on the tarmac. There were blinking lights lining the runway. Jack could see them through his outline of the villain.

The King ran toward the plane and leapt up to Jack's window. Instead of hearing contact, Jack watched the powdery gray lines poof into clouds.

"Shit," he said, fighting off the haze.

"It's okay, buddy," Tom said. "Just get some sleep."

"No," Jack said feebly. "N-n."

He trailed off, closing his eyes. He was dreaming before the plane left the ground. Worst of all, he missed his favorite part of the flight.

"Jack, this is Joe. Joe, this is Jack." Joe's agent was a creepy man. His beard was sad and patchy and gray. He wore a suit that was much too tight, and accentuated his fat, hairy neck. His teeth and fingernails were the same shade of yellow, and Jack guessed he could probably open a can of soup with either. His smile was made mostly of gums, and he didn't open his eyes all the way.

"Great to meet you, Joe." Jack was suddenly annoyed with himself. In all the research he had done, piecing together every bit of information he could find about voodoo to create the man's villain, he never once thought to look up Joe McDermott. He was as underwhelming as his agent was overwhelming. He wore his hair in the same fade that every guy of the day wore his hair. He was clean-shaven and wore horn-rimmed glasses. He was glad Tom came with him, because Joe was so forgettable that if Jack went to the bathroom he may get lost on the way back. Aside from the fact that his teeth looked like they were fighting to be at the front of his mouth, there was nothing that separated Joe from anyone else on the planet. "This is Tom Dwyer. You've been emailing one another from what I hear."

"Only positive things," Joe said. He was British, and that gave Jack the much needed something with which to connect him.

Jack sat at the table across from the agent. Positioning was important. It wouldn't help his cause much to have to hover over the table to point out different features of the cover art. Sure the agent would have to see, but the agent wouldn't need to be convinced. Jack laid his folder on the ground, propped against his chair leg.

"This place has the best crab in the world," Joe told them.

"I love crab," Jack said. He'd never had crab. He never liked seafood in general. God put them in the water to hide them from us. That's why cows are so slow, and chickens can't fly. That's his opinion on it. But as they tell you when you go to an audition, whatever they ask you to do, you say yes. If you can't do it, learn how.

"Great," Joe said. "I went ahead and ordered for us."

Ballsy move, although it is expensive. Jack thought.

"Should we get into it?" Joe's agent said.

"I'm okay with that," Jack told him.

The waiter brought their drinks and told them that their food would be right out.

"So what do you have for me, Jack?" Joe leaned back in his chair.

Jack picked up his folder and untied the thread keeping it sealed. Inside there were only five pieces of paper. Just like there always was. The first was an outline. That was for Jack. The second two were full-color printouts of the front cover turned face down. He never gave it away too soon. Timing is everything. Those were for the writer and agent. The last two were the full cover—front, back with filler text, and spine.

"I talked to my wife about his project when I finished the first draft of the cover," Jack said, launching into his speech. He found that he didn't need his outline. "I told her the title and showed her the draft. She listened to what I didn't like about it, and then made me realize what I should change. She said that evil wasn't just bad. Anyone can be bad. But people who are bad can be corrected. They can be talked down and convinced to be good. But people who are evil, they're bad just for the sake of being bad. There's nothing at stake for them, but spreading more evil." Jack handed Joe and the agent the printouts of the cover.

Joe rested his elbow on the chair, rubbing his chin with his hand. There was an obvious change in his posture in that moment.

"How many really evil villains are there?" Jack asked. "Maybe The Joker. Randall Flagg. Voldemort. Not too many others come to mind. I think we have a golden opportunity to join in the ranks of evil with this character. There's already this idea behind who the character is with the numerous portrayals of the voodoo priest with dreadlocks in a tuxedo and top hat. Just like The Joker, but when that movie came out, The Joker became this phenomena that everyone had to be a part of. I don't remember going to a Halloween party without at least one person in dirty green hair and face paint that year and the next. That's what I want for the King. People already have the idea in their minds what he's capable of doing. We just have to knock it out of the park. What I've done is taken two very important figures in the Voodoo religion, and—"

"It's a religion?" The agent asked.

"Yeah," Jack said. "It's basically a more fun version of Catholicism."

"I didn't know that."

"Not many people think of it that way," Jack explained.

"I was raised Catholic," Joe said.

"Well this should be fun for you," Jack chuckled. "But it's more than just face paint and sacrificing chickens. Now the old man you see is taken from the Voodoo gatekeeper. St. Peter for the Catholics. Only he is depicted as an older man with a cane in more secular venues. He's name is Papa Legba. But for our purpose he's just a mask. For this guy," Jack leaned in close to Joe and held a finger above his villain, "this is Baron Samedi. Or the Grim Reaper if you prefer our Catholic comparison. The fourth horseman. He is charming, conniving, drunk, horny, and of course, the ruler of the dead."

"Yeah," Joe said, not taking his eyes off the paper.

Jack put down his outline. He decided to skip the background information, and slid the printouts of the full cover to the center of the table. He leaned in a little closer and lowered his voice. "Now what I'm going for is someone who cannot be talked down, who can't be reasoned with. His skin is gray, it's not painted. He's the reason people paint their face and hands. The rib cage on his hat is small, the implication being that he killed a child and is wearing his bones as an accessory. Not just that, but he's carved ridges out of them to make them sharp. He has the staff as he is typical to carry. It's his tool for hypnosis and hexing, but ours comes with something a little extra. I put this mallet head on the end as a way of bringing down his victims."

"What's this?" Joe pointed to the box dangling from the King's belt.

"That's where he keeps his heart," Jack explained. The tinge of doubt crept into his mind. *Fuck, I forgot to fix it.* "It's a steel box. I was thinking the legend could be that he needs a heart to get out of the box, but we reveal that he takes the heart from his victims to live longer."

Joe sounded a noncommittal, "Hmm…"

"It's an idea," Jack said.

"And what's the symbol on it?" Joe tapped the paper.

"It's called a veve. It's the symbol of Baron Samedi. Papa Legba has one too."

"Have you ever done anything like this before?" Joe asked.

"I've done covers, but never a full book."

"Well, I only ask because with graphic novels the covers are usually a preview of the artwork on the inside the book. This is an actual picture. The old guy seems like a drawing but your Baron Samedi is real."

"I actually thought about that." Jack hadn't thought about that. He only said it to give himself more time to think without showing his hand. He cleared his throat and paused as if thinking how to properly word what he was about to say. Nothing came to mind, so he just started. "Baron

Samedi is of the Lwa spirits, which means he's basically a saint. He's responsible for overseeing the dead, he even has the ability to reject the death of a person if he sees fit." Then it hit Jack like an almost physical surge of momentum. He suddenly became more excited. "So I was thinking he's more than just a human. So we probably shouldn't draw him the same way we draw the *people* in this book. He should be on a higher level. So if we keep him looking more real until you finally decide to take him down, it'll show him as immortal. We can fade him into a drawing as he becomes weaker and weaker with each volume."

Joe's eyebrows went up. "Now that's interesting."

Jack's leg bounced with excitement. *Reel him back in, Jackie boy.* Joe and his agent couldn't tell that he was obviously proud of the bullshit he just sent their way, but Tom knew right away. "I'm sure when we pan out the story, we can come up with some other ideas. Those are just a few I thought up."

The waiter brought their food, breaking the silence at the table. Jack noticed the wide gauges in her ear lobes, and the tattoo of a bird on her neck. "Wow that's cool," she told the table. "Who's is that?"

"It's his," Tom pointed to Jack. "He's an artist."

"Is it a movie?" She asked.

"It's going to be a graphic novel," Tom told her.

"That's awesome," she said. "If you guys need anything else just let me know."

"You got it," Tom said.

The four of them fell into a conversation about Jack's career—what he had done, where he went to school, how long he lived where he did. Jack noticed that Joe kept the print out on the table, sneaking the occasional glance down at it.

When they had finished, Jack offered to pay the check but Joe took the leather folder before he could bring his wallet to the table.

"No. This is my turn. You did something for me, I'll do something for you."

They did the dance of the check payer for a moment longer. Jack didn't want to be rude after all.

The check was paid and Joe's agent told them that they'd make a decision by the end of the next week. "I'll send you an email by Friday at the latest."

"I'll keep an eye out for it," Tom said.

"If you have a chance, you should see the city," Joe told him. "It's a beautiful place."

"I can tell," Jack said. "I thought it would bum me out being so rainy, but it's actually very nice."

"We'll be in touch," Joe told him.

"I think I got it," Jack told her over the hotel's phone.

"That's great!" Cindy's voice peaked the speaker in the phone.

"I know. I'm not going to be able to sleep until I hear from them though."

"Well, at least you're used to it," Cindy said. "Do you want me to get someone to prescribe something to help you stay asleep?"

"Maybe when I get back I'll see someone. I brought some liquid melatonin with me."

"Ew," Cindy said. "Did it give you a weird dream?"

"Actually, yeah. How'd you know?

"I used to take it in college to keep my schedule right. I'd have all kinds of weird things go through my head. What was your dream about?"

"When we boarded the plane this morning I dreamed that a drawing of the King came to life and was outside the plane staring at me."

"Elvis?"

"No," Jack said. "Not of rock. Of evil. I made a sketch of him before I left."

"That's weird. What'd he say?"

"Nothing. He was outside the plane, just standing there."

"No wonder you can't sleep." Her words were caked with sarcasm.

"Oh, hush you," he told her.

"Seriously, don't kill yourself. We'll get through this."

"Walk me through your day," he said.

"Well, I had breakfast alone."

"Yay!" Jack whispered.

"Shut up. Then when I got to work I had two more clients in my database for Monday."

"No way? That's awesome."

"I know," she agreed. "One came into the gym after her appointment just to meet me. It was sweet."

"That's cute. What's her, uh, her injury?"

"She fell off a horse and broke her wrist and ankle."

"Yikes, how'd she fall?"

"Gravity."

"Oh, burn," Jack said. "What are you doing tonight?"

"Samantha and I are going to a basketball game," Cindy said. "I'm getting ready now."

"You pencil in your unibrow yet?"

"That's always first, I'm changing clothes at the moment."

"Don't smudge it. You may make Anthony Davis upset, and they may not win if you go in there looking shotty. Make him proud."

"I'm a little bit in a hurry. Her boyfriend is taking us to eat before."

"Do I need to let you go?"

"Sure, I'll text you relentlessly at the game."

"Please do."

Cindy said, "I love you so much, Jack."

"I love you too, Cin."

Jack leaned back on the bed. He watched the ceiling overhead. A number of thoughts ran through his mind but more than anything else he reminded himself how much better things are now. *Cindy's happy. I'm going to have the job of a lifetime. Everything is working out. I'm finished paying dues.* He exhaled now that he had gently draped a wet blanket over his momentary happiness. The feeling of bliss was like an oasis mirage, there one second, then once the struggles of everyday life had been momentarily abated, it disappeared.

Back to your regularly scheduled program.

3

A Week Later

Jack sat it his computer, staring at the screen. There were only two revisions to the poster of *Coda's End*. They wanted the words to be a darker shade of off-white. Jack had taken the original color from the dirt road behind the main character, but it took nearly no effort to add little color to the title across the top. The second was that they needed the image to be saved as a bigger file. The rework took a total of thirty minutes, including his meandering daydream time. As he exported the PDF file to his desktop, his phone rang.

"Hello?" Jack said, not recognizing the number on the screen.

"Hello, Jack," the voice was high-pitched and had an accent.

"Who is this?" Jack asked.

"It's Joe," the voice said through his cell phone.

"Sorry, man," Jack said. "I don't know why I didn't recognize your accent."

"I don't have an accent, do I?"

Jack straightened in his chair, looking around. He stammered.

"Only kidding," Joe said. "I just wanted to let you know that Levi and Tom are talking out the contracts. We chose your design."

"Jesus, that's great news," Jack said. His heart raced. Tears welled up in his eyes. His hands shook. He calmed his voice. "You're not kidding me, are you?"

"Yeah," Joe said. His mood had changed completely. "Sorry I just wanted to call you and tell you myself. We've decided to go another way."

"What?" Jack's heart stopped.

"I'm just kidding again."

"Ha!" Jack shouted. "I like the other one better, but good one."

"Ah, yes."

"That's great, man. Thank you. Thank you so much."

"It's a pleasure. I'm excited to work with someone of your talent."

"So when do we start?"

"Well, everyone has to come to an agreement first, then when that's all taken care of we'll get to work. We are pretty much waiting for the paperwork to be filed."

"Oh, okay," Jack said. "I guess we wait then."

There was a heavy pause on the line, then Joe said, "Well, I'll let you continue on with your day. Your agent will be in touch with you sometime today to talk about strategy and payment and that sort of thing. I just wanted to be the first to congratulate you."

"Thank you so much, Joe. I'm very excited about working with you."

"No problem. Say hello to the wife for me."

"You got it," Jack said. He hung up the phone.

Suddenly overwhelmed with excitement he ran into the kitchen. He found two pots and banged them together, yelling at the top of his lungs until tears welled up in his eyes. He had to be loud. Creating an uproar had always been his way of uncapping. He didn't care who heard, and at this moment he was trying to make them wonder what was going on with that old, wooden house in the woods.

Jack dropped the pots. They banged loudly on the floor. He bounded over the couch. His foot caught on the top and he went to the ground. Keeping his stride, he rolled out of the stumble and ran outside. He ran like a kid, with no direction or care for what he may destroy in his path. He just ran hard and ran loudly. Onlookers be damned. He was certain that he looked like someone in trouble, but he knew he wasn't. He sprinted around the house and down the pier. Then fully clothed he leapt into the river, flipping and flailing his arms and legs. He landed on his side and swam as fast as he could until he was out of breath. He screamed at the top of his lungs until he dry-heaved. Afraid that someone might hear him—now that he was out in the open he felt self-conscious about someone watching him make noise—he put his face in the water and screamed more. The hysterics caught up with him and water filled his eyes.

After a few moments of splashing around in the river, finally feeling the near-freezing water, he paddled back home. He pulled himself up onto the pier and lay there heaving air. He sprawled out and stared at the afternoon sky. When he could feel his toes again he stood up, shivering, and walked back inside, stripping down to his soaked boxers.

"That was a shitty trick," he told the house. "He better cut that crap out if I'm going to be drawing his book." Then mocking Joe's accent, "Oo, er, oo I'm so British. Dickhead. Oh my God, I can't believe this is real." He tossed the wet clothes into the washing machine on his way to the closet for something else to wear.

His cellphone buzzed.

"Ring all you want. I don't care anymore."

It did keep buzzing. He glanced down once his shirt was on and saw that the call was from Tom.

"You son of a bitch!" Tom said. His voice matched Jack's mood perfectly.

"I take it you heard?" Jack said.

"You're goddamn right I heard! Who says snooping never came to anything good? I sure as fuck didn't."

"I never heard you say it anyway."

"Oh, Jackie boy. And they waited until the exact end of the week too. You realized that, too, right? British dickhead. They had me thinking they were calling to renege. That would have pissed me off for good."

"You think it was a hard choice?"

"Nah," Tom assured him. "I saw the pictures. He knew

before leaving that table you were his guy. His agent just wanted to make you sweat. They'll probably try to dick us out of some money by the end of it."

"Can they do that?" Jack asked.

"I don't think so. I'm just trying to stay grounded. But who cares? This is *huge!* Total game changer."

"That's what I'm hoping," Jack agreed. "No more taking the job I need and only taking the ones I want. I can finally sleep tonight. Cindy wants a baby. I think now we can start really trying to get pregnant again. Or get her pregnant. Whatever the right way to say that is."

"You sure?" Tom said the words, but his voice added a hint of, "Don't you remember what happened last time?" to his innocent phrase.

"Yeah," Jack said as if there were no reason to ask. "It's not like that could happen again. She's at a much better place. Security everywhere. We were ready then. We're in an even better place with one another now."

"Yeah," Tom said. "But I mean pregnancy is just a gateway drug to having a kid. Are you sure you want that? Besides, you don't even know what it's going to look like until it's too late."

"Probably half like me, half like her."

"Well half of that is good."

"I knew you had a thing for me."

"Yeah, you keep swinging. Look, congratulations and all that shit, but we have to earn it now. They're supposed to email me the contracts in the morning. I'll look over it and we'll write our names on it and get rich."

"If that's all it takes, man, we should have done this years ago."

"No one ever told me."

"I'm going to celebrate. Let me know when the contracts come in."

"I'll give you a call."

The sun ducked behind the trees just as Cindy's car pulled under the house. Jack met her at her car and carried her to their bedroom. He explored his wife, kissing her more than anything. For the first time since it was put on her, the scar on her stomach didn't strike up a thought of regret or anger. He almost didn't see it. It was just there, playing its part in telling her story. Their story. It didn't affect him anymore, because he knew that part of their lives had ended earlier that day. There would be no more struggle or worry about where the money would come from. Not for years to come anyway. By then she could even have her own facility.

When they finally stopped, Jack rested his head on Cindy's stomach.

"You got it, didn't you?" She asked.

"We got it." Jack's smile stretch to its full length.

"That's wonderful, Jack. I'm so happy."

"I am too."

Cindy pulled herself closer to him. "I should've known something good happened today. There are pots on the kitchen floor."

"I've been thinking all day about what we're going to do to make this place even better."

"What were you thinking? After we clean up the kitchen, I mean."

"We can make the gym area upstairs just my office, and you can do your stretching outside or at a real gym."

"Shut up. Seriously, tell me."

"We could refinish the floors. I got a splinter when I hung up the phone. Some of the walls need to be painted. That green in the living room looks like smashed peas. Get some bikes. I saw a trail across that bridge right before you turn in to get here. There were people riding along the river. It looked like a fun date idea."

"Yeah? What else?"

"I thought since now the money would be a little more stable we could have a baby."

Cindy leaned up. "Really?" she said softly.

"Yeah. We're in a much better place than we were. On all accounts."

"Okay." She made a conscious effort not to go into the kitchen and bang around for a while. "I'll figure out when I'm ovulating and we can start as soon as possible."

"Or we could just play it safe and always be at it. Win, win. It doesn't feel like homework if we do it that way."

"Come here." Her smile was wide and genuine. She kissed him. "Let's eat, and then we'll get back in bed."

They did.

Once they were too tired to move again, Cindy and Jack both slept until morning without waking up for the first night since moving to Louisiana. The house creaked and popped like every other house in which he had slept, but the two of them remained asleep.

Instead of her normal facedown position like she had assumed since she was a baby, Cindy slept on his shoulder. He was awake before her, and he lay in bed as she slept. He felt her breath, and heard her soft, quiet snore. The smell of her shampoo wafted into his nose.

They stayed in bed for the majority of the weekend, leaving the house once to see a basketball game Sunday afternoon with Samantha and her boyfriend. Jack could feel his life changing already. He welcomed it.

They were up before the sun. They lay in bed, holding hands like they used to when they would stay up all night.

"It's like you always have to go to work," Jack said.

"I know. Someone has to save the world. And I can't do that either, because these injured retirees need help getting back to their normal speed."

"They can't even outrun smell."

"I know, baby, but they need me."

"What if I started paying you to stay here with me all day?"

"Because then you'd never get any work done."

"Fine," he said. "Behind every great woman, there is an adequate man painting pictures of creepy stuff. Oh, the money came in for that movie poster, I thought I would take your car to get your tires rotated and checked."

"That's fine," Cindy told him. "Sorry in advance for leaving the seat too close to the wheel."

"Just don't let it happen again."

"Did you ever hear from Tom?"

"He said he got the contracts and he'd look over it by Monday. So I guess I'll be hearing something today."

"Everything takes so long," she pointed out. "I would go crackers waiting for something like this. I hate waiting. I know you already have it, but you could be painting already, but there's just so much paperwork you have to do first."

"Maybe we'll get a tablet."

"You should. Works wonders for us," she lifted her head from his chest. "Oh, no. The sun's coming up."

"That bitch."

"I have to get up now," she groaned.

Cindy stood and Jack dragged her back in bed on top of him one last time before the new week began. After they got ready for the day together in the bathroom. Jack walked her through his day telling her he was going to start drawing characters. He still didn't know anything more about the story, but it couldn't hurt to have someone waiting to be added to the King's story. They made breakfast together. When they finished, Jack walked Cindy to his car and watched her leave. Then he went upstairs.

Jack stared down at his notepad. And back at the computer screen. And back at the notepad. He tapped his pen. Sniffed. Cleared his throat. *How do I start this?* Jack wasn't a writer, but he knew how to paint. Creating images was his job. This was concerning. Surely he should be able to make a few drawings. His foot bounced up and down. He knocked over the white canvas he had laid underneath the table over a week ago. *Maybe I should warm up first. Have a bit of a stretch before working out.*

He assembled the easel and replaced the canvas. He went into the plastic bag for the paint and used the egg carton from the kitchen trash to keep the colors separate.

Back upstairs he painted. After five minutes his bare chest was covered in blacks, purples, and browns. He wanted to start on Papa Legba, saving the King for last, but he didn't. He couldn't. He fought the urge, but like whiskey will lure an alcoholic back to the bottle against his will, the King drew the brush to the left of the canvas. Jack couldn't so much as paint the flames surrounding the King without having to go back.

At one in the afternoon he laid down the egg carton and brush. There was paint on his face and in his hair. He looked at what he had done, and his chest puffed up a tiny bit. The detail on the painted King's face looked exactly like the layout on the computer screen. The top hat was even better. Something about the wet paint gave the sharpened ribs a gleam that creeped Jack out. He loved it. The paint stopped at the King's shoulders, but already the painting was alive. The disembodied head sneered back at Jack from the canvas.

Jack didn't want to, but he forced himself to stop. He got into the shower with it on his mind. He got dressed with the television filling the house with noise to distract him, but finishing the painting lay on his mind like a thick blanket. Jack would get little pieces of information from the television, just enough to know that something was there, before his mind filled with ideas about the painting. What brushes he would use next, what colors he needed, what he was about to run out off. He couldn't fight them off. He even started talking to himself about what he could do in order to keep his thoughts straight. In the end he had to throw the egg carton away before he could walk out of the house. Even then he was miles away from home before he could pay attention to anything else.

"Jack heard back from his agent," Cindy told Samantha, Jennifer, and a couple of the other therapists she had already befriended in her short time at Louisiana Bone and Joint. She paused with a completely neutral expression on her face. An inaudible drumroll as the audience waited for her to open the envelope. "He got the job."

Everyone in earshot cried out, or cheered, or congratulated her loudly in some way.

"I'm so happy for you!" Amanda Livingston told her, touching her arm. "You're finally married to a successful artist."

"Well, he was already successful," Cindy said.

"But now he's going to have a cover of a book!" Amanda said. Cheers went up.

"He's had hundreds of book covers, too," Cindy corrected again, trying not to dampen the excitement. It felt good that they genuinely cared. She didn't want to squash it.

"Oh," Amanda said. "I didn't know that."

"Yeah, the last three Steven Bell books were his. Well the last two and his new one."

"No way," Amanda's husband, who was a doctor upstairs, said. "I have one of those."

"So what *does* this mean is different?" Samantha chimed in.

Cindy paused, thinking. "More money."

Cheers and woos filled the gym. She wanted to add that he would be drawing the entire book, but she thought it be fine to save it for later conversations. Spread it out.

The intercom buzzed from the reception desk. "I have Mr. Geller for Samantha, and Mrs. Rosenburg for Cindy coming in."

"Thank you, Brad," Jennifer told the speaker. "We're ready for'm."

"I think you have a crush on Officer Brad," Cindy said when the group dissipated.

"What?" Jennifer asked on the defensive. "Why do you say that?"

"Don't feel bad. I do too," Samantha said, showing her it wasn't a negative thing.

"It's kind of obvious," Cindy added. "Because all those security officers sound exactly alike, and not just to me. But you know every single time when you're talking to him. You don't thank any of the other officers, either. I'm just saying. They're going to find out."

"You should tell him," Samantha said.

"I can't tell him," Jennifer said. "I work with him."

"Not really," Samantha said.

"You do see him, but not a lot." Cindy added.

The door opened and Mr. Geller, Mrs. Rosenburg, and Brad the security officer came into the gym.

"Thank you, Bradley," Cindy said.

"Hey, no problem," Brad rumbled, glancing at Jennifer. He knocked on the surface of the reception desk and left the area.

"No ring," Cindy sing-songed. "I think he did that because he *wanted* you to know."

"He touched your desk. You must be a slip and slide right now," Samantha joked.

Jennifer tilted her head and made an expression of exhaust. "Don't be gross."

"Next time he comes in, you should ask him," Samantha said, leading little Robbie Geller to a plinth and grinning ear to ear.

"Ask him what exactly?" Jennifer said.

"To marry you. I don't care." Samantha turned away grinning.

"How are you feeling today, Mrs. Rosenburg," Cindy asked.

"Much better than last week," she said. She kissed the charm from her pocket as she did every day before her appointment. "Little darlin', yaw working magic on me. That first night I couldn't get into or out of bed, but yaw gonna have me running marathons before I can say no."

"You know I'd never make you run unless you wanted to," Cindy said.

"Well unfortunately yaw got me feelin' like I's in good hands. If yaw said to, I'd go and do it just cause yaw gotta sweet face."

"You're going to make me blush, Mrs. Rosenburg." Cindy helped Mrs. Rosenburg onto a table and handed her a band so she could start stretching.

"Yaw can still call me Beth, Cindy. I prefer a first name basis so I don't feel so old."

Cindy typically only called her older patients by their last names, but for the adamant ones she made an exception. Beth Rosenburg was definitely one of the adamant ones.

The lights flickered in the gym. It was almost imperceptible, like a simultaneous blink for everyone sharing the light.

"I hope it ain't raining," Mrs. Rosenburg said. "I didn't bring in an umbrella."

"The AC probably turned on upstairs. Nothing to worry about yet," Cindy assured her. She opened her tablet and checked Mrs. Rosenburg's account even though she had memorized everything in it, when the tablet displayed an update notification. Because she was so used to doing so on her own tablet, Cindy absent-mindedly tapped "update software" on the screen. "Oh. No. I didn't mean to do that."

"What happened?" Mrs. Rosenburg asked.

"Oh, nothing with you. I just updated my tablet, and I'm not sure if we're supposed to do that or not."

"Oh, darlin', yaw had me worried."

"Hey Samantha," Cindy called across the tables. "Does it

matter if we update these things? I accidentally accepted one."

"Really? I didn't get one," Samantha answered, checking for one on her own tablet. "I guess it's okay. No one has ever said anything to me about it. I didn't know these things could update."

"Maybe I just dreamt it. Nope." Cindy showed Samantha the black screen with the silver apple and a status bar below it growing from one side to the other. "I guess it's not going to explode. I should be okay."

"You'll be in my prayers," Samantha said.

"Mine too," Mrs. Rosenburg assured her.

"You two are too sweet."

"Do we need to wait for that thing to juice up?"

"I think I have everything we're going to do today memorized. We should be good to get going without it. So where do you want to start?"

The bright part of the statue bar completed its trek across the screen. The screen went black and then acted as though it had just been turned on. The tablet asked for a password. Cindy gave it what it wanted and logged back into the Louisiana Bone and Joint application, which was the lone app on the screen other than settings. Nothing noticeable had changed so she continued her appointment when Mrs. Rosenburg without a hitch.

"Jackie boy! Can you hear me?"

"Yeah, hang on, Tom." Jack closed the door, separating the shop and the lobby of the mechanic's building. "Alright I can hear you."

"Hey, buddy, I got Levi and Joe on the phone with me."

"Hey, mate," Joe said.

"How's everyone doing?" Jack asked, not knowing what else to say.

"Doing well," Levi and Joe said together.

Tom started the business talk going. "They called me and thought it would be good if the four of us set up a meeting so that you guys could work on the story together." Tom sneezed and cleared his throat away from the phone. "Sorry guys, fucking pollen is everywhere."

"Okay, um," Jack said. "Were you thinking I'd fly up again?"

"No, actually," Joe said. "You seem to have a huge advantaged living where you do, and I don't want to miss out on something that could be helpful to the process. So I thought I would come down there and get the full experience of the New Orleans culture. A lot of the ideas you incorporated with the cover design helped you out jolly well. I'd like to see what we could come up with together."

"So do you not have the story completed yet?" Jack asked.

"We have a very detailed outline," Levi told him. "Graphic novels are a little different than novels. A lot of the story telling is done with the imagery. You struck us as capable of handling that."

"I guess we'll find out."

Everyone laughed.

"I was thinking I could fly in by the end of the week. You could show me around."

"That's totally plausible. It's Monday today, so would Wednesday be too soon?"

"Perfect." There was excitement in Joe's voice.

"Now will you both be coming or just you?"

"It'll be just him," Levi said. "This is the point where the agents step aside and let the artists be artists."

"Finally, a break," Tom joked. Everyone laughed again.

"Do you have my email address?" Jack asked.

"Er, yes," Joe said. "And your phone number is now in my contacts."

"Great, just give me a call when your flight leaves, and I'll pick you up from the airport. We'll take it from there."

"Again, perfect. I'm online booking a flight right now. This is much easier than I thought it would be. Especially being over two thousand miles apart."

"Well, I don't like to work hard. Easy is preferred."

"Ha ha, right," Joe said. "I'll email you later when I get the flight and hotel arrangements settled on, and I'll see you this Wednesday."

"See you then," Jack said.

Jack hung up, not knowing if that was what he was supposed to do. He knew that Tom would call within five minutes with advice on how to act when Joe arrived in town or a comment on his weird accent. Probably both.

Jack dropped the phone in his pocket and waited, looking through the glass of the mechanic shop.

Jack rebounded off the front door of their old house. It was chasing him. He turned back to the street. There was nothing there in the afternoon light, but he could still hear the sound of children laughing all around him. Jack twisted the doorknob, breaking it off like a dead tree branch. It crumbled in his hands like a clump of dirt. He pounded the door, calling for Cindy.

"Babe," he said in a panicky calm. "Can you come to the door? Come let me in, please."

Behind him came a feeling that something was moving in on him. The thing that was chasing him. Jack turned away from the street. He rammed his body against the door in an attempt at breaking it open. With each pound his body made against the door, a fresh set of splinters stabbed deep into his arm and side. When the blood stained the door's cracked blue paint, he stopped. He turned around.

Two glowing green dots, shrouded in black smoke, watched Jack from the road. The smoke took the shape of a head around the eyes. It spread downward forming the vague shape of a neck and shoulders.

The pain from the splinters was washed away with the onset of fear. His chest tightened as if a hand wrapped around his heart and squeezed. Jack sprinted for the back of the house. The green eyes chased. The black smoke faded to gray like the skin of a corpse. The laughing from the children grew louder in Jack's ears.

Jack ran the length of the privacy fence. He turned the corner and the smoky head and shoulders waited there. A shrill buzz ripped from the mouth like an electric alarm. The noise sounded almost insect-like. Jack's bare feet slipped on a black residue on the grass. He scrambled to his feet and ran the opposite direction.

Another set of eyes appeared at the opposite end of the house.

Jack leapt up the privacy fence and pulled himself over. Splinters dug into his hands, feet, and chest. He fell onto the ground and raced to the back door. Jack pulled the doorknob, and it crumbled in his hand. The fractured windowpane beside the door was still broken. Now it dripped black liquid. Jack pounded on the back door calling for Cindy. He saw the rock next to the porch and made for it.

A pair of green eyes materialized above the fist-sized stone. Jack ran and snatched it up before the smoke could form into a shape.

Jack swung the rock into the window, shattering it completely. Blackness poured out of the hole. The smell of paint overwhelmed his senses. The black paint filled the backyard, covering Jack's feet.

The smoke and glowing eyes formed a face in front of Jack. It was the face of the King. But only what Jack had painted. The head was equipped with the top hat, dripping with blood. The rest was just an outline in ashy gray lines. Below the shoulders, the head dripped black paint on the ground. The eyes bulged madly in the King's skull. Jack backed away but slipped on the black paint and fell to the ground.

At the sight of his own painting, Jack shrieked.

Children laughed all around him, but no one was to be seen. It felt like the children were peering at him though the cracks in the fence and laughing at him.

The King's evil leer penetrated Jack.

The head flew toward Jack.

Jack flinched awake in his bed next to his wife. He was sweating and breathing heavy as though he had just finished a race. He looked out the window and saw the reflection of the moon on the river. He calmed and slipped back into unconsciousness.

4

Two Days Later

"Wow, baby," Cindy said. "I thought you only did those when it was finished."

Jack turned around to see Cindy in khakis and the company polo. "I couldn't wait. I was just really excited about the project. You haven't worn scrubs since you started this new place have you?"

"Nope. We're a highfalutin organization, babe." Cindy hugged him from behind and propped her head on his back.

"No scrubs? No chaos? It's like you guys aren't even in the real world."

"Who needs the real world?" She kissed the spot between his shoulder blades. He shivered like he always did. "This is still really good, you know. Even though it's not finished I like it better than the computer. It feels more alive as a painting. Like it's more than just an image, don't you think?"

"It does," Jack agreed. "I feel like there is more to a

painting than a print out on a piece of paper. I certainly connect better with these."

"We sound pretty pretentious don't we?"

"Yeah," Jack laughed. "I guess we should've moved to Portland."

Cindy walked around to his side, her arms still around him. "What are you going to do if it changes?"

"Don't get paint on your clothes."

"It'll wash. I prefer this to clean clothes." She hugged him tighter.

Jack smiled at her. "This one is just for us," he explained. "I thought since both of us liked it, we could find somewhere to hang it up."

"Maybe downstairs somewhere. I definitely don't want him looking at my ass when I'm doing yoga."

"You can't blame him. Those are tight pants, and some of them are very transparent."

Cindy grinned and rolled her eyes. "When does Joe's flight land?"

Jack checked his watch. "Four more hours."

"Do you want me to bring something home to cook for you guys?"

"Actually, he wanted to stay in a hotel. I offered the spare room but he was adamant. He thought it would help the creative process if he spent nights in the city, considering that's where most of the story takes place. I guess I respect that."

"Good, then we won't wake him up," she kissed his neck.

"We always have the option to call him in the middle of the night. I can figure out his room number if you really want that."

Jack turned to face her. The two of them started dancing in the attic with no music. They swayed to the sound of the creaking boards. Cindy turned around, her back to his front. She felt safe that way, with him behind her and around her. Nothing could touch her with him there. She reached back and ran her fingers through his hair.

"I have to go," Cindy said sadly.

"Is it another man, Lucinda?"

"His name is Mr. Franklin. He's very quiet, and he buys me pretty things."

"He sounds like a loser. Probably wasn't even president."

"He was busy doing other things. That's all."

Jack grabbed her hand and walked her to her car. He kissed her goodbye and she told him to have fun on his little play date. Jack turned to go back inside. When he did, he noticed a wooden paddleboat seesawing in one place on the river. It was waterlogged and nearly black in the morning glow. He walked down the pier for a better look. So far as he could tell there was no one in the boat.

"Hello?" He called out to the empty boat.

Someone must not have tied that thing down very well.

He walked back to the house and up the stairs. He stepped onto the first rising and looked back at the boat. It was farther down the river, and the tension Jack felt eased dramatically.

Jack continued painting until ten thirty when he took a

shower. All the colors he had used that day washed off his skin and down the drain in a milky gray and red stream. Soon enough he was a brand new version of himself. Cleaned and dried, he left the house. On his way to the airport he thought about the mostly-finished painting drying on the easel in the attic. He thought about where he should start tomorrow, where the first stroke of his brush would go, what colors he would use. He walked himself through the remaining pieces of the puzzle, telling himself which shades would go where and what mixtures he would need to create the color exactly. He subconsciously made swooping gestures over the steering wheel. In his mind he could see the finished product. He was already applying the finish to the canvas.

Before he realized he had even made a turn, he was pulling into the airport. *God, I hope I didn't kill anyone. Surely I'd know if I did.*

Jack parked the car in the first lot he saw and walked through the vestibule of travel brochures to the main lobby of the airport. The building was a noisy, rumbling space. He asked someone behind the front desk to direct him to the terminal where the Seattle flight would be unboarding.

Is that the right word? he asked himself. *They didn't seem to notice anything wrong with it. Must be close at least.*

He arrived forty-five minutes early, but by the time he reached the terminal he had to wait only a few short minutes before the plane landed. He sat in a cushioned chair away from the gate. A woman in a clean, navy blue skirt and jacket walked up to him. She stood for a second waiting to meet Jack's eyes. When she did, she asked if he would like a drink while he waited for his flight. He declined, and as she left, Jack began to nod off. His head and eyelids started to fall. He jerked up and wiped his eyes.

"Didn't even know I was tired," he whispered to himself.

He leaned forward and put his elbows on his knees. He looked like a basketball coach during a close game.

A voice coming from the intercom system announced the arrivals of Kansas City, Seattle, and Minneapolis. Jack stood from the chair and peered over the heads in the crowd looking for Joe.

Jack saw him wearing a pair of black sunglasses over his prescription glasses. He waved Joe down. Jack held out his hand. "How was the flight?"

Joe shook it with a stronger grip than Jack expected. "I only caught the takeoff and landing. Slept the whole time. I'm only wearing these so you won't think I'm high."

"I do that, too. Get high, not sleep on the plane." They laughed, although Jack guessed neither of them really knew why. They walked out of the terminal. "Do you need to get a bag or anything?"

"No, this is all I have." Joe pounded the side of a nearly empty duffle bag. "I'm only here for two days then I'm going back. I'm hosting a conference about crossover writers this weekend back home. But don't worry, I'm sure we'll get everything we need to do accomplished. There's plenty of time in the next two days."

"I don't doubt that. Hungry?"

"Famished," Joe said. "I'd like to try Café du Monde."

"Okay," Jack said. "We'll get something to eat in the quarter and go there for dessert."

"Do they not serve food?"

"Not really, it's pretty much beignets and coffee."

"Oh," Joe said, confused. "And they stay in business?"

"When you see it, you won't be surprised. Even less so when you try it."

"Alright," Joe said enthusiastically. "Let's be off then."

Mrs. Rosenburg had had another fall the night before. The fall didn't affect her replaced hip—her newly replaced hip—but when she lay on the plinth doing her warm up stretches, Cindy saw a dark purple bruise spreading out of her sweatpants.

"What happened, Beth?" Cindy sounded shocked.

"Oh, I just dropped off the couch in my sleep. Nothing to worry about, little darlin'."

"Are you okay?"

"I'm fine, a little sore. Just hafta walk it off."

"Are you sure it's not bothering you?"

"Child, I have had both these things replaced. I know what it feels like when something is wrong." Mrs. Rosenburg pulled the charm out of her pocket and kissed it as she had a number of times before. Quick as a gunslinger, she had it tucked away in her pocket.

"I guess you would know pain when it hits you," Cindy said. She was curious about the little thing in Mrs. Rosenburg's pocket now. "Can I ask you something, Beth?"

"Sure thing, child."

"What is the significance of kissing that coin?"

Mrs. Rosenburg paused for a moment. "This?" She retrieved the coin.

"Yes," Cindy said. "I don't mean to pry or anything, but you seem to have a pretty strong attachment to it."

"It's my lucky charm."

"Do you mind if I see it?" Cindy asked. Mrs. Rosenburg handed the small metal octagon to her. There was a carved symbol on the face of the coin. It displayed three pitchforks crossing each other. One straight up, and two crossed either in front of or behind, Cindy couldn't tell. There was a jagged line running behind it and small dots surrounded the edge of the coin. "This looks very familiar for some reason. Where is it from?"

"My grandmother passed it down to me."

"What kind of coin is it?"

"It's a voodoo charm."

Suddenly Cindy realized from where she recognized the coin. She saw the same exact symbol in the shop where Jack had bought the pewter statue of Papa Legba and Baron Samedi. It was burned into what looked like a medicine cabinet hanging on the wall. "Do you believe in voodoo, Beth?" She asked.

"Now before you go thinking old Beth is crazy, let me just say it is a legitimate religion that even the pope sees merit in. My whole family was raised to believe it, and I don't want no one thinkin' less of me for it."

"Come on, Beth," Cindy said. "I think you know me better than that by now. My husband has been doing a lot of research on voodoo recently. It's a lot like Catholicism. I was curious, because he recently started working with it, and now I have a patient who believes in it."

"Well, I do. And it's very important to me. I don't mean to get all snappy. I just don't go pokin' fun of everyone else, but they all seem to come at Mrs. Bethel." Cindy handed her the coin. Mrs. Rosenburg kissed it again and put it away in her pocket. "It's where I come from, and ain't nothing more sacred to a person than their ancestry. It's the only thing you can't change about yourself. It's who you are." She swelled with pride.

"It's very interesting," Cindy reassured her. "Anyone who would make fun of you for it has priorities of their own to sort out before they're flawless."

"They's jackasses. Besides it sure makes me happy."

"That's all that matters anyway." Cindy smiled at Mrs. Rosenburg.

"It's not like the movies, you know."

"Oh, I know."

"That helps me keep them from makin' fun of me though. I just threaten to hex them like some kind of grudge-holdin', angry witch, and they's running off like lightnin'."

Cindy grinned. A laugh slipped through her teeth. She was worried Mrs. Rosenburg would think she was laughing at her. "That's a woman that knows how to make the best out of a bad situation. At least you find the fun in it."

"You got that right, little darlin'," Mrs. Rosenburg hollered. "So we moving anythin' up today? I'm feelin' as spry as I used to be."

"Well, we're going to do a few more pounds on your squats," Cindy said, checking her tablet. She had another new slot for a patient, but there wasn't any information, not even a name. There was only a gray row where it was typically white, or gray with patient information. She tapped the row but nothing happened. It only said, "New patient added Apr. 12." Cindy had enough time to read the information in the row when the application unexpectedly closed. "That is, if you think you're ready to go up of course. It's only five."

"Oh, I'm ready, little darlin'."

"Well, keep stretching. If anything hurts, stop and let me know, okay?"

"Okay then."

"I'll be right back." Cindy walked over to Samantha who stood near a patient on an elliptical machine. "Hey, does this happen a lot?"

"Let me see," Samantha said, taking the tablet from her. She tapped around for a moment and noticed that Cindy had a new patient.

"It's a new slot," Cindy told her. "But there's nothing in it and nothing happens when I tap the section."

"Oh, yeah that's not a problem. It just means the information hasn't been completed yet in the computer system, but you've been given a new patient." Samantha handed back the tablet. "What does that make? Fifteen now? You're no longer a new girl."

"I always knew this day would come," Cindy feigned

wiping at a tear.

"Heads up," Samantha told her. "Mrs. Rosenburg is going to leave you behind."

Cindy watched Mrs. Rosenburg getting up from the table. "Oh, geez." She started running across the gym.

"You know," Joe said. "The way people talk about this city and its relationship with voodoo, I almost expected every hotel and shop entry to be lousy with brick dust and chicken bones."

"I know it sounds crazy," Jack said. "But not everyone here is barefoot and toothless, either."

"Just like not everyone from England is all 'God save the queen' and bad teeth," Joe said.

Jack joined him in laughter, thinking that one of those seemed to be right anyway.

"So," Joe began. "I really loved your idea about the chest hanging from the King's belt, and how he's taking the hearts out of people to survive. That gives him a drive that I didn't."

"Really," Jack said. He was a little shocked. That was the only part of the interview where Joe didn't seem impressed at all. It was the only time when the conversation came to a grinding halt. "I wasn't sure if it was okay to add my own twist or not, but my gut told me it'd be worth a shot."

"Well, you hit it right in the bollocks. I've noticed that with this subject, there is always a sort of trickery going on behind the audience's back. That's why I had you come up to Seattle. I wanted to wait and talk to you before I committed to the idea I created on my own. I like this idea much better. It's creepier and it gives the reader something to wonder about throughout the book. 'If it's always there, there's got to be a reason why.' That's what they'll think."

"What do you think about the way the chest looks though? I'm wondering if we could make it a little more interesting. Make it stand out more."

"I'm sure there is something we could add to that. We'll trapes around the city and see if we can't find something. Throw enough shit against the wall and something is going to stick, right?"

"That's right."

"So what I have here," Joe opened an accordion file folder and laid a stack of papers on the small table, "is the first book mapped out entirely. The reason it took so long to get back is that I wanted to make sure I could incorporate your changes and still have somewhere to go. The other guy didn't have any, and that was somewhat troubling. I'd prefer to work with someone who has too many ideas than none. Coming up with the story was easy once the sparks flew. Everything just sort of fell out of my head."

"Happens to me all the time. So basically, you've got the story here, we just have to fill in the blanks."

"Essentially, yes."

"And if we wind up changing the story, what happens then?"

"Then we just change it. Just like writing a novel."

"Just like that?" Jack snapped his fingers.

"Just like that. We should actually expect to do that a few times before it's all said and done. The first drafts are never any good."

"So we get as many chances at this as we want."

"Absolutely, it's very low pressure. We just have to finish it by the end of the year."

"I think we can do that in eight months," Jack said. He was feeling a lot better about this job. He didn't have any problems going in to this lunch, but he was getting less and less room to complain as the progress continued. "Anyway, continue. I didn't mean to interrupt."

"Not a problem, mate. Stop me if you have anything to add. I have my notepad out in case we need it. Now, first we have your cover, of course." Joe flipped the top page over and laid it next to the stack. That page simply read "COVER" written in pencil across the center. "We're going to open up as an old man comes down the Mississippi in a rickety old boat. I've put all the direction into each frame like you see. He'll have an inner monologue, which I've added to each frame as necessary you can see all through these pages. All the dialogue will be in bubbles like you see all the time."

"Okay," Jack said, imagining the King's grimacing face trapped inside the panels.

"So, anyway, we have an old man on a boat. He's paddling and paddling through a hazy, foggy night. He holds a lantern up before him to have a better look at where he is. He sees a pier leading to a house or business whatever you prefer. He doesn't stop. He just throws the box onto the pier, and continues on down the river.

"In the morning," Joe walked his pencil through a number of panels that said "DAWN," "BRIGHTER," "BRIGHTER," and "MORNING" along the top of the next page. "Our protagonist, Robert Taylor, comes outside for a bit of fishing. He's got his pole, his tackle box, his bait, and whatever else you think he would need. We see him walk from a business to the end of the little dock here. He sees the box and there's a note on it. The note says 'I hereby grant you the gift of this box and everything inside. It is all yours.' See that's the secret. The only way to get rid of the King other than killing him is to gift him to someone else. Robert opens the box and sees a face staring back at him. He drops the box into the river and runs away. Then there are a few ominous frames where there's sort of this smoky light coming from under the surface of the water. That'll be the King coming out of the box. Then the next page will be our title page. It'll have the credits and such there."

"So you want it like a movie. Action before the credits. Get'm while their guard is down."

"That's my style."

They continued through the stack of papers. Joe explained the movement of each panel. Jack offered tweaks and subtle changes, and Joe jotted the notes on the paper when it was necessary. Jack sketched a number of characters on a pad he had brought with him. They went back and forth with ideas on how to make certain faces look when a note called for something specific. They settled on the look of most of the characters right there at the table in the middle of town.

Eventually the final pages from Joe's folder were turned face down. Beignet powder covered the table and coffee stains tarnished the edges of the papers. Jack's hands were stained dark gray from dust falling off the charcoal.

"And if you remember nothing else," Joe said. "Just keep in mind that the King will do absolutely anything to the people in Robert's life. He will stop at nothing to torment him and all the people he loves. After all, as your wife pointed out to you and you to me, he is evil. Bad for bad's sake."

"Very cool story," Jack told him, genuinely impressed.

"Well, it's up to you to make it even better."

"Great. So where do you want to go from here?"

"I was thinking I'd let you have the rest of the night to yourself," Joe said, glancing down at his watch. "I didn't expect us to work through the whole thing in one day. I'd like to walk around the city and take some pictures. I saw an interesting painting on a building with some creepy character playing a warped and curvy piano in the woods. I rather liked it. I have a feeling the more I poke around, the more I'll learn about what we're doing. What was the place that you went to when you found the statue you were telling me about?"

"I actually can't remember the name. It was some shotgun store between Canal and the next street further over. That's only about two blocks away. I think the word museum was in the name, but I'm not one hundred percent sure. There are tons of shops like that around here though.

Even stores that look like they don't have anything, they're worth going inside. I can look it up when I get home and let you know."

"No, no, that's okay. Canal you said?"

"Yeah, it's the one with the trollies running through the middle of the street. You can get something no matter where you go, but it's on the avenues between the streets where you'll find the authentic places. Off the beaten path, that's what you're looking for."

"Okay," Joe jotted down what Jack said. "If I find anything I'll send a picture of it to you."

"Please do."

"It may not be usable but it'll be better to have it than need it. Anything else I should know about the city?"

"I think it's best you know as little as possible going into it," Jack said. "See things with new, discovering eyes. You'll take it in better. Just be slow about it so you don't miss anything. Oh, put your wallet in your front pocket at night."

"Thanks." Joe had a nervous look on his face after that. "By the way do you know where the Hilton is?"

"Yeah, just keep walking that way." Jack pointed down the street over Joe's shoulder. "You can see a sign from here if the people weren't in the way. Is that where you're staying?"

"Yes," Joe said. "There should be a British Plaza in that area I'd like to see. Hopefully it'll be something like home."

"I'm not sure," Jack said, knowing it wasn't what Joe was expecting. "For dinner you should go by Drago's. That's right outside your door. It may also change your mind about that Seattle seafood. That's one thing we do right here."

"Ha, I'll take you up on that."

"Honey, I'm home," Cindy called in the voice of a 1950s trophy wife.

"Hey, Cin," Jack called, walking down the steps to the living room. "How was your day, babe?" He kissed her and she set down all of her things.

"It was wonderful, as usual. Mrs. Rosenburg came in with a huge bruise on her hip."

"Yikes, what happened?"

"She was probably just talking back."

"Sounds about right."

"No," Cindy said. "She was asleep on the couch and apparently she just rolled off."

"To be perfectly honest, if I knew it would get more attention from you, I'd jump hips first off the couch."

"Shut up," she grinned. She pulled him closer to her and kissed him.

"What do you want to do for dinner?"

"I was thinking you could call Joe and see if he wanted to have dinner. I don't think I've ever had more than a passing glance with someone who had an accent. And that was at Disney world. Epcot. Whatever the difference is."

"He's getting lost in the city right now. He said he wanted to poke around. Part of his process I assume."

"How'd it go with him?"

"Pretty simple. He walked me through the story and we—"

A muffled crash sounded upstairs.

"Is there someone in the house?" Cindy asked.

"Just us." Jack stared at the ceiling.

"Should I call the police?"

"No," Jack said, in a don't-be-silly tone. "Probably just the house settling or something."

"But it's forever old, how could it still be settling?"

"It's okay," Jack said. "It's nothing."

"Could you do me a favor?"

"You want me to go look?"

"Please. That's so sweet."

Jack walked upstairs, and Cindy nervously watched him from the foot of the steps.

"Oh no," Jack said. He sounded sincerely upset.

"What? What happened?"

"My painting." Jack entered the attic. The room was open and there were only a few things in it—Cindy's yoga mat rolled up in the corner, his computer sitting on the table in front of the printer, and the now bare easel with the tarp spread out underneath it. He could see everything and there were no people in the attic. "It fell over."

The painting lay half on and half off the tarp mat on the floor. He picked up the canvas, leaving a tiny black smudge on the wooden floor from the still damp canvas.

"You scared me," Cindy said. She climbed the steps after him. "Is it alright?"

"Yeah," Jack said. "Just smudged the black on the hat a little. I can fix it. No one would notice even if I didn't. Better get a rag or something to get it off the floor."

Jack racked the painting on the easel and grabbed a warm rag from their bathroom. Cindy went into the kitchen, looking for something to transform into dinner.

Jack climbed the steps to the attic again with the rag. There was a dull shade of green in the room that he had never noticed before. He wiped his eyes, and it was still there. Something flickered in his eyes from outside. Something was moving out there. Jack tightened up. He became aware of how tired he was. He slowly walked to the window. The flashes came from the river. The irregular surface reflected the sunlight into his eyes. For a moment he saw the shape of a person standing on the river. He jerked back, and then realized that the trees blocked the afternoon sun, creating nothing more to be afraid of than a shadow. Jack turned back to the room, but the greenish hue was gone now.

Probably just a weird trick of the light, he told himself.

Jack returned his attention to the spot on the floor with the offending stain, but it wasn't there. He lifted the tarp to see if maybe he had covered it in the commotion. Nothing was there. He eyed the floor suspiciously. He spun circles around himself, finding nothing. He toweled the spot on the floor where he thought the stain had been and walked away. He examined the rag on his way down the steps. Aside from the normal amount of dust, the hand towel was clean.

Am I seeing things? He wondered.

5

That Night

Jack was dreaming. No. No, dreaming would have been too nice a word. Jack was being terrorized by his subconscious. The sheets clung to his sweating body. The face he made in his sleep would have broken Cindy's heart if she wasn't sleeping face down in her pillow. The corners of his mouth were turned down and his brow furrowed. His throat let out a weak whimper.

In his nightmare he was drowning in the river behind his house. The water froze his skin and prevented him from breathing with any more regularity than a few random hitches.

Finally his head broke free of the water only to be forced back under by the black rubber sole of a shoe. A brief moment of lucidity swept over him when he realized his eyes were open underwater and everything was clear as the movies made it seem. From that moment he knew he was dreaming, but before he could make an effort to wake himself, the thought was jarred out of his mind when something grabbed his ankle and yanked him down.

He flailed his arms and legs, desperate to free himself. He reached down to untangle his ankle from whatever had latched onto him. His hands felt wildly down, finding purchase on a naked, skeletal hand. He ripped at the bones until they released the death grip fastened around him tight enough to bruise. When the hand was loose the bones separated and floated around him to the surface of the river. He could see the shape that had kicked him down, peering down like an animated watercolor painting. The top of the water distorted the sight to something hazy and unreal to Jack.

He decided to swim.

Still underwater, Jack flailed his arms and legs in an effort to out-swim the thing's reach. He got far enough away to break through the water and swallow a massive lungful of air. The clouds started to rain. He turned and the foggy shape was no clearer to him than before. It was the vague shape of a person colored so deeply that whatever stood on the pier trying to drown him could have just been an inkblot. He raced further away from the shape.

Jack swam to the bridge he had seen, which led to a bike trail. He thought certainly someone would be there to help. He stopped.

No.

Jack was stopped.

The feeling was as though he were in a pool with a generated current rushing against him. He paddled and paddled, knowing without a doubt that if he didn't get away, he was going to die in this river. The unmoving current of the river had become unrelentingly stubborn to his attempts at crossing its width. He was going to die here. And Cindy would probably find him, pale, bloated with some far-off dumb look on his face.

He paddled harder, but only went backwards. Something pulled him. Not the way the hand had pulled him under, but as if something had latched on to the water around him and now dragged everything toward the shape on the pier. There were faces before him in the river. White, skeletal faces.

Jack turned away from them, accepting his fate head on, ready to right whatever was terrorizing him. His vision warped. A cone of vapor led from a glowing green light just to the side of the shape. The light is what dragged him back. The light brightened and heated Jack's face. The green light mesmerized him, eliminated all his attempts at survival. It began to boil him. He knew that surely he would be liquefied. Something kept him there. The light was ending his life, daring him to break free of its spell, and at the same time, crippling him into oblivion. Jack rose out of the freezing water, beginning to sweat. He stared into the light, waiting for the darkness to envelop him. All sound left him. The only sensation to be had was the sight of the green light and the vapor surrounding it.

Then the sensation of falling.

❖ ❖ ❖

Jack was erect, seated on his side of the bed when he opened his eyes. He jerked awake and gasped so hard he nearly choked on the breath he took. Jack fell backwards onto the bed, the sensation of falling shocking him even more into consciousness. Something banged upstairs.

Shit. What the hell was that?

He slid on his pajamas and walked as quietly as he could up to the attic. The wooden step sent up a creaking alarm, letting what, if anything, was up there know exactly where Jack was. He peeked around the doorframe standing on the second step, and saw that the easel with the painting of the King of Evil cover had fallen over. He reset the painting back on the easel, and made for the bathroom. There was a scratch in his throat and clearing it only made the cruddy feeling hurt worse, so he zombie-walked into the kitchen and drank out of the orange juice carton. He shook the last remaining drops at the bottom before dropping the carton into the trashcan.

Need more for breakfast. Make a note.

"Where's my list?" he asked the interior of the refrigerator. "Phone...car."

Do I want to go all the way downstairs to get it? No. But it's in Cin's car, and she might leave with it. You don't have a landline anymore. What if Joe sends you a picture of something really helpful?

"Shit," he grumbled. He stood in the light from the fridge for a moment longer on standby, waiting for nothing in particular. "Okay, fine."

Jack quietly took the keys off the counter, and snuck out

the door. Cindy was a heavy sleeper, but after the years of sleeping in the same bed, he still made his way around her quiet as a mouse. He eased the front door closed, then turned and dropped down each wooden stair, his feet pounding with ever step closer to the ground. Upstairs Cindy was sound asleep.

He opened the yellow Kia. The chiming noise that greeted him felt as if it were coming through an amplifier. Every tiny beep was a snare drum in his head.

"Ahh," he lazily argued with no one.

Annoyed with the sound, he climbed into the car and shut the door.

Why am I in here?

"Phone?" He called out. "Where are you?"

He felt around between the seats and in the cup holders with his eyes closed. He felt for the glove box knowing he had never opened it before. He felt around inside anyway and closed it. He opened his eyes and saw that his phone rested quietly on a pad on the top of the dashboard. It was right where he always put it, even when he wasn't driving.

"Stupid phone," he said picking it up.

He pulled up the application he used to make the grocery list, and typed "orange juice." Then he left the car. He clicked the lock on the key fob, and made to rejoin Cindy in bed. He thought he might even try her face down approach.

Something big, something very big, moved in the driveway.

It had watched him the whole time he had been outside.

Whatever it was saw him leave the car and ducked off in

the trees to one side of the driveway. Jack was suddenly wide awake.

"What the hell's going on, man?" He asked the movement. "Who's out there?"

He opened his eyes wide, suddenly full of nervous energy. He sniffed loudly.

"Hello?" Jack called.

Not knowing why, he stepped toward the driveway. He activated the flashlight on his phone and aimed the beam in the direction from which he thought the movement came. The hair on his neck and arms stood at attention, but he didn't shake. He somehow managed to keep his nerves settled enough to seem like a threat to who or whatever had made its way down his driveway.

"Look, whatever is going on, just fuck off," Jack said. He sounded angrier than he was. *Whatever gets the point across.* "I'm calling the police."

He wasn't going to actually do that until something erupted in the darkness. A cloud of black smoke went up through the overhead canopy of tree branches a dozen yards away, and a noise like a thousand cicadas buzzing together in one gigantic mound tore into Jack's ears. Something started to choke.

"Hey," Jack called out. "What the hell is going on?"

The thing ran on all fours through the woods. Jack caught a glimpse of long matted black hair. It sprinted in all directions as though it were trying to confuse Jack and make him lose sight of it. Everywhere the thing in the trees ran, a trail of smoke ran up behind it from the ground. The thing hissed, and coughed, and buzzed.

Then the woods were quiet.

Jack heard footsteps, and something tripped. It hit the ground hard. The sound of something being cooked sizzled into the air. The thing buzzed again loudly. Jack moved closer to the look between two pine trees. Whatever it was leapt face first at him. The reflection of the flashlight bouncing off its eyes was the only thing Jack saw. He felt a head or fist covered in wiry hair hit the side of his face like a steel sledgehammer. It knocked him to his back. The phone fell to the ground with the flashlight facing downward.

Jack watched as whatever it was bolted down the driveway. It wasn't the way a horse galloped, or a dog ran. It was like a bear hobbling awkwardly down the street. It wasn't a bear though. It was much thinner. The hair on its back was patchy like a dog with mange. It wasn't any animal he had ever known either.

Was that a person?

He followed it. He watched it duck into the trees lining the driveway. Jack quietly went to the spot where the thing had hid. In the black, a circle came into view. It was a hole in the ground with flecks of ember around its circumference.

Jack's heart drummed. His pajama pants clung to his sweaty legs. His eyes latched onto the hole in the ground and refused to go anywhere else. Jack's wide eyes stared.

When his mind was finally able to take back control from the fear, Jack called the police.

❖ ❖ ❖

"I just came down to get my phone out of the car before my wife left in the morning. I didn't want to forget to grab it. I can't really explain what I was thinking. Then I heard it moving around in the driveway. It jumped in between the trees somewhere around there. You can see the ground looks like something was wrestling around in there."

"Where is that?"

"Right there," Jack pointed to a burned pile of pine needles and leaves that had been kicked up. "It looks like something was struggling to move around. And that's what it sounded like, too."

"Okay, yeah, I see what you're talking about. What exactly was it?"

"I—do we have panthers here?"

"Not usually."

"It looked like a black panther or a skinny bear. Its hair was falling out though. I could see the skin on its back when it ran away."

"Where did it go?"

"Just back down the other direction toward the road. Do you mind getting him to turn off the lights? I don't want to worry my wife if she wakes up."

"No problem." The policeman called his partner in the car and a few moments later the lights died and the woods feel into darkness once again.

"Thanks," Jack told him. "We had a run-in before we moved here. Someone tried to break into our house. Broke a window on one of our last night's there."

"And was that resolved?"

"We came here."

"You never found out who it was?"

"No."

"Would they have followed you here?"

Jack waited, thinking of every possibility. "This wasn't a person here."

"But could that have been the same person?"

"I'm pretty certain no one knows where we are. We haven't even lived here very long. A few weeks. We don't have anyone who wants to hurt either of us anyway."

"No one?"

"No."

"Okay, I'm sorry," the police said, opening his notepad once more. "So tell me again, what did it look like?"

Cindy stirred in her sleep. In her head she was being chased. Her shoes beat on the gravel driveway of her house back home. *No,* her mind corrected. Even in the dream she didn't think of that place as home. *Back where we used to live.*

Most of her dreams vanished as quickly as they appeared, but unlike the others, this one clung to her memory like a white piece of paper to a windshield. And that's what it was like: she was watching them come for her as if through a window.

She ran from them, everyone she had befriended, worked with, or met in the last three years of her professional career. The rain pounded down on them. Their eyes bloodshot and angry, everyone from her past marched after her from the street up to her old house, all of them carrying blades. Even Mark carried a small, red pocketknife she associated with boy scouts. His menacing eyes towered over the crowd. Knives of every size glinted in the sudden flash of lightning striking down between her and the angry mob. Cindy called for her husband. She ran up the driveway as if through deep mud. Her legs churned through the gravel and dirt but they wouldn't go fast enough.

The neighbors came out of their houses. All their faces had the same expression of hatred towards her. They slowly closed the space between them and Cindy. She shrieked for help. She reached the door, knowing it was locked, and pounded. She hammered so hard that she thought she might break the door down.

Jack opened the door, and she ran inside to the opposite end of the house. Instead of closing the door Jack opened it wider so he could see.

"Baby, close the door!" Cindy screamed.

"I can't," he said.

They entered the house, putting an end to her husband. The first ones started for his stomach, but eventually they became less interested in where the knives went and focused solely on getting the blades in him. She watched as they tore him from her life. She hid behind the couch, watching. Suddenly a green light appeared above the destruction of her husband. It waved back and forth above the massacre.

From the light, her vision blurred. It began at the green pinprick and emanated slowly outward like a smell. It spread toward her, blurring her vision, consuming her thoughts. She couldn't look away. She wanted to run from the people flowing into her house. The light held her there, gaping. Somewhere behind the blurry spectrum of her sight, something reached out. She felt something. A tickling sensation, like the pad of a finger sliding across her skin, moved from her neck along her jawline toward her chin. As soon as she registered that someone was touching her, the sensation was gone.

Then they came for her.

Cindy jerked her head from the pillow. There was a tiny pool of drool where her mouth had been. She wiped it off and flipped the pillow. Outside the bedroom window there was light. Blue and red waves washed across the treetops. Cindy felt for Jack. He wasn't there. There was a warm sensation beneath her jaw. She put her hand there. She didn't feel anything. "Jack?" She tried to say. All that came out was a breathy exhale. Her head slowly found the cool side of the pillow. She was back down for the night. She had no other dreams, none that she would remember, just like most nights. And she slept without waking up.

6

The Next Day

"Hey," Cindy said quietly. Her head lay on his chest. "You gonna get up?"

"What time is it?"

"It's seven forty-five. I have to go soon."

"You want anything to eat?"

"No, just want to lay here a minute if that's okay."

"It is," he told her, his eyes still closed. "Are you alright?"

"I am," she told him. "I just had a very bad dream last night."

"So did I," Jack said. His eyes cracked open to look at her. She rubbed her fingers down his side. A powerful tingle ran through him and he had to fight off twitching. "What was yours about?"

"Everyone from our last neighborhood was chasing me with pocketknives."

Jack's eyes sprung open. "You didn't wake up?"

"Yeah, I did. I realized it was just a dream. I was afraid because you weren't there."

"Well, you made it back to sleep."

"That was my way of asking you why you got up last night."

"I woke up and remembered I left my phone in your car."

"So you went outside to get it in the middle of the night?" She rolled onto her chin to meet his eyes. "I always leave it for you before I go."

"Yeah, I don't know why now."

"You put your pants on too, I assume."

"I'm sure I did," Jack said, laughing.

"Did I see police lights outside?"

Jack waited, wondering if it would be prudent to keep it from her. He decided it wouldn't. "Yes," he said nervously. "I saw something really weird in the driveway."

Cindy leaned up on her elbows. "Like what happened before? Jack, please don't tell me we have to move. I can't move. I love it here so much."

"No, baby," Jack said. It came out louder than he expected and he cleared his throat to downplay the volume. "It was *not* a person. It's not like last time. We're totally safe."

"What could've been in the yard that warranted the police?"

"I don't know if we should talk about it. It may freak you out."

"Was it an alligator?"

"No," Jack said. He smiled at her cuteness. "It was furry."

"Like a bear?"

"It was smaller than a bear. It was sort of like a panther."

"They don't have panthers here, do they?" Her voice became high-pitched.

"The cops didn't think so."

"It wasn't someone in a suit?"

"I don't think so. It walked a little too well hunched over."

"You know, we're making money now. There's nothing protecting this house. We should consider putting in a security system. I think since we're trying to have a baby, it would be good to at least price some things out."

"I completely agree. I was thinking about pricing a gate for the driveway."

"Oo, swanky," Cindy grinned. "Are we suddenly rich?"

"I've come into some money recently," Jack said. He added a smirk to his high eyebrows. "I don't think it will happen the same way it did before we left, but I don't want it too regardless. I noticed that there is a fence around the property last night when I was showing the police what happened. The fence sort of disappears in the trees. I didn't realize how much we bought. It's pretty shitty, but it'll keep people from coming in. The only thing is the driveway is totally open. Makes me wonder what the fence is even there for."

"I guess to narrow down where the panthers would be coming from."

"That makes sense," he said as if there were no other answer.

"Maybe we can get an alarm for the windows and doors, too?"

"We'll get a dog and put an alarm on that, too."

"What kind of dog?" Cindy asked.

"I was thinking a bulldog. A nice and slobbery pooch." Jack shook his face mimicking a dog. He could tell Cindy wasn't coming along with him. "Or a Great Dane. Big Scooby Doo."

"I like that better. Bigger. Scarier. And Maybe I can ride him to work one day."

"You know, now that we're rich, you can just pay homeless people to carry you to work. Write it off as charity work."

"Shut up," Cindy said, laying her head back on his chest. She lit up her phone screen, checking the time. "I have to go now, sir."

"Okay, I get it," Jack said, rolling out of bed. "You don't love me anymore, and you're off to bend people for money."

"Yep. That's it." She wrapped her arm around him and walked him to her car.

"You're beatin' feet. Blowin' town. Gonna find you someone who'll treat you right. Do anything you ask."

"You would," Cindy said. "If I asked."

"Yeah," Jack said, putting aside the joke to make a cute face.

"I love that that's our back yard," Cindy told him as they walked down the steps outside their house. The sun was high in the bright blue sky. The river water was so clear that the tree line reflected perfectly on its surface. A couple of teenagers rode cruiser bikes on the dirt bike trail across the bridge. Cindy was suddenly overwhelmed with the urge to call in sick and buy a couple of bikes.

"It's alright," Jack acted unimpressed even though he was eager for he and Cindy to get on the path. "When are you coming home?"

"It's my late day, so I'll be back around six."

"Anything in particular you're feeling for dinner?"

"I'll text you."

"Okay. I love you, Cin," Jack said, and kissed her.

"I love you, too."

"Yeah, my name is Jack Simmons. I just moved to Metairie a few weeks ago. I'm looking to price a number of different things for my house. I checked your site, and, lucky you, you guys do literally everything I'm looking for, and some I don't even know what it is." The website looked somewhere between hokey and professional but the nine point two overall rating sold him. NetProperty Security was a regional company, and they had clients in Texas, Alabama, and Arkansas. The reach also impressed him. Either way, he had been on the computer for more than an hour researching companies before he realized what time it was. He had to call someone and get to work on the novel.

"Well good morning, Mr. Simmons. My name is Wade."

"Hey, Wade. Just so I don't feel weird talking to you, you can drop the Mr. Simmons and call me Jack."

"Okay, Jack," Wade said, obviously forcing a happy tone. "Do you have any form of home security at this time?"

"Yes," Jack said. "It's a Remington 870."

"I've never heard of them," Wade said. "Are they a nationwide company?"

"Oh, no. It was just a joke. I don't have any real home security."

"Oh, alright, Jack. What were you looking to have installed?"

"Well I definitely want an alarm system. We recently moved here and we had an incident at our last home that has kind of opened our eyes a little."

"I'm going to make a profile for you in our system. It's not any requirement to purchase, I just want to make sure I get it all down for you."

"Okay, that's fine."

The sound of typing came through the headset. Jack waited for his turn to speak again.

"Now, 'Simmons,' is that with two Ms or one?"

"Two," Jack said. "None in Jack and two in Simmons."

Wade sort of chuckled politely. More typing ensued. "And is this a good number to reach you at?"

"Yes," Jack said.

"Could I get you to verify the last four digits for me please?"

"Uh, yeah. Two three two five. How do you know the first six?"

"Our system tells us when you call."

"Oh, that's creepy."

"It's just caller ID."

"Oh," Jack said. "Duh. I guess that's not very creepy."

"What's the address, Jack?"

"Four-ten Partridge Corner."

Typing. "Metairie?"

"Yep."

Typing. "Great news, Jack. We are able to cover you. You aren't too far out that the satellite signal won't be unreliable in an emergency."

"That's obviously what we want," Jack said. "But here's the thing, we don't want to stop there. I see here that you also do driveway gates, yeah?"

"That's correct. We work exclusively with a company called Barrington Gates. They're also a regional company. They will come to your home. Take measurements. Have a consultation about what you're looking for as far as design. Pretty much just walk you through the whole process, start to finish. They even run wiring so you don't have to worry about that."

That's good, Jack thought. *I wouldn't have been able to do that anyway.*

"I assume they're just a reliable as NetProperty or you wouldn't use them, right?"

"Absolutely," Wade told him. "They do fine work, and offer lifetime service repairs. But they can walk you through everything you would need to know for that. I'll make a note here to make sure and have one of their representatives call you later today."

"That'll work."

"So you want an alarm system. Were you considering any video maintenance?"

Jack waited, looking at his computer screen. He thought of the thing in the yard. "Would they work in the dark?"

"Yes, once light becomes scarce around the property, the cameras switch to nighttime mode. Even the lower level cameras do that."

"Well I wouldn't need them inside. We have a raised house and it's pretty dark all over with the trees and cars being underneath and all that."

Typing. Typing. Typing. "Yes, well don't worry about a thing, that's something the technology takes care of for you." Typing.

"Let me ask you something. Do you guys get a lot of panthers in the area?"

The typing stopped.

"You alright, Cindy?" Samantha handed her a plastic bottle of tea and a packet of sugar from the break room. She stirred the creamer in her mug of coffee.

"I just didn't sleep right last night." She emptied the packet of sugar inside and shook the bottle. She wiped the sleepy out of her eyes. "And I really didn't want to leave the bed this morning either."

"Oo," Samantha crooned. "Did the lovers put in a good

night's work?"

Cindy reddened. "Not that. I'm talking about in the middle of the night. When we fell asleep. We both woke up. I had a bad dream. Jack saw a bear or a cat or something. We just had an off night."

"A cat, huh? That's terrifying."

"It was a big one, I guess. He called the cops. Then this morning we laid in bed and had this great conversation about dogs, and the baby."

"Y'all are so weird."

"I know. I just didn't want to leave, and now I'm trying to work up the momentum to work today."

"What happened there?" Samantha touched Cindy on her neck. There was a brownish gray bruise along Cindy's jawline.

"What do you mean?" Cindy tried wiping at the place where Samantha had touched her.

"There's a bruise or something there."

"I don't know."

"Does it hurt?"

"No," Cindy told her. She pressed the spot, hoping to spur on some pain. She couldn't remember being struck there or falling. "I didn't even know it was there. Probably just slept weird. You know I go to it face first."

"Oh I forgot to tell you," Samantha said, dropping the subject of the bruise. "Mrs. Rosenburg rescheduled her Friday appointment for this morning. Said she is going gambling this weekend and wanted an early start. That should whip you into a frenzy."

"Great. I actually look forward to seeing her now." Cindy picked up her tablet and logged into her schedule for the day. "She reminds me a lot of my last patient before I left."

"Wasn't he a total bro though? A white guy?"

"Sort of," Cindy said, thinking of a way to explain what she meant. "Well he was definitely white, but it's the way they talk. They're both kind of crude. They make me laugh, and work hard to recover. It's like the one good thing from that place followed me here. Wait, Mrs. Rosenburg is white isn't she?"

"I don't think so." Samantha thought about it. "I want to say she's Hispanic or Cuban or something like that."

"She's not black," Cindy said.

"Is she white?" Samantha turned to Jennifer at the other end of the receptionist's desk. "Hey Jen, what would you say Mrs. Rosenburg is?"

"Um, probably old?"

"No, I mean like what race she is?"

"Oh, I don't know. There's a term for what she is. It's something like reporter or news anchor. You know how they like to be diverse with who they put on the air so they look like they could probably be all the races?"

"What's her file say?"

Cindy picked up her tablet and logged in. "I don't know where to find that."

"Let me see," Samantha leaned over her shoulder and scanned the patient information screen. She hadn't actually looked for a patient's race before, so it took her a moment to find the link market "E:O" She pointed to it on the screen. "Is that it?"

"I don't know," Cindy said, and clicked. "Ethnicity: Other. I guess she's something we don't offer in our files. Maybe we should update patient info."

"Maybe she's a coonass," Jennifer said. Cindy and Samantha both laughed loudly. "I'm serious. I have a lot of coonass friends. They all look vaguely like an intersection point of a racial Venn Diagram."

"It's not that," Cindy said. "I just don't think they're going to add 'coonass' to the ethnicity possibilities."

The intercom beeped. "Mr. Geller is here for his last appointment," an enthusiastic, deep voice said.

"Well, bring him on in, Brad." Jennifer said. "We're ready for him."

"How can you even tell?" Samantha asked. "They all sound exactly the same."

"That's probably offensive to their people," Cindy said.

"Ask him," Samantha said. "We'll leave you alone so you can have your privacy."

"I just don't want to make work uncomfortable."

The door opened then. "Here you go," Brad said, leading Robbie Geller into the gym.

"You know what, Jen," Samantha said. "I really don't know. Cindy could get the bands from the closet for Robbie. You know, Jen I bet Brad would be able to help you. Why don't you ask him about it?"

Jennifer looked at her with an open mouth and wide eyes.

"What's up?" Brad asked, leaning on the counter. He smiled at her.

Samantha and Cindy walked away smiling.

"I never did get that new patient information," Cindy told Samantha. "I can't do anything to move it along and it just stays there. I've gotten two since then but it's still there in line."

"Hmm," Samantha said, looking at the screen. "Robbie, start on the treadmill and I'll be right with you. Do you want your towel and water bottle?"

"Yes, ma'am," he answered.

"I'll be right back, hun."

Cindy showed her the tablet. "You think it would help if we turned it off?"

"Couldn't hurt. I don't think they've been off since they come out of the boxes."

"I'll give that a try."

Jack blew through the opening pages of the novel. He was halfway through the sketches for pages ten and eleven when his cell phone rang. A picture of a laundry dryer displayed on the screen with "Agent Tom Dwyer" superimposed on it.

"Hey, man," Jack said. He activated the speakerphone so he could continue working. "You got some other life changing bullshit you want me to work on now?"

"Well said babe. Listen I just got a check in the mail with

a list of shit you're doing for this project. It's a lot larger and a lot longer than I expected. Did you know about this? It has your signature on it, but this is the first I'm hearing about it."

"Yeah, Joe was going to pay someone to color the book separately and I told him I'd do it. He didn't know I didn't realize I wasn't supposed to do it. I would've accidentally done it anyway without ever sending him the sketches."

"And he gave you an extra fifty for it?"

"Like I said I would've done it for nothing if he hadn't said anything."

"But. That's just my job."

"Better watch out. You've got competition, Tommy boy."

"Well, either way the check is here. How do you want to do it this time? Piece it out or take the lump sum?"

"Can you put fifty in the checking and whatever is left in the savings?"

"Sure," Tom said. "Fifty? You throwing a hell of a party?"

"Something like that. I'm going to make a few renovations to the house."

"Sex swing?"

"Maybe. We want to class the place up."

"What were you planning on doing?"

Jack stopped working for a moment. "Can I be honest with you?"

"Jesus," Tom said as if regretting saying anything. "Uh, sure. You can tell me anything."

"I saw something last night in the driveway."

"Oh, you're serious?"

"Yeah," Jack said. "It was big. At first I just thought it was an animal, and if Cindy asks you that's what I said it was too. But I don't know. The more I think about it, the more it was definitely not what I thought it was."

"You don't think it's the guy that tried to break in do you?"

"How? No one knows we left. Cindy didn't give the institute our address, just told her to forward her mail to her mother. You have no reason to tell someone."

"What about Joe?"

"I didn't know him when that happened, and he doesn't know where I live now."

"Does anyone know you're there? The cops, and the woman that sold us the house."

"It's probably just a dog. They have them everywhere in rural areas like that. Don't poop your panties over it. You're probably just coming down from the honeymoon phase of the move and now you're finding all the weird stuff that happens there. Nothing to worry about."

"That actually makes sense."

"Good, because I don't know what the hell I just said."

"You're a winner."

"So fifty in checking, and the rest in the savings?"

"That's right."

"How's it coming? You running into any problems."

"I actually love it," Jack said, turning back to his work. "I didn't think I would this much, but it's a new kind of designing. I'm used to getting a page to tell the story, now I get over a hundred. It's like I get to be invested in something now."

"And it's all because of me. Can you believe that?"

"You did all of this," Jack humored. "Your mom must be so proud."

"I'm sure she'll find something to bitch about."

"Uh, oh, mommy issues."

"She never touched me and that always screwed with my self esteem."

"Okay, this could go off the rails quickly. I'm going to get back to work."

"You're no fun without the woman. Check your account in the morning to make sure I didn't skip town with your dough."

"I'll have the police on standby."

"Oh, real quick, I have an email from a band about an album cover. It's the Blood Moon Vodka kids. It's a quick buck. Interested?"

"Sure, get them to send the single and some ideas they have."

"Right on. Later."

Jack hung up the phone. He had managed to power through the rest of pages ten and eleven while on the phone.

This sketching is the easiest thing I've ever done. Maybe it's time for a little lunch. Then I'll come back and introduce our fancy protagonist and his slick post-adolescent hipster fade.

He stood from the computer and stretched his back. A few unconcerning pops echoed through the attic. Jack lumbered over to the window and leaned on the sill. He looked down at the small yard leading to the river. The sun shined on his face through the tree branches overhead. He closed his eyes. The daylight warmed his face.

Then the light on his eyelids changed.

A quick interruption of shade went across his vision. He opened his eyes again, looking around. He was on the third floor and it wasn't likely to him that someone walked across the window. Nothing was there. Only the trees.

Then he saw it.

If he hadn't been looking for something, it wouldn't have been there at all. A small, black tendril of smoke rose above one of the branches. He narrowed his gaze and slowly scanned down the tree trunk until he saw a tuft of wiry, black hair. It didn't move from where it was, only blew in the wind. Then it did move. Jack saw a single yellow eye staring at him behind a hollow eye socket.

Jack's hand slipped off the windowsill and lost contact with the eye. He stood erect and searched wildly through the leaves for the eye again. Nothing came. Then he saw it again. The yellow circle of the iris split and elongated. The alarm that stiffened Jack's body ebbed out of him.

Goddamn it. It's a fucking caterpillar on the tree trunk. You need to relax.

"I need to eat," he told the attic.

His stomach moaned and growled all the way to the kitchen. He opened the kitchen and found that he and Cindy had decorated with mostly empty cabinets. They used the same motif for the inside of the refrigerator.

"We need more food it seems."

Jack grabbed his keys and left the house. He stopped under the tree where he thought he had seen the yellow eye. There was nothing all the way up to the top. Not even a bird nest. The trunk was a lot darker at the top than the rest of the tree though. As if something had been there and left a black spot.

Or it's just in the shade. Just chill out. You're allowing what you saw to freak you out.

He shook his head, somewhat embarrassed at his silly behavior. Just for good measure he looked around at the other treetops. He did eventually find a bird's nest, but nothing more. Then he got into his car and drove to the grocery store.

"So did you get a chance to call the security company today?" Cindy called from the closet. The afternoon sun was falling below the horizon. She put on her 'Go Pels!' crop top and a pair of shorts. She slid her bra out of one of the sleeves and dropped it in the hamper in the corner of the closet. Jack suddenly wanted to buy everything the team gift shop had.

"I did." Jack said enthusiastically.

"What'd they say?"

"I called a company that took care of everything we needed," he sounded preoccupied. "Cameras, alarms, a gate at the end of the driveway."

"Yeah? Bad news?"

"No, they said they can do it."

"Oh you said it like I wouldn't like what I was going to hear."

"I got distracted by your bellybutton."

"You've seen my bellybutton," Cindy said, grinning. She ran her fingers around the edge.

"Yeah, but this time it made a face at me."

"Shut up," she said closing the closet door before walking into the kitchen. "When are they coming to hook everything up?"

Jack rolled off the bed and followed her through the house. "They're sending someone to do a consultation in a week."

"Seems like a long time to wait."

"It's the earliest they could come."

"They must be popular."

"That's what I gather. Highest rated I could find."

"Only the best for our family. Wow, baby," Cindy said, standing in the cool glow of the open refrigerator. "Did you rob a Winn Dixie?"

"No, they were closed so I knocked over a Wal-Mart truck and had my way." Jack grabbed a bottle of hot sauce from the door and shook it. "Sriracha!"

Cindy snickered. "Why so much food?"

"You and I used to not eat together, and I think we got in a bad habit of that. I was just thinking with new jobs and a new home we should have a new way of doing stuff. Shouldn't be too hard considering we've been here a couple weeks now and we've eaten together almost every night. Now we just have to get groceries like we do, instead of for one of us."

Cindy smiled at him. Her heart warmed.

"Plus we got paid today so I put it all on my card."

"They sent a check already?"

"Yep."

"What'd Tom say when it was more than he expected?"

"He said that I should obviously be doing his job instead of him."

"He'd keep his cut though."

"Of course."

"So what do you feel like making tonight?"

Knowing that if what he said wasn't what she originally went into the refrigerator to get he wouldn't be making it anyway, he said, "I have bought everything we have ever made together and a few things I have never made. I say you should surprise me. Go way back and see if I can remember how to do it. Better yet. Make up something."

Cindy pursed her lips in thought. She realized then how lucky she was. How much better they were than a year ago. "How about…" She trailed off. Jack raised his eyebrows. "Let's go to bed."

"Breakfast in bed?"

"Sure," Cindy said, kissing his neck. "But bed first."

As the sounds of Cindy and Jack filled the house, the

pewter statue upstairs on the computer table started to glow. The radiating green light began as a hued shadow and grew until everything in the room could be seen. The right side of the statue, the side with Papa Legba, darkened. Wisps of smoke danced up from the pewter surface. Green light from the statue brightened to a brilliant white. At its brightest then, it quickly faded. The light in the statue dulled everywhere except for the eyes. The cold lifeless eyes of the statue burned a deep green for a moment. Then the attic fell into darkness again.

7

Two Weeks Later

Jack continued working despite the constant interruptions and distracting noises from the workers installing the security system. He had finished the painting of the cover and it now hung next to his desk on the single nail sticking out of the wall—the only noticeable relic they brought from their old lives in the move. He thought he would have more trouble from the guys building the huge brick base for the gate at the end of the driveway the week before, but he had forgotten they were even out there until Cindy came home and made a comment about how fast they were. It was the guys inside the house that distracted him. The painted canvas tapped the wall as the workers banged on the house, affixing the cameras to the exterior walls. Jack was annoyed. The only thing keeping him from snapping was the certainty that his wife and their future family would be safe once the job was done.

"Mr. Simmons," the NetProperty Security installation man said from the door. He was mostly bald but where his hair started, it continued down his neck, into his shirt, and down his arms. His blue button-up was covered in dirt and sweat, and it stretched tightly against the man's gut. "Could you show me where your breaker box is? We're ready to hook everything into it."

"Sure," Jack said. He managed to keep cool through the whole ordeal. Nothing good would come from yelling and screaming. It would only slow them down. "It's in the bedroom near the living room next to the closet."

Jack led the worker to the center of the house and showed him the gray panel that covered the electric switches. "That what you're after?"

"Yes, sir." The man was breathing heavily and dripping sweat onto the floor. "We're going to hook up the power without a switch so the gate and cameras can't be turned off. When we're done with that we'll be out of your hair."

"Really? One day is all it takes?"

"Pretty much. We set up your account and have everything ready for you before we even come. Once we install the box in the living room it's just a matter of running cables and screwing in the cameras. Before I leave I'll give you your log in information and you can monitor everything from your computer."

"That's easy enough."

"I'll have to show you how to set up the door panel but other than that we're pretty much finished."

"Well, great. Just come get me before you go."

"Oh, if you want a separate monitor specifically for the cameras we can get you one. It's just a hundred dollars."

"Will a TV work?"

"We could make a TV work."

"We have an extra one in one of the other bedrooms. I'll pull it out while you're doing that. Let me know if you need anything."

Leaving him to his work, Jack ascended the stairs.

In the weeks between the meeting with Joe and now, Jack spent his time taking all the heads from his former boss and severing them so that he could call upon them when the King made an entrance onto the page. After he found the wrinkled and weathered release form his boss signed all those years ago, Jack started work with that worry gone from his mind. He decided to get the tedious task of making the skin tone on all the pictures the same color out of the way first. Once he was satisfied with each head's color, he started dropping them onto the page. For time's sake he only used the heads instead of the full body. After Jack added a head to the page, he drew in the body with a digital drawing pad. This made the job much easier. Much quicker as well. He had burned through half the book in a matter of days.

It wasn't until this morning that he hit a snag in his work. He had turned the page in Joe's notes and saw that for the first time in the novel, other than the cover, the reader would see Papa Legba turning into Baron Samedi. He didn't stop because he couldn't do it. He knew he could make the drawing. He did the same thing on the cover without giving it much thought at all. But now—now that he actually had to put the transformation onto the page—Jack couldn't make himself start. The problem came from deciding whom to draw first. Once he started on Papa his hand would move toward Baron's floating head on the opposite side of the frame. Then when he tried drawing the body underneath the head, his hand gravitated back toward Papa. It was like the two were fighting for his attention, bickering in his subconscious. It made Jack angry.

He stared at the mostly empty panel on the computer screen.

Do we really need this to be a full page?

"Of course," he mumbled to himself. "It's the first time you see it happening so you have to make a show of it. It's a critical plot point."

He glared at the computer screen.

You won't beat me.

Jack concentrated solely on the floating head in the panel. He moved in close enough to the screen that he couldn't see the outline of Papa Legba. Jack was able to think about only Baron Samedi long enough to draw the outline of his full body before his hand went to the other side of the electronic pad. He hurriedly scribbled Papa's features before his hand went back across the pad. His head dropped. He flexed his hand in hopes of working out whatever jitters this was. Soon the plastic pencil in his hand crept closer and closer to the flat surface of the pad. He watched as it moved almost on its own. He could vaguely feel his hand moving, but he wasn't making any conscious effort to move it.

His hand scribbled, jerking back and forth across the pad.

He watched as it made a seemingly furious effort to create the images. Then it stopped and he dropped the fake pencil. Eventually, he looked up at the screen, and there they were. Papa Legba and Baron Samedi waited on the page just as he imaged them. The picture captured every detail he imagined them to have. Not just captured but drawn better than he would've thought he could have. Even the vapor-like visual effect had a different quality to it. It was as though the vapor were shining in a ray of sunlight. Only the light in the picture would be from the light from overhead streetlight he hadn't yet added to the picture. Little flecks of bright blue and white glimmered on his computer screen.

Jack picked up the pen to add in the streetlight behind Papa when his hand froze. All of a sudden he didn't want to add anything else to the picture. It wasn't just that he didn't want to. Every time he picked up the pencil, he forgot what it was that he was going to draw. He sat there picking up and putting down his pencil for what seemed like ten minutes before he stood and decided to find the old television Cindy used in college to use as a monitor for the cameras.

"What room would you like the monitor in?" Jack asked the worker from across the house. He rummaged through the spare room.

"It's all wireless so you can put it anywhere you want it to be."

Hmm, Jack thought. *That's pretty high-tech. Well, maybe not. Everything else I have is wireless. Where'd we put that TV? Oh yeah, we put it in that shed with the lawn mower.*

Jack debated on telling the man in his house that he'd be

right back. No telling what someone would do if left alone in a stranger's house. He reached the door before coming to a decision and didn't.

I'll only be out a minute tops, he thought.

Jack walked across the yard to the metal shed. He opened the wide door to a cloud of dust. Waving the dust out of his face, he saw a reflection in the television's screen. It was small and Jack easily carried it with one hand. The sound of a cicada ripped through the shed. Jack jumped and nearly dropped the TV. Jack looked around to see if he could find the little bug making such a heinous noise, but the sound died away after a few moments. He waited for the buzzing to continue.

That scared the shit out of me.

His heartbeat slowed as he crossed the yard and climbed the steps to the house, navigating around the other worker screwing in the last of the cameras.

Jack laid the TV next to the box in the living room. The man in the spare bedroom was still working so Jack went upstairs to continue drawing until it was his turn to participate again.

"Okay, Mr. Simmons," the heavy, hairy man began. "This is your control panel. You can use your computer to do everything for this. It's our latest model. Our technicians realized that most people only use this on their way out so they beefed up what you can do with it. That's why the screen is so advanced. Anyway, from here you can activate everything from the gate to the cameras to the alarm. Now, do you remember the PIN you set up your account with?"

"Yes, I do," Jack said confidently. It was the month and date of Cindy's birthday, then the month and date of his birthday.

"You'll use that for pretty much anything. The gate has a four-digit code. Just enter it and it'll open. Come look at the panel." He pointed to the small blue numbers on each button on the twelve-button panel. Half of the numbers also had a blue word beneath them. The words: ARM, TEST, CAMERA, INFO, DISARM, were printed below the numbers one through five, and below number nine HELP was written in red. "Each of these buttons with a word on it will perform a task. So to arm the system you would put in your code and press one."

"No pound or anything?" Jack asked.

"Nope. Just your code and one of the buttons. Arm means the system is ready. Test will sound the alarm just in the house, not at our headquarters. Camera can turn off and on the cameras. Info will allow you to check on any alerts. That could be malfunctions in the line or a message from NetProperty. Disarm disables the alarm. Help is your emergency button. If anything happens whatsoever you can call or put in your code and press nine. Sometimes if there is a break in the criminals will round up everyone and make sure no one calls the cops. This gives you a way to call for help without using the phone. Just tell the criminals you have to deactivate the alarm or the police will show up and press help. All this info is in your manual."

"Well here's hoping to never needing to use that," Jack said.

"We hope so," the man said. "Okay, let me show you the camera display."

The hairy man led Jack back through the house to the monitor he had set up.

The sounds of the facility rang in Cindy's ears. It was music. The somber, baritone voice of a doctor explaining the results of an MRI test to a family in a waiting room rumbled thought the open corridors. She passed a nurse station where the chatty attendants and far away chirping machines created a rhythmic beat down the hall. If she had been seated, she would've tapped her toes to the distant beeps of a patient's heart rate monitor.

Cindy continued through the hospital, listening to the sounds of her work.

She turned a corner where the only thing between her and the entrance to the gym was a few hundred feet to walk.

The hallway ended in a T-intersection just beyond the gym's double doors. The florescent lights made the white floors and tan walls too bright. A bulb flickered once and then stayed on. Cindy put her hand on the lever to open the door when a doctor walked across the intersecting hallway with a patient. Before she could depress the lever, something about the patient stuck out to her. The little old man struck an oddly familiar chord with Cindy. Not odd because she couldn't figure out why the man looked familiar, but because who the man reminded her of.

The little old man was the exact living image of the old man from Jack's new cover. Papa something. She couldn't quite remember the last name. Something weird with an L. As the man and doctor walked across the hallway, Cindy thought it was unmistakably Papa-something. The way he walked hunched over a cane, the overalls he wore, everything down to the yellow plaid shirt and straw hat, it was all as though the Papa stood up from the painting and walked into the hospital. The only thing he was missing was the corncob pipe balancing between his lips. Cindy guessed the only reason for its absence was that smoking wasn't allowed in the hospital.

She watched, blinking her eyes with her fingers on the lever. It wasn't until they were out of sight that Cindy came back to the present from the image of Jack's cover in her reverie.

Finally, Cindy entered the gym greeting Jen as she picked up her tablet.

"Hey, Jen. Did we get a new patient today?"

"I don't know. Check to see if there's anyone else in your appointments."

Cindy logged in and pulled up her calendar. "Nope. Not me anyway."

"Why do you ask? Is someone missing from an appointment?"

"No," Cindy said. "I just thought I saw someone I

knew." Come to think of it, had she really seen it? Maybe she just eased into a daydream without realizing it. She couldn't count how many times she had pulled up to work in the morning without even remembering when she got into the car. Maybe she was just thinking about Jack's work and saw a doctor crossing the hall. *But that's silly*, she thought. *I've never added images to reality. I've only zoned out. He had to be there. What's the alternative? Jack's pictures are coming to life? Does this hospital have a psyche ward?*

"Well, maybe they're coming," Jen said.

That strangely worded sentence caused Cindy's heart to jump. Partly because she was zoning out again. Luckily she was looking at the tablet screen when she did or Jen may really think she was crazy.

"Coming?" Cindy asked.

"Yeah, maybe they're setting up an appointment and haven't been completely processed yet. Or maybe they're just visiting. That happens a lot for knee replacements and other stuff where they take time to choose a doctor before a procedure has to done."

Cindy looked at the tablet's screen where the bar that said, "New patient added Apr. 12" and nothing else. A parade of thoughts clouded her mind. Was she certain she wasn't seeing things? Did Jack use someone's likeness to draw the Papa? Was the little old man *really* there? More than any other thought, she remembered what Jack told her over the phone while she was getting ready for the basketball game. *When we boarded the plane this morning I dreamed that a drawing of the King came to life and was outside the plane staring at me.*

Could his drawings actually be coming to life? She remembered the man in the voodoo shop introducing her and Jack to Papa Legba and Baron Samedi. She shoved the thoughts to the back of her mind.

Don't go losing your marbles, Cindy. You're just thinking too much. Probably doesn't even look like the picture.

"Maybe that's what it is," she finally told Jen. "Hey, do you know why this won't go away? It's been there for weeks now."

"What is it?"

"It's a new patient bar, but it won't update."

"Let me see," Jen reached for the tablet. She saw the line in question. "I think you can just delete it since it's an incomplete file. Yep, it's gone."

"Are you serious?" Cindy asked. "I didn't even see that."

"Yep. The system glitches all the time. Just gotta delete it when it does that."

"That has been bugging me. Thank you."

"No problem," Jen said. "Now it looks like you have an opening for a new patient."

"Well, that'll make three after this afternoon. Losing two to a full recovery."

"That's the worst, isn't it?" That wasn't a joke that Jen normally would have told. She was always so optimistic about the betterment of the patients. So much so that even making a joke made her uncomfortable. Cindy remembered what Jack had said at the restaurant their first day out of their new house. *It's like your bubble takes over everyone else's.* Cindy shook it off. *Jen probably just hadn't had lunch yet*, she told herself.

"Yeah, I still have Mrs. Rosenburg though."

"Then maybe you don't need any new patients," Jen laughed.

"She is a handful," Cindy agreed. Looking down at the tablet's screen, she dragged the display down with her finger, causing the information to reload. Part of her expected the blank slot telling her of a new patient added on the twelfth of April would pop back onto the screen. The circular loading icon disappeared meaning everything was up to date. Cindy was relieved to see the blank bar didn't reappear. "I'm covering your break today if you'd like to go ahead and eat. It's only five minutes ahead of schedule and I don't have a patient for another hour and a half."

"You don't mind?" Jen asked.

"Of course not."

"Okay, I think you guys talked me into it. I'm going to ask him on my way out."

"Well, don't tell Samantha. She'll psyche you out."

"Hey, Cindy?" Samantha called from across the gym.

"Go," Cindy said. Her face and tone were animated. "Run, child. Fly!"

Jen stood from the desk, laughing. "Thank you."

"Yes, dear," Cindy sing-songed back to Samantha.

Jack stared at his creation. He had managed to power through only one page since the men from NetProperty noisily packed up their things and left the house. Baron Samedi stared back at him from the computer screen.

"This is the best thing I will ever do," he said to the empty house. There was something about the spread that felt alive. It was the way Cindy made it seem when she saw the paintings. Like there was something more than just a picture on the screen, almost as though a physical energy kept pulling Jack back to it.

The sound of Cindy's car pulling into the driveway seeped up through the floorboards. He listened with his eyes on the screen as her footsteps came closer to the front door. He had gotten so used to the sound already that he knew the second he would hear the door open below him. When it did, he called down to her.

"Hey, babe," Cindy called back. "You in your office?"

"Yeah, do you mind coming to look at this?"

She started up the stairs. "You didn't make a mess did you?" she playfully asked.

"I just wanted to make sure this is going as well as I think it is."

Cindy crossed the attic and kissed him. She turned to the screen and her body jumped. "Jesus," she said. The word came out without her being able to catch it.

Something wrapped around her stomach as the image locked onto her from the computer. She saw it all at once. Unlike the cover, this image showed Papa Legba's mouth open in a grotesque yawn, and then the hazy effect floating across the screen drew her eyes toward the King. "Yikes, that's creepy. Is that the first time you see the change happen?"

"Yeah, I figure this has to be the most powerful part of the whole thing."

"Well, you've accomplished that."

"Great," Jack said. "I don't know why, but I couldn't get past this one today."

"How much more do you have?"

"About a quarter of the way."

"Almost done."

"Yeah, I don't like not having color. This is the boring part."

"But it's also most of the work. After this, it's all downhill."

Cindy followed the black haze across the frame back to Papa. It *was* him she had seen in the hallway. The shirt and overalls were black and white, outlined sketches, but somehow it was obvious to her. The thought just came to her. Not as a sentence she said to herself in her mind, but as a complete thought all at once. That was the real Papa Legba she saw in the hospital. Not an older man that looked like him. It was actually him.

"What do you want to eat tonight?" Jack asked her. "I'm starving."

"I don't know," she said, her eyes fixed on the image. Something about it kept bringing her eye back and forth between the two in the picture. "I'll have what you're having."

Jack looked from her to the computer and back to her. She never blinked, only squinted her eyes a little more as the seconds ticked by. "Is it that good?"

Jack was dreaming. He was back at their old house, waiting, for what he didn't know. He sat at the dining room table staring at the shed in their backyard through the large panel window. The sky was white. Not blue or cloudy, but a white filmy color over the scope of his vision.

Someone came inside. It wasn't Cindy. Even though no one said anything, Jack knew it didn't sound like her. In the time before they moved, he was able to tell when his wife came home even when she said nothing at all. He had grown used to and tired of the silent way she had entered their broken home. This wasn't her. This was somehow worse.

"Leave," he said, not getting up. For some reason he didn't care that someone had infiltrated the house, and asking who was there felt whiny, even in his head. His voice was cold and noncommittal. "Get out of my house."

The footsteps continued through the living room, toward him.

"I said get out," Jack said, finally turning to see who waited for him.

He saw the clothes first. The black, ashy tuxedo was incomplete in its texture, like the imperfect surface of a charcoal drawing. The figure stood there in the doorway, its face blocked by the frame.

"What do you want," Jack asked.

The figure leaned into the kitchen, slowly revealing the sharp, gray face of the King. His lips parted to reveal big teeth. The smile was dirty and wet, like the underside of a boat. The ribcage clinging to his hat dripped red. His eyes bulged, and his shoulders rose and fell with every uncomfortably loud breath. His whole body twitched, half hidden in the doorway. Jack couldn't see what he was doing, but the hidden half of the King was fumbling with something behind the doorframe. He could hear something that sounded like laughter. Something that morphed between a child's laughter and an adult's.

"I can see you," Jack's voice trembled in his throat. It hurt him to talk. "What are you doing?"

The King stepped forward, wielding his heavy mallet.

"What are you doing to do?"

Jack wanted to run out of the house for the police station, but stayed as if naked and glued to the chair and any attempt to get up would result in ripping his skin.

The King lifted the mallet over his head and swung it down onto the table. The thick wooden dinner table disintegrated into sawdust. Jack didn't move. The maddening gaze from the King's face fixed on Jack. It burned into him. He could see everything. He knew what Jack was thinking, how he felt. He knew what Jack would think before Jack thought it.

The King opened his mouth, and the deafening buzz of the cicadas tore at Jack's eardrums.

The mallet went up and crashed down on Jack's face.

❖ ❖ ❖

Jack was standing near the bed. His legs gave out and he fell to the floor. He managed to grab onto enough of the bed to slow his descent without waking Cindy. He rubbed his eyes, not believing where he was now. He struggled with the fact that he was now lying on the wooden floor. He weakly made his way to his feet. Without thinking about it, he slid his pajama pants up to his waist.

There's no way I'm good enough to give myself nightmares, he thought.

He crept up the stairs to the attic and quietly powered on his computer. The painting of the cover had fallen off the hook and now lay tilted between the wall and the monitor on his desk. Jack grabbed it and hung it back on the nail. He found the page with the panel of the King staring around the corner of a building at Robert Taylor. His creeping face and bulging eyes aimed at Robert as he sipped coffee at an outside table. The face was right, but the look wasn't. The dream was more like a chalk drawing.

There was a pad of yellow paper lying next to the computer monitor. He had used it to pencil out the drawing by hand before adding them to the computer. He flipped through about twenty sheets before he found what he was looking for. There were a number of other drawings on the page that had been tried and scribbled over with the black pen Jack used. Somehow that made the King's face look even worse. It was as though the King had done that himself, even though Jack knew that wasn't true. It was like the King was saying, "Look at what I did. I brought these images to life, and I buried them in ink. I created them and killed them in one easy motion, and guess what Jackie Boy? I'm going to do that same thing to you. You're not in charge here anymore. I'm running this freak show. Now draw the rest of me so I can bury *you* in black."

Jack held up the note pad next to the image on the screen. The glowing face on the computer was obviously a doctored photo of his old boss, but the one on the pad looked exactly like the dream. The King's creepy bulging eyes burned at him from the yellow paper. His teeth looked decayed with the thick marks of the pen between every one.

"I guess I can freak myself out," he mumbled.

He heard something outside then. Something running into the post of the steps leading up to his house. Something followed, a groan of pain Jack thought.

He moved to the window and peered out into the black yard. The river reflected the moon up to the attic window. He didn't see anything to fuss over.

Probably just something fell out of a tree. Wouldn't the alarm go off if it was something else? It can't be screwing up already.

Jack picked up his cell phone and walked downstairs. On the porch he activated the flashlight and scanned the backyard. Nothing stood out to him until the light fell over the shed. The doors were wide open.

"Hey," he called out with a little more anger than he meant to add. "What's going on?"

There was no answer. Just the open black space where the door should've been.

Damnit, he exhaled, starting toward the shed.

The pain from the rocks underfoot bolted up his legs, and

he switched from a normal walk to a clumsy tiptoe until he reached the doors.

He used the light from his phone to make sure no one or nothing waited for him in the dark corners of the shed. He found nothing. He closed one side of the double doors once he was satisfied. The lock dangled from a hole on the sliding mechanism that kept the doors shut. It was open and somehow completely unscathed.

I didn't leave it unlocked, did I?

"I wouldn't do that."

What about the obvious thing you're not thinking about? You just spent thousands of dollars to protect you Cindy and the rest of your future family, and it doesn't even work outside.

Jack looked out to the river. There were no boats as far left or right as he could see. There were no swimmers or interruptions of any kind along the river's surface.

Who's going to come down the river this late? No one. Stop freaking yourself out. It's probably just that panther.

Jack reached for the other door when either a high-pitched growl or a low-pitched buzz swelled to life behind him. He turned around with enough time to see the reflection of its eyes coming toward him. Jack's stomach turned to stone. His chest hardened to concrete in an instant. Jack was paralyzed with fear.

He tried to move, but a root caught his foot and he stumbled backwards. The thing leapt at him. The black shape, like a missile, flew toward him as he went down. A weak moan of terror escaped Jack's lungs. He kicked up a leg and caught whatever it was in the stomach, hurling it upward and beyond him into the dark shed. The thing cried out as it hit the side of the riding lawnmower.

Jack scrambled to his feet and shut the opened side of the double doors. Fear gripped him, shooting piercing pains into him with every thump of his heart. He tried to fasten the sliding lock but the door kicked open and into his face. He stopped it and fought the thing in the shed, throwing all of his weight against the door. One of its claws came through the crack between the doors. It ripped at the side of the door. The needled points took out long divots in the side of the door. The dirty claw was unbelievably sharp. The dirt clumped together on its arm dropped to Jack's bare feet and burned him like embers. Jack cried out. The phone fell out of his hands and landed with the light pointed to the ground. The thing behind the door started wheezing. The breaths were quick, shallow hitches.

Is this fucking thing laughing?

The point of the claw came further out between the doors. The weapon now pointed at Jack. It no longer looked like a set of claws. Now it was four long spikes. Like sharpened fingers reaching for him. It swiped at him. Jack recoiled away and immediately rammed his body against the door, cutting the hand open at the wrist and sending it back in the darkness. A silent cry of relief found its way out of Jack's mouth.

Jack threw the lock into place and listened as the thing in the shed pounded on the door. Jack's eyes narrowed as he watched the lock on the door bounce up and down with each attempt at escape. He listened as the thing—which he no longer believed to be a panther—tired itself out. The beating became more and more sporadic until it stopped all together, leaving nothing to be heard but the thing's tired, labored breathing.

Thank God this shed isn't as shitty as the one we had. It would have torn right through.

Jack's hands were shaking with adrenaline as he dialed the police.

"My name is Jack Simmons. I have…" He thought for a moment as he caught his breath. What did he have? A person? An animal? "I have an intruder on my property. It's dangerous. It tried to stab me. *Please hurry.* I have it trapped in my shed. I live at four-ten Partridge Corner in Metairie. Please hurry."

Jack dropped the phone in his pajama pockets.

Thank Christ I put those on when I got up.

That low cicada buzz sounded again, far away and low like an eighteen-wheeler driving toward him on the road. It rose in pitch and intensity. He felt it vibrating in the ground. The lock dangling from the door trembled. The doors rattled as the sound grew. Jack covered his ears, but it didn't help the shrill, screaming dissonance.

The noise suddenly stopped as if choked off before it wanted to. One more loud bang on the doors. Then a pounding on the ground. Then the smell of fire. Jack waited for the smoke.

"Burn it down. I don't give a shit. Burn it down with you in it."

The smoke didn't come and before he realized it, Jack

had gone from waiting for the smoke to waiting for the police. He walked to the control panel, keeping his eyes fixed on the shed, and opened the front gate.

Nothing moved.

Nothing sounded.

He was alone in the yard.

Cindy immediately started to argue.

"No," she said to herself, but her patient couldn't hear her. "No, I don't work here anymore. I *won't* work here. I *can't!*"

"What's the matter, Cindy?" One of her old colleague's voices came from behind her.

"No, I'm not working here. I left. I *moved*. I don't live here anymore."

"What *is* the problem, *Cindy*?" A hand grabbed her by the shoulder and whipped her around. Where the therapist stood was a normal person, but the face was a clean slate, pale and sunburned with no eyes, nose, or mouth. "Don't you like it here?" the voice coming from the face asked. "You didn't move. No one ever wants to leave here."

"No," Cindy said. Her throat hitched, and tears spilled onto her cheeks as she ran out the door. She collided with Tiffany Maxey just as she crossed the threshold of the door.

"I'm sorry, Mrs. Simmons," Tiffany said, holding her by the forearms and helping her to her feet. "But he can just wait." Tiffany squeezed Cindy's forearms.

"*Stop it,*" Cindy yelled. "*Stop it, Tiffany. You're hurting me!*"

"God, it's about time, bitch!" The man in the truck behind Tiffany said. "Get your ass in the truck. I got shit to do."

"No," Cindy repeated, gritting her teeth. "No, no, no."

The car rear-ended the truck again. The wife got out and stabbed a hole in the tire. Cindy watched the truck's driver's side dip and rock on its shocks.

"No, no, no, no."

"And you got that bitch with you, too, don't cha!"

Cindy shoved Tiffany away from her and cowered against the wall of the University Blvd. Physical Therapy Institute. "Please, no."

"Come here." The wife pulled Cindy up by her hair.

She felt the knife go in again. Cindy screamed. It was exponentially worse than the first time. She felt it in her spine. The knife left and came back into the same spot. She fell to the sidewalk. The wife kicked the knife, purposely this time.

"Fuck you, bitch!" the man shouted. The door to the truck slammed and the manual window rolled down. "I'm gonna kill you!"

The truck roared to life.

The wife screamed something unintelligible toward the truck's grille as it revved over and over. Then the trailer park tradition of the double-finger salute. Cindy heard the man yell from her place on the sidewalk.

She watched between the wife's legs as the truck ran up

on the sidewalk toward the wall.

He was still leaning against the shed doors even though nothing had moved behind it for five minutes. That didn't stop the sweat from trickling down his back and into the waistband of his pants. His pulse was a thunderstorm. Finally the police arrived to his yard.

"It's over here," Jack waved his arms to signal the police car.

Two cops with flashlights got out and trundled across the front lawn. They looked like two sequential pieces of a Russian doll. Both of them had the same buzzed haircut, and mustache. Both were somewhere between muscular and overweight and both walked as if coming here this late at night was enough to warrant and ass-whoopin'. The only difference Jack could see in the night air was that one of the cops was slightly taller and slightly wider.

Whoa, slow down, guys. It's not an emergency.

"It's in there?" the bigger cop asked.

"Yeah," Jack said. "Have your guns out. I'm serious." He hoped that would send them into some semblance of a rush, but they continued their easy pace to the shed.

One of the officers drew his weapon, and the other kept his hand by his holster like a real life gunslinger.

"You ready?" Jack asked.

"Go ahead."

Jack flung the doors apart and jumped out of the way.

The metal door clanged on the side of the structure. He expected to see an image of hell's flames conquering the shed, or the demon panther ready to strike. At the very least he expected to see a litter of scrawny, mangy, panther things with needles for fingers in the corner. He didn't expect to see the inside of the mostly empty shed staring back at him in the glow of the moon.

The cops moved in like a team of soldiers after an explosive blew open a wall. Jack waited outside the range of the shed doors. He thought that if the thing saw him, it would want revenge. After a few seconds the bigger cop asked Jack to come look at what lay on the ground next to the lawnmower, or more accurately, what lay in the ground.

"Was that here before you trapped it?"

"No," Jack answered. He smelled the lingering aroma of something burning. "I've never seen that in my life."

A hole about a foot and a half wide all the way around had been burrowed through the dirt. Flecks of embers glowed dully around its circumference. A few inches into the ground, muddy water blocked the view of whatever may still be inside.

It dug out, Jack thought. *It's still here.*

"Looks like whatever it was dug its way out," the big cop said, shaking the dirty water off his arm as he stood from the ground. "It curves back at the bottom. It must have dug toward the river. What do you think could've dug that far that fast?"

It's still in the hole. You reached your arm in there with that thing still in the hole. Jack imaged the thing laughing at them the way it seemed to when he was alone with it.

Jack waited as the pregnant pause filled the air. The two flashlight beams fixed on the opening in the ground. The embers slowly died away.

"We're going to take a look around outside, Mr. Simmons," the smaller cop said. "Looks like you scared it off. Dansby, check behind the shed. See if you can see anything."

It's still out there, Jack thought. His hands trembled.

Cindy was bawling into her pillow before she realized she wasn't dreaming anymore. They were big teenage, heartbroken tears, and Cindy didn't even try to stop them. It wasn't only that her worst fear was remembered and played before her more vividly than she could ever recall, but done so with an even more horrifying ending, and at the moment all she wanted was to burn that city to the ground.

She slid her arm across the sheets, looking for Jack. Before she could discover he wasn't there, a hand slid across her bare back.

"Hey, hey," Jack said quietly. He was kneeling beside her on the floor. "What's the matter, Cin?"

Cindy turned back toward him and pulled him over onto her. She squeezed him tight around the neck. She hoped she wouldn't have to say anything about her dream. That wasn't likely though.

"Talk to me, Cin. What's the matter?"

She wiped her eyes with her free hand. "I just had a bad dream."

"What happened?"

"I don't remember. I just... I just remember that it was horrible."

Jack climbed in bed and pulled her to him. He listened to her sniff a minute or two more. When she finally let go of his neck, he rolled over to his side of the bed. "If you want to talk..." he trailed off.

"I don't," she said. She was looking out the window. The fleeting blue and red dancing lights on the trees hypnotized her into closing her eyes again. "Let's just go back to sleep."

She moved closer to him on the bed and rolled over to lay her face into the space between their pillows. When she did, a burning throb welled up in her forearms and shoulder. As she fell faster and faster into the darkness of sleep, she wondered what could've happened to cause that soreness. She hadn't worked out since moving to Louisiana. She hadn't even found a gym yet. Before she could connect the dots, she was asleep. *You're hurting me*, she thought as she slipped back to sleep.

"Don't forget you have to show me how to use that thing," Cindy told Jack. She was chewing on the remaining half of Jack's bagel and watching Jack pressing buttons on the control panel.

"The thing is, I'm not one hundred percent sure it's

working correctly." It was unusually cold for April, and Cindy, who got cold even in the middle of summer, added a thin white undershirt to her work uniform. With her free hand she played with the end of a sleeve. It made her look like a teenager.

"We didn't waste our money, did we? I will pitch a fit if you want."

"Let's save the fit for now. I can't really tell what the problem is. I may not have set it right last night." Noisy beeping filled the living room. Jack and Cindy grimaced. Jack put in his code and pressed DISARM.

"Works now. Maybe you were just tired. Or forgot. You never said anything to me about setting it, so you probably just forgot. It's no big deal, babe."

"Remember the panther thing I saw?" Jack made an effort to hide the tremble in his voice and fingers. Cindy was smart. He wouldn't be able to hide this from her. *I just need sleep. I haven't had a full night of it in too long.* He was more than tired lately. Fatigue had set in and took over most days, and it always seemed to drag him upstairs to work on the book. It was as if the King was controlling him like a marionette. "It came back."

"I knew you were up last night. You had me freaked out. Up running around all night while I'm trying to sleep."

"I had to protect the princess."

"Oh, you," she exhaled, too tired to play the game she had started. She walked to the control panel and dipped under his arm so he would be holding her when she stood up. "So, Captain. What do we make of this?"

"You know the PIN we use for everything?"

"Fourteen eighty-four."

"And you see these words." Jack pointed to the blue words written on the buttons and the red HELP on the nine.

"They're right there. Couldn't miss 'em."

"Basically you put in fourteen eighty-four and press whichever one you want to make the control panel do. Easy as that. Oh and 'help' is not a help screen, it's a call for help. If you want a help screen, press info. He got weird about me knowing it, so I'm telling you too."

"Why don't we just call for help on the phone?"

"In case they round us up and take away our phones we still have a way of getting ahold of the police. It also deactivates the gates so the police don't have to smash it down to get in."

"Awfully convenient," Cindy said, eating the last of the bagel.

"I thought so, too. Especially considering how expensive it was to put it in."

"It's funny how that worked out. So now that I'm off to work I just press fourteen eighty-four," she said as she pressed the numbers. "Then to arm it, one."

The house beeped again.

"Yep," Jack said. "That's it."

They stood in the house as the intervals between beeps and the beeps themselves became quicker and choppy as it counted down from thirty. Jack met Cindy's eyes and the two were in a showdown. Twenty-two and twenty-one went by before either blinked. As thirteen changed to twelve Jack raised a mischievous eyebrow. When five was on the screen, Cindy could no longer stand the noise, so she entered their PIN and disarmed the alarm.

"Wow," Jack said, unimpressed. "That was a close one."

Cindy playfully punched his arm and pulled him close to her. She kissed him. "What are we going to do about that thing you keep seeing?"

Jack swallowed. He became aware of the sweat on his palms. "We're going to homerun kill it."

She snorted, and pushed him away in embarrassment. Her cheeks warmed slightly. "I'm serious. I don't want to have to worry about something getting me if I go out to the car in the middle of the night. Especially now that we're trying to have a baby."

"I can get traps for it."

"Do they make panther traps?"

"They make deer and bear traps. I'm sure there's a way to split the difference."

"Or you could just get a bear trap. If it can trap a bear it can trap a panther."

We may not need it to trap a panther. Jack asked, "Do you know what a bear trap does?"

"You tie a rope to a tree and bury it with leaves. Then when it steps in the rope the tree yanks it up by its feet, right?"

"If we lived in a cartoon, yes." Jack grinned at her. He continued when he realized the impatient look on her face wouldn't go away until he did. "Here, though, it's a big clamp that breaks their legs so they can't walk and you come back and shoot it."

"*No,*" Cindy's face became one of surprised anger. "You can't kill him."

"Would you rather it be roaming around out there?"

"No." Cindy scrambled for a better idea. Nothing came to her immediately. "*Oh,* when I was a kid my dad got a raccoon trap that wasn't much more than a little cage with a one-way door. Maybe they have a bigger version of one of those."

"I will ask them if they have something for a big raccoon."

"You see? And nothing's dead. Win, win."

"You make the world a better place, madam."

"And now I'm off to work, sir." She kissed him goodbye. "I love you."

"I love you, too."

Cindy stopped at the control panel. "What does 'camera' do?"

"Hmm?" Jack asked, and remembered all the options from the panel. "Oh, it turns on and off the cameras."

"Why would we want to turn off the cameras?"

"I guess in case we wanted to do it outside?"

"That doesn't answer the question." Cindy gave him a seductive look as she left the house.

Jack watched her go.

Then something came to him.

The thing he saw last night was not a panther. In his hazy morning routine, he had partially forgotten about that. It did look like one when he originally saw it, but it certainly wasn't last night. He remembered the sharpened claws. But they weren't claws. They were like sharpened...fingers? That wasn't it. Nothing had fingers like that. Or claws for that matter. It was like a hand made of finely sharpened daggers.

Jack shuttered. Then he realized how he could get a better look at the thing that attacked him the night before.

The cameras.

He took the steps, two-by-two. We he got to the computer he moved the mouse and entered Simpsonsdidit1st. When the password screen disappeared the King's face glared at him with his too big smile and bulging eye from around a brick building. Jack remembered the dream he had and suddenly in his mind, the picture was alive and swinging that huge mallet at him. Jack jerked back in the chair and nearly went to the ground. His eyes resettled on the screen and he was able to calm himself.

He searched through the papers on the table until he found the login information for the NetProperty website. He logged in and began the long, monotonous process of finding the footage he was after.

"Have you heard the news?" Samantha said the moment Cindy opened the door to the gym. She and a couple of the other therapists were huddled around the receptionist desk. Cindy didn't know what had happened, but the looks on their faces said that good news was on its way.

"No, what?"

"I got a date," Jen said. Her excitement was nearly uncontainable.

Cindy made all the right faces and sounds of elation. "Go on, tell me what happened."

"Okay, okay," Jen said, calming herself. "On my way out, I saw him at the little booth they have to stay in, so I walked over, but he wasn't alone. I had to talk to him through the microphone thing they use to talk to the people in the cars. I was so nervous. I asked if he knew how to change a tire to get him out of the booth. He followed me to my car and started looking around for the flat. When he realized there wasn't one, I just asked him."

"And he said 'yes,' of course," Cindy said.

"He did," Jen affirmed. "He got all nervous, and his hands started shaking. It was so sweet. Instead of putting him through more, I gave him my number that I had ready and told him to text me. We're having dinner."

"Oh my God," Cindy said. "That's amazing."

"I know," Jen said. "I don't know that I'da done it if you guys didn't talk me into it."

"You wouldn't have," Samantha said.

"Just remember that when you're choosing your bridesmaids," Cindy reminded Jen, with a smile. "Where you going?"

"Shrimp Gumbeaux Co."

"I don't think I've heard of it," Cindy said.

"It's in New Orleans. It's the one with the big shrimp stirring a pot of gumbo wearing a chef's hat on the sign out front. Gumbo is spelled G-U-M-B-E-A-U-X."

"Oh, I think Jack and I went there out first night out."

"It's really good, right? My favorite place in town."

"We have three of the nine o'clocks ready for their appointments," the voice from the loudspeaker said.

"Okay, we're ready for them."

"Which one was that?" Samantha asked.

"Not Bradley. That's all I know. He's on a different floor today."

"Well, don't be so sad," Cindy said. "We're still here for you."

Cindy picked up her tablet to prepare for her day of patients. If she didn't get anyone new, this would be her short day. Only three patients had been scheduled for her when she left work the day before. She logged in with low expectations, and when the information registered she saw the familiar screen with her daily schedule lined up for her. One unnerving thing stood out to her, the bold words like a visible shriek to her eyes at the top of her list: New patient added Apr. 12.

"No!" Cindy mumbled. "I thought I got rid of that."

The chill running through the building was enough to allow the heater to come on. Cindy stopped in her tracks, trying to find the delete option in the "New patient" screen. At first she couldn't, but then she saw that it was there, but the link was dulled out and when she tapped it, nothing changed. Heat, both from the air conditioner and her annoyance, caused a sticky sweaty feeling all over her. Cindy realized she was standing right below a vent and moved to the side. She rolled up her sleeves, hoping to cool off quicker.

Then she noticed the bruises on her arms.

"What the fuck..." she whispered to herself. She twisted her arm to see if the handprints circled her arms completely, and they did.

"What's the matter, Cindy?" Samantha's voice pulled her from her momentary lapse in personal awareness.

Cindy raked the sleeves back down to her wrists. "Nothing," Cindy said, stammering. "This thing has that blank new patient bar again."

"Again? I didn't know you got rid of it."

"Well, Jen got it to go away, but it's back again."

"Let me see." Cindy handed her the tablet. Samantha's eyes lingered a little longer than Cindy would've liked on her shirtsleeve. Samantha tried a few things. "I don't know," Samantha said. "I'm not very good with these."

She took a step back with her eyes still fixed on the screen. Something that seemed normal enough in a normal situation, but Cindy knew immediately why she did it. She handed Cindy her tablet.

"I just don't know what to do," Samantha said, watching for any movement of the hem of Cindy's sleeve as she reached out for the tablet.

Cindy reached for it, knowing that the bruise began high enough on her forearm to stay hidden. "I don't either. I guess I'll just have to put up with it."

"You should tell someone," Samantha said, her eyes locked on Cindy's. "You don't have to put up with anything."

"I'll ask Jen to fix it again. Do you have an aspirin?"

"Not on me. Maybe in my purse."

"Me too. I think I got a headache. I'll be right back."

Cindy knew that Samantha was watching her leave for the break room. She had no idea what the hell happened to her arms, but she knew that saying that would only create a massive red flag. With the tablet in hand, she grabbed her purse and walked to the bathroom just outside the gym around the corner.

She exited the gym and turned to her right down the corridor where she had seen the old man that looked like Papa Legba. A thought came to her, one that didn't seem as crazy as it would have only a few weeks ago.

What if this is voodoo? What if Jack and I are under some kind of curse?

She put her hand on the door and pushed it opened. She sat her purse on the sink by the door and rolled her shirtsleeve up. All she found was white skin and a few freckles.

"What?" she asked herself.

Jack had given up on finding what he was looking for in the footage. At first he thought he picked the wrong day, but there was only the one to choose from. Certainly there would be a shot of the police car or at least the lights on the trees, but he found nothing. He had gone through everything time and time again on fast forward until he realized there was a timer on the bottom right corner of the footage. After he noticed that, he noticed that right about the time he and

Cindy finished dinner and they took each other to bed, a gap interrupted the flow of the footage. There was a brief moment of dull sweeping lights on the trees from the car backing out of the driveway. If Jack hadn't noticed the time jump from a little after nine o'clock to fifteen minutes after two in the morning, he wouldn't have ever noticed it while rewinding and fast forwarding the boring shots of his yard.

So you disarmed and rearmed the camera system. No big deal. Just pay attention next time. At least no one got hurt.

"But what *was* that thing?" he said to the empty attic.

There was no question that five hours was plenty of time for the thing to swim up or jump the fence—whatever it did to get on their property again—but Jack had never seen anything with claws like that.

Jack decided not to call NetProperty and chalked the mistake up to his own ignorance.

He had put it all aside and reclaimed his momentum at the helm of the computer. The progress itself had not gained much speed from the day before. Jack kept stopping to check the drawing, and compare it to the likeness he remembered from the dream he had the night before. He thought about the last time he had a nightmare. He was drowning in the river behind his house. Something had grabbed him. Hadn't something weird happened after that, too?

Wasn't that the first night I saw the thing in the woods?

He remembered the eye he saw in the tree.

Was that a dream or real? It was real. It was just a caterpillar though.

He found himself staring into the eyes of his drawing on

the yellow note pad.

This can't be real.

The King stared up at him with that creepy look. The same look from the dream as he glared around the corner with those bulging eyes.

Can it?

Jack had no time to answer himself before the phone rang. The harsh vibration caused the phone to move across the table. He answered without looking at who was calling.

"Hey, Jack," Tom said.

"Who's this?" He sounded preoccupied even to himself.

"It's Tom. You alright?"

"Oh, sorry. I wasn't paying attention. Yeah, I'm fine, why?"

"You just sound like something is going on. Do I have your attention?"

Jack was coming around. "I'm just working on the sketches."

"How's that going? I haven't heard from you in a couple of days."

"Not too bad. I hit a snag yesterday, but I think I'm getting past it."

"It was just an important part in the story. It needed to be a big deal, for some reason I just couldn't hammer it home like I wanted to. I think I was just psyching myself out."

"What happened?"

"I don't know," Jack said, but he could remember. He picked up the notepad again and looked at it. "I just wanted it to be perfect. I spent all day on a full-page spread. I'm past it now though."

"Yeah?" Tom waited for Jack to say something. "Boy, you're really a different person without Cindy around. You know that?"

"What do you mean?"

"You're just being distant and weird on me."

"Sorry," Jack said, laying the notepad back on the table. "Can I tell you something?"

"Anything." Tom wanted to make a joke about Jack coming out of the closet, but Jack's tone suggested now would not be the time.

"I keep seeing this…thing around the house."

"There's a thing? What kind of thing?"

"I only see it at night. I thought it was a panther the first time I saw it."

"Jesus. Why didn't you say anything?"

"I didn't know what it was. I thought I ran it off. That was a few weeks ago. It never showed back up so I thought I scared it off or something. It came back last night."

"A panther? I didn't think Louisiana had those."

"I didn't either, but last night it didn't look much like a panther."

"What did it look like?" Tom said. Jack could tell he was on the edge of his office chair. The cigarette was probably hanging on the edge of his lip.

"Like a skinny bear."

Tom guffawed into the phone. "You're fucking with me. You had me there for a second."

"I'm completely serious," Jack said after Tom's laughter

subsided enough to get a word in. "It really was. It attacked me last night. It had claws. Long, thin claws. Almost like needles."

"No shit?"

"No shit."

"You call the police?"

"Yeah. I trapped it in that shed that came with the house."

"So they got rid of it?"

"No," Jack said. "It dug its way out."

After a moment Tom said, "You're not fucking with me?"

"I'm serious. It's got me a little on edge today, honestly."

"You set a trap or anything? What if it comes back?"

"I was going to go at lunch to see if I could find something just in case. I told Cindy about it. She wants to catch it instead of kill it or hurt it."

"That's so her," Tom said. "Look, I don't like the idea of something getting you out there in the woods. Why don't you let me come down there and set up a few traps? I can have that thing bagged on the wall before you finish the sketches."

"You don't have to do that. You have a job to do, too. You don't have to babysit me just because I'm literally your only working client."

"Holy shit, you're hysterical," Tom said with no emotion. "I'm serious. Something with claws is out there, and I want it on my wall."

Jack remembered the stuffed animals on the walls in his

office. The creepy dead faces. It was the plastic eyes that unnerved him. He wondered now, how many of the plaques on Tom's walls were for his skills as an agent, and how many were for some hunting competition? Jack realized then that this was the first time that had really talked about Tom's hobby as a hunter. "Are you getting jacked up on testosterone just thinking about it?"

"Not particularly," Tom humored. "But if it has claws and only comes around at night, I don't want it fucking with my well being. The offer is just as much for me as it is for you."

"You are the charmer," Jack said. He was staring at the yellow pad again.

"I can be there by sundown."

"You sure you want to do that? What about your other client?"

"My other *clients* have my number. Besides ninety-fine percent of my job takes place on a computer. You have the Internet still, don't you?"

"Yeah."

"Then I'll have everything I need. Unless you and the wifey want some alone time, I don't have any objections."

"You fine with a couch? Folds out."

"I can do that. I'll be there two, three months tops."

"Fine. But after that, you gotta start paying rent."

"Alright," Tom said. "Let Cindy know. I don't want to cause a scene."

"Yes, sir," Jack droned.

"Get to work, asshole. We need to be making some

money."

"Kay," Jack said, deliberately feigning his enthusiasm and not very well. "Love you."

Jack put the phone over the yellow pad and continued working on his sketches.

"Good afternoon, Beth." Cindy's excitement was authentic. She wanted to see Mrs. Rosenburg. In the time between finding the bruises on her arms, and hearing the guard announce her arrival she was starting to buy into the idea that the cause of her problems lately were somehow rooted in Jack's new involvement in voodoo.

"How you doin', darlin'?"

"Just swell," Cindy said. "I'm actually glad to see you. Let's get you on the table and start with some stretches. Get that hip ready to go."

"Oo, child, you are feisty today."

"No," Cindy said, waving her off. "I'm just excited to see my favorite patient."

"You up to something, child." Mrs. Rosenburg pulled the coin from her pocket.

"Do you mind if I see that again, Beth?"

"What you up to, darlin'?" Mrs. Roseburg handed Cindy the coin.

Cindy studied the coin, turning it over between her fingers. "You remember me telling you about my husband?"

"A'course," Mrs. Rosenburg said. "You's the first one

that ain't had something smart to say about me and that coin when you first saw it."

"Have you ever had something..." Cindy mentally reached for the words she was looking for, "...strange happen?"

Mrs. Rosenburg looked at Cindy sideways, with narrowed eyes. "What you mean, darlin'?"

"Well," Cindy paused. She handed the coin back. "Something strange has started happening since Jack began his work. I know it seems crazy."

"It ain't crazy. What you mean strange?"

"I've just been having weird dreams." She waited to see Mrs. Rosenburg's reaction. "Jack, my husband, has been working on the art for this book, and the character is based on voodoo religious figures. I was just wondering if anything like the Hollywood voodoo ever happened to you."

"Oh, child," Mrs. Rosenburg said. She put her hand over Cindy's "It's just bad dreaming. Ain't got nothin' to do with voodoo. You done let your imagination get silly, and it done ran amuck in your head."

"So you've never had anything crazy happen?"

"Crazy like what, child? You mean do I feel the overwhelmin' power of God in my soul? If you do then, eyah. Do I speak in tongue? No. Have I ever seen a skeleton walkin' around in a graveyard? No. Like you said, it's just like the Catholics, only the Catholics don't have the same reputation."

"You're right," Cindy said, hoping she didn't offend Mrs. Rosenburg. "So if you don't mind me asking, what does that symbol mean?"

"It's a symbol of good health," Mrs. Rosenburg said. Cindy was happy to see that she was still willing to talk to her about it. "Everyone in my family who ever owned it lived past a hundred."

"So it works?"

"I ain't dead yet, darlin'," Mrs. Rosenburg said and began stretching.

Samantha drove home from work with so much on her mind that she could've ran another car onto the sidewalk and into a building without noticing. Front and center were the images of the bruises on Cindy's arms. She didn't understand why Cindy would go through such incredible lengths to cover them up. She didn't know what kind of concealer Cindy used to cover them up when she went to the bathroom to nurse her headache, but she had to admit, it worked. Samantha had looked almost constantly to where they were along her forearms. She wouldn't forget anytime soon how vivid the details were. She could almost see the palm print from the hands that did it. Cindy could put as much concealer on her arms as she wanted too. Samantha saw, with her own eyes, the marks on her arm. She knew they were there now.

Unless it was something she could wash off. Samantha admitted in Jack's favor.

But what could have been that color? Sure, Jack was a

painter, yes. She would allow that possibility. But why would he have grabbed her with paint before she left for work. That wasn't something Jack would do, was it?

I don't know, she thought to herself, slowly as if trying to get a feel of what it meant. *Come to think of it, I don't know Jack at all outside of Cindy. He's probably a totally different person with her. Everyone else is. She does have a way of spreading herself into other people's moods. Could Jack actually hurt Cindy?*

She didn't like the idea of anyone hurting her best friend from college—her best friend in adulthood come to think of it. She had technically known Cindy longer than Jack, but Jack was obviously closer to her now.

That doesn't mean anything. Husbands hit their wives all the time, and it has never mattered who knew who longer before and it won't matter now.

Samantha pulled over to fill up her tank before she went home. She wore a heavy grimace on her face brought on by the deep thought she was diving further into. She could talk herself around in circles until she passed out from starvation, and if she didn't get her mind onto something else, it was plausible that she would literally do that. Because before she realized she had been standing next to her car from more than a few seconds the nozzle clicked. The tank was full. She had to move on.

Do I actually believe that Jack is capable and willing to hurt Cindy? Nothing else matters but that. Do I believe it's true?

Did she?

She stared at the total of her purchase as she waited for the receipt to print. The displayed 24.10 went blank then returned to zero.

But my receipt.

Her receipt was in her hand. She hadn't remembered taking it.

I'm going to hurt someone one day, she thought. She dropped the receipt in the glove box, and sniffed her hands. Not enough gas on them to worry with at the moment.

Samantha sat in her car staring at the dashboard.

Do I actually believe that?

She thought of all the games they went to together. The dinners they had with Samantha and her boyfriend. Everything they had done over the previous weeks leading up to this. She thought of every dumb, head-over-heels look they gave one another over their shared stadium armrest, or glass of water at the table. Would anything Cindy had said allow her to believe that Jack would do anything to hurt her? Or anything violent at all for that matter? No. Had they fought or ever showed a reason to in the entire time Samantha had known them together? No.

Then crank the car, drive home, and forget about it. Cindy is smart. She wouldn't allow anyone to run the score up on her and get away with it.

Samantha put the keys into the ignition and thought she put the subject to rest.

Then why did she try to hide it from me?

She was able to focus on the road just enough so that she wouldn't injure anyone. When she pulled into the driveway of her rented house, the image of Cindy's bruised arms was the only thing on her mind.

8

The Next Day

"How'd you sleep, Tommy?" Jack handed him a mug of coffee.

"Like a vegetable, Jackie boy." He sipped the coffee. His disheveled hair made him look like a completely different person from his office persona. The wrinkled T-shirt and basketball shorts were a first as well. The bones in his neck popped and cracked.

"On the couch, really?"

"Your guess is as good as mine," Tom said, lazily swiping his hand over the sheets. "This thing is better than my bed."

"Think we caught anything out there?"

"I do not," Tom said. He had spent hours setting up traps all around the yard. Jack had never seen one work, so Tom showed him. He pressed the tip of a fallen tree branch into the center of one of the traps. The metal clamp came together, cutting the wood in two. He had worked well into the night mapping out the yard and plotting each one. He had even laid a trap that wouldn't hurt whatever was out there, one of the one-way-door traps Cindy mentioned. Deep down Jack didn't think that's what he wanted. "They never come out the first night. Still smells like me out there. Gotta give it time to settle. Maybe by tonight if the wind's blowing enough we'll get something."

"Strangely enough, I think I feel better already."

"All I ask is that you let me get it mounted."

"And all I ask is that you don't make me watch when you do it."

"You know what I mean." Suddenly Tom turned his head away from Jack who was leaning against the hallway doorframe.

Cindy slid her hand around Jack and kissed him on the back of the neck. "Come here. I have something to show you." She pulled him backwards by the tail of his shirt toward the bathroom. He turned to her, and she kissed him again, resting her hands on each side of his face. "I love you, Jack."

"I love you, too, Cin," he said giggling with her.

She reached behind her, keeping her eyes fixed on him. She handed him a white, plastic stick. He looked at the display. Having no idea what the blue lines meant he said, "So, is this good news?"

"I'm pregnant, Jack."

"Oh my God," he said as the tears came. He hugged her tightly. This was it. The only remaining change their new life in Metairie required to actually make them complete. There would be no more worries, no more uncomfortable memories to rehash from their old life. Their lives started over right then. New jobs. New home. New baby. Everything was right.

"Don't touch me with that," she said, struggling to breathe against his shoulder. "Because I peed on it."

"Gross," he tossed it in the sink over her shoulder.

"Much better place for it than the garbage," she said sarcastically.

"Oh, so you're pregnant and this is how it's going to be now? Pointing your finger and barking orders?"

Her eyes narrowed and Jack wouldn't have taken her seriously if her thin lips didn't turn up on each end. Jack pulled her to him. He took a deep breath of his wife's scent. "You had sex a bunch of times, and now you're pregnant. Not everyone can do what you have done here today."

"Shut up," she said, playfully hitting him on the back.

"How are you feeling?" Jack's tone was suddenly serious, as though this were the most important question he had ever asked her.

"I'm happy, Jack. Everything is exactly how I want it to be."

"That's all I want."

"Please go back to screwing around. You're much less fun this way."

They laughed together standing in the center of the bathroom.

"Should we tell him or no?" Jack asked. He flicked his

head toward the living room.

"Of course we should. He's our friend."

"Yeah," Jack said. "But is he 'the first one to know' caliber friend?"

"Come on," she said. She turned him around and they walked together down the hall.

"So how's she taking it?" Tom toweled the sweat from his head with a handkerchief as he and Jack strolled down the sidewalk of the city of New Orleans.

"Well, I mean you saw her," Jack said. His stomach still hurt from the enormous breakfast the three of them shared in celebration of the news. He felt like he would explode egg, sausage, bacon, and biscuit all over the sidewalk. The strange thing was that Cindy ate twice as much as he did twice as fast. He bet she could've put away even more if she had the time. He would have to remember to restock their supplies on the way home.

"I saw her destroy that breakfast."

"Eating for two, or whatever they say. Sometimes she just doesn't know when to stop cooking, then she feels bad for wasting, and it just spirals out of control. We had breakfast all day once."

"You don't think it was a little bit of panic?"

"Not unless she panics every morning. That's just normal breakfast at our house."

"Every morning is like that?"

"Every morning we cook, yeah. Sometimes we act like we're on the phone with a bunch of other people when we drive through at Dunkin Donuts. I don't think they believe it anymore. We should definitely know what everyone wants by now if we ordered the same thing that often. We wouldn't need to take the order from the phone."

"You guys were made for each other. You're both just weird enough to not be caught by normal people."

"I don't think it's weird," Jack said, keeping his eye out for the store he and Cindy had found before. "I think it's funny. It's endearing. And I also think it's only one of us. I just got lucky enough to snag her for myself. I think this is the place up here."

Jack led Tom around the corner to the store where he and Cindy found the pewter statue, which now stood cracked and discolored on his worktable. They ducked into the shop and Jack looked for the man behind the counter.

"Whoa, this is charming," Tom said, testing the sharpness of a stone tooth with his finger. "This is where it all started, huh?"

"Right here. The guy behind the counter is different though. I was hoping I could talk to the other guy. He seemed to be in tune with what was going on."

"That guy probably is, too."

"Maybe. I think I'll find what I'm looking for first."

"Anything in particular?"

"The box I'm using for the belt isn't creepy enough," Jack said, kneeling to get a better look at some things on a lower section of a bookshelf. "I realized yesterday that the hat takes your eyes away from the box. Since it's not as important, I have to beef the box up."

"That's a good idea. I wouldn't have thought about that."

"What do you think of this?" Jack held up a pink and light blue jewelry box. Bright green feathers dangled from each of the corners.

"I can't tell if you're serious."

"I'm not," Jack said, dropping the box back on the shelf.

"What about this," Tom said. He held a small chest that might have been big enough to hold a couple cigarette lighters end to end, but would run out of room for anything else. The outside was black, and there were cracks coming in from all around. In some places the cracks were wide enough to see what was inside. Tom handed it to Jack. It had four tiny legs—one at each corner—to raise whatever was inside away from the ground, in case a half-centimeter flood ran through the owner's house, Jack presumed.

"Actually, that's pretty cool." Jack took it to the new guy behind the counter. He was only new in the sense that Jack had never seen him before. The man could have owned the first ever junk store for voodoo-related knickknacks in the state, and Jack wouldn't have been surprised. His eyelids had wrinkles. Jack asked him, "What is this?"

The man took that box with wildly shaking hands that had cracks as deep as the wrinkles on his face. He held the small box away from him and examined it. He spoke with a thick creole accent. "This is a case."

"A case?" Tom asked. "What are you going to put in a

little thing like that?"

"It is..." the man trailed off, reaching for the word. "Ahh," his whispered in frustration. He mimicked the sounds and motions of playing a harmonica.

"Oh, it's for a mouth harp," Tom said. "That's cool."

"Yeah," Jack said. "How much?"

"You think you're going to get a heart to fit in there?"

"*Quoi?*" the man asked.

"How much?" Jack said. "Uh, *combien*? And I don't have to fit a real heart in it."

"*Quinze.*"

"That five or fifteen," Jack asked Tom.

Tom picked up the case and showed Jack the price tag underneath. "I'd say fifteen."

"Of course."

"Yeah," Tom said. "So what's the plan then?"

Jack handed the man a five and a ten. "I think I'm going to make it bigger, obviously, then put a skeleton around it. It'll be like the ribcage on the hat."

"Yeah, see it is both of you. It may not be weird exactly, but it's something strange."

"How about we settle on quirky?" Jack said. He was turning the harmonica case over in his hand and watching the red felt lining disappear and reappear from behind the shadowy holes in the wood.

"Meh," Tom offered. "You said 'tomato,' I say 'let's call the whole thing off.'"

"I like how you can see into it."

"You going out on me?"

"Nah, I'm good."

"You sure?" Tom asked. "That's how Lennie looked at those rabbits."

"No, I'm fine." Jack scoffed, putting the case in his pocket.

"I don't want to have to shoot you."

"I'm good," Jack said with an exhausted laugh. "You hungry? My treat."

"If you're buying, then hell yeah."

"Well, I figure I should thank you for giving me the chance to have a kid."

"Well the commission is fine, but that works too."

"That's sweet of you."

"Hey Cindy," Samantha's voice was wobbly as if doing it's best not to fall off a tightrope.

Cindy's voice was chipper as always. "Hey. What's up?" She was ignoring the weight of the tension between them. It hung on the two of them like a thick syrup. She wore a short sleeve undershirt so there would be no mistaking the long sleeves for a cover-up. Now that they were in the middle of talking about what happened, she wanted it to be over quick. Not because it was awkward, but because she was freezing.

"Look, I just want to apologize about yesterday."

"What happened yesterday?"

"You know," Samantha said. She put her fingers over

Cindy's tablet and made her lower it. Their eyes met. "I don't know what I saw, but we both know what I thought."

Cindy's mouth went up on one side. She had practiced this in her head all the way to work. "It's okay. I would have thought it, too. It was just paint. Sorry I was acting weird about it." Cindy opened her arms for a hug. Samantha obliged her. "Don't be mad at me, okay?"

Samantha hoped Cindy didn't feel her body tense when she said it. "What happened?"

"I did something bad, Samantha."

"Like Hitler bad or calling me 'Sam' in front of a stranger. You know I hate that."

"I just didn't tell you something. I only found out this morning."

"What?"

"I took a picture of it." Cindy reached into her back pocket and pulled out her phone. She unlocked it and pointed the picture that was already pulled up toward Samantha.

"What the hell is this?"

"A pregnancy test," Cindy started overdramatically sobbing. "I'm…with *child!*"

"You ass," Samantha said, relieved that it was not only not bad news, but also it was the best news she could have expected. "I'm so happy for you, Cin."

Samantha had heard what had happened. Only through passing comments that sent the dinner conversations spiraling into a physical awkwardness she pieced together with conversations on double dates, and once when Cindy went to the bathroom Jack filled her in on as much as he could at a basketball game. He spared anything that wouldn't be allowed in a PG-rated movie, but Samantha understood that it was a touchy subject. She fought the urge to tell her that this time it was going to happen for them. That this time there would be no interruptions. That this time she would have a baby. She hugged her best friend as though she'd never be able to again and repeated, "I'm so happy."

Those three words were enough to put Cindy completely at ease. It's all she wanted.

The only thing Cindy worried about was Samantha saying anything more. She didn't want any words of encouragement, because that would just remind her of what happened before. It would remind her that she had lost a life already and of what that life could have been if she had just stayed inside, or if the institute four years ago would have just hired a few more people to take at least one burden off of her shoulders.

Cindy didn't want to have to pretend it didn't happen. That made her feel weak, as if she was incapable at the point in her life of taking care of her own child before it got the chance to walk on its own, or sit up by itself, or open its eyes.

All she wanted was for her best friend to say that she was happy.

Without a moment's hesitation, Samantha delivered.

❖ ❖ ❖

"I don't know, Tom," Jack said looking over the seat of the Xterra to the onesie Tom had picked out for Cindy. He was currently wearing the baby suit loosely on his hand. It was black and in bright pink graffiti-style letters the thing said, "My MOM'S a bad BITCH" in fake spray paint. There was a hoodie the baby could wear that was a matching pink and resembled a shaved head with a spiky Mohawk blazing down the middle like some sort of tiny dinosaur costume. "That's a little more weird than quirky."

"It's from me. You had nothing to do with it. You are exempt from all blame that may come our way. Besides, she was so happy this morning I don't think she'll even notice we're alive for another month or two."

"You actually may be right on that one."

Jack activated the gate at the end of their driveway and waited for it to close all the way behind him before moving the Xterra any farther down the narrow strip of unpaved dirt.

At first he didn't notice anything new with the trees or his surroundings other than the overcast sky shining through the gaps in the branches. This was the first day it wasn't sunny in the entire time they had lived there. So much for April showers. It wasn't until Tom pointed out that something was different that Jack even looked for anything out of the ordinary.

"What the fuck happened here?" Tom said, gesturing out the windshield.

Jack looked around with a feeling just shy of panic. All he saw was trees. "What is it?"

"The traps."

"What's wrong with them?"

"What, you don't see it?" Tom said. "Someone threw them up in the trees."

Tom pointed to four different spots ahead of the car. A large trap dangled at every point, each coated with a red liquid so dark it may as well have been black.

Jack sank, accidentally pressing the brake. The car jerked. More came into view as the car traveled through the row of trees. For every twenty feet he moved the car forward, Jack saw another of the ten traps Tom had laid out the night before. They drove under one, and a drop of dark red landed on the windshield. He couldn't be totally certain, but Jack would have sworn he saw a plume of steam or smoke flurry up from the place the drop had landed. He activated the wipers with the fluid and the drop smeared, faded, and disappeared.

"What happened?" Jack asked.

"Looks like whatever it was came back."

"Did he get loose and just keep getting caught in them?"

"That's what it looks like. You said it was a panther?"

"I said it *looked* like a panther, yeah."

"It's been throwing them up in the trees. There's no denying that. I could see it throwing *one* in the tree in an effort to get it off, but I've counted eight so far. Oh, God. Look at that." Tom pointed straight ahead.

"Holy shit," Jack said. The car stopped.

The last of the traps were hanging from the last tree before the trail through the woods opened to the house. The blood dripped in more of a flow than any of the ones before. The two clamps twisted and dangled in the wind. Whatever left them—or put them—up there had been in the area recently. In the mouth of each trap was a clump of once-living fur, rodents, with the blood of both of the animals drained onto the dirt path below.

Jack didn't believe what he was seeing. He couldn't. The way the rodents hung there, it was as if whatever put them there was trying to send them—no, to send *Jack*—a very specific message. *I'm not done here.* It said. *There's so much more to come.* One of the traps snapped and two chunks of fur fell to the ground in front of the Xterra. Jack's eyes followed it to the ground. When it hit the dirt, Jack noticed the hole in the driveway. Jack could see the gleaming orange flecks of burning debris around the edges. There was more this time. Jack understood that they had just missed whatever had done this. He wondered if he had made the right decision not telling Cindy the full truth about what was out here. She was happier than she had ever been, but if maintaining that risked her being hurt, or worse, the means wouldn't justify the end.

Then Jack remembered how it was so easy for her to believe the thing was just gone. Cindy wasn't that naïve. She was happy. That counted for a lot. He decided to at least tell her it wasn't gone. Jack heard the buzz of the cicadas through the glass. He could feel the floorboards vibrating as the sound grew.

Both of them leaned back in their seats when the sharp, thin hand reached up from the hole. It was ashy and gray. It looked like it was made from wood that had recently been used in a fireplace. The fingers were long and filed to points. The skin wrapped tightly around the bones, leaving little else between. The hand slammed down over the animal and dragged it underground. The buzz grew again and cut off. Jack thought he could almost hear it chewing.

A cone of sparks and flames rose from the hole. It looked to Jack like the back end of a bottle rocket as it took off into the sky. There was no boom or colors after that. Just a smoking black spot in the ground where the hole had been. The ground was loose at the top. Steaming water bubbled up through it and sank beneath. The hole became nothing more than a wet spot on the ground.

"That's not a panther, Jack."

"I see that." They were both still focused on the wet spot. Their eyes and mouths were wide. Their hearts pounding.

"What are you going to tell Cindy?"

"I'm working on that."

"You can't let her think she's safe. Not with your kid. Not after what happened."

"I know, Tom."

The wet spot on the ground didn't change or dry up.

Jack drove the car forward. Neither said it, but they were both absolutely committed to the idea that the hole would open back up and swallow the car. When it didn't, and they were certain it wouldn't, they breathed regularly again.

"What do you want to do?" Jack asked.

"We should probably call the police."

"I'm worried they're going to get a boy-who-cried-wolf

vibe from me. There's nothing to show them. And there wasn't last time."

"Yeah, but we both saw it this time."

"Yeah," Jack said, finally snapping out of his awe. "Yeah, I'll go inside and call them."

"Make it an emergency."

"Definitely. I don't want her to come home with the police in the yard."

"I'm going to leave the traps where they are. I'm going to see if I can find where it came from. Tracks, hair, whatever. You got a gun here?"

"Yeah, a few."

"Go get them."

They got out of the car, looking around for anything that wasn't supposed to be there.

"Come out when you find your gun. I wouldn't mind an extra person in case we have to shoot something."

Tom opened the door to his truck and pulled the shotgun that was stowed behind the seat. He unsheathed it and made sure it was loaded and that the safety was on for the moment. He knew horror stories of families coming up one or even two short, and becoming a member of that group wasn't on his bucket list. He heard Jack's footsteps upstairs in the house as he followed his weapon around the yard.

Dead leaves crunched on the ground, stepped on by a squirrel. A bird flew out of a tree. Tom jerked the gun toward and followed the bird with the crosshairs until it was out of sight. The woods were still then.

He listened.

He smelled.

Tom heard something splash on the surface of the river. Maybe a fish leaping up to snap at a bug. Maybe a stick falling off of a tree branch. Maybe a panther.

Tom held the shotgun on his shoulder, pointing at the ground. He slowly moved across the yard, always keeping his right foot behind him. Now was no time to screw up a shot because of bad posture. He needed his stance as close to ready as he walked. A ripple disrupted the river. He saw where it was coming from even though he was about twenty feet away from the edge of the dark water. The tiny waves rolled around the reflective surface from somewhere behind the shed.

Another splash, followed by a tiny stampede of watery hills.

Tom whistled, thinking it might scare the thing off, or coax it around the corner of the shed. The whistle was loud and piercing, and as soon as it sounded, a flat smack, like an open hand on a face, popped the river. Drops of water fell where Tom could see them. The thing was playing in the water. Not just playing in the water, but also playing with Tom himself. He was taunting Tom, luring him into the water. Tom was no fool, but he was pissed. He flicked the safety off.

Whatever it was in the water had changed the game before Tom even knew he was playing. Instead of being lured out into the open, it now lured him into the water.

Tom whistled again.

Another splash, as soon as it left his lips.

Tom moved forward and raised the gun before him. He whistled again and peered down the barrel.

Another splash, somehow even quicker than the first.

Another whistle, and this time the splash came at the same time.

Tom saw the hand making the splash. That's what it was, not a claw, or a paw, but a dark, dirty hand. He saw it between the cracks of two trees. Too much overgrowth leaning over the embankment blocked Tom's view of whatever stood there in what seemed to be waist-deep water. He saw just enough of the hand to believe he was dealing with a person, not an animal. Tom eased his finger off the trigger. But only a little.

"What's going on?" Tom called.

Splash. The hand slapped the water in sarcastic defiance of Tom's question.

"What are you doing?"

Splash.

"Come on out where, I can see you."

Splash, splash, splash.

"What—"

The brush moved out of the way like a curtain being ripped down.

The man standing in the water was hardly more than bones. His tuxedo, which Tom thought would've fit himself at elementary graduation, dangled off of him. His skin was some hybrid white-gray color that made whoever this was look dead. Matted facial hair clung to his chin like seaweed. He was grinning like a madman. His smile, his face, his chin were sharp and pointed. His lips were red like a healing wound ripped apart before it could fully mend. His black eyes were bloodshot like a drunk.

This thing jetted out a laugh. Quick. Two short, high-pitched *hnyuh* noises.

"Who—"

The person disappeared in a black fog and reappeared kneeling with his mouth on the barrel of Tom's gun. The vibration from the thing's *hnyuh hnyuh* laugh travelled through the steel and into Tom's hands. His eyes seemed too wide as the man's vision burrowed into Tom.

"*Get off,*" Tom shouted. He jerked the gun away, but the lunatic bit down and came along with it.

The lunatic punched Tom in the leg. The muscle in his thigh went numb.

"Fucking stop it."

He punched Tom again.

"*Asshole!*" Tom yanked the gun ahead, bringing the lunatic with him. Tom kicked at him. He stood from his kneeled position, the weird cartoonish laughter stopping.

The dirty man punched Tom between the eyes. Tom fell backwards, the gun finally pulled loose of the man's mouth.

The man picked up a handful of dirt and threw it into Tom's face. He kicked Tom repeatedly, switching between hip and ribs.

"Knock it off or I'll shoot you!" Tom pointed the gun at

the man's face.

The man's mouth opened and eyebrows went up in an is-that-right expression.

He kicked at Tom again.

Tom locked the gun on the man's face and pulled the trigger.

The gun clicked and water sprayed from the barrel.

"Oh, no, no, no," the man said. His voice was low and had a touch of a Cajun accent. "You shouldn't have done that." The man kicked the gun from Tom's hands. He dropped to the ground, one knee on his chest, the other between Tom and the gun, and punched Tom again. "You should not have at all."

The man punched at him again, and Tom flinched backward.

The man's fist became black fog. The fog entered through Tom's mouth. The man with the wide eyes and dirty tuxedo said, "You gone come with me."

Tom was suddenly on his feet. He was walking toward the water behind the lunatic. He tried to cry out. "Jack, help." In his weakened state it fell to the ground like a rivulet of drool. His head fell and he could see that he was walking on the river. Not *on* it exactly, but *over* it. His feet were not touching, but he felt the sensation of each step he took.

"Look at me, boy," the lunatic said. "Ain't no one gone save you. I promise. You mine now."

Tom dropped beneath the surface of the river.

The lunatic stared up at the window. He could see Jack moving back and forth between the attic windows.

"I'm coming for you, boy. You took the bait. Now you gone find out money ain't the root of all evil. I am."

The lunatic eased himself into the dark water.

"Come out when you find your gun," Tom called up the steps. There was more, but Jack swung the door closed, keeping it out.

In the other house there was a closet downstairs that kept a gun, but this one didn't have that. Jack and Cindy agreed that their bedroom closet was the best place in their new home for it. He leapt onto and off of the bed in one wide stride and landed on the opposite side at the closet door. He flung the door open.

There was no light inside. The closet was unsettlingly black. He reached for the light switch next to the door, and flipped it. Nothing happened. Nothing that Jack could see anyway. Light came from the closet casting his silhouette onto the floor of the bedroom. But Jack only saw the oily, black nothingness where clothes and junk should've been. He went to step inside, but there was something physically holding him at bay. Something wouldn't allow him to get the gun. He leaned forward, reaching for the back corner of the closet where he knew the gun stood, waiting for a chance to be used for the first time. Jack couldn't move beyond the threshold of the doorframe to step into the closet.

He tried striking whatever stood blocking him, but his fist only caught air.

Am I high?

He stepped forward again, but was stopped.

"Oh, fuck this," he snapped at the darkness.

Jack stomped up the steps to the attic. Something weighed on him, something slowing him down. He put the painting of the King of Evil back on the hook, and picked up the second shotgun from between his desk and the wall. He nearly fell over when he lifted the enormously heavy object. Out the window Jack watched Tom cross the pine needle-covered yard like a soldier infiltrating an enemy base. He heard a sharp loud whistle muffled by the glass. He didn't know Tom was the type of guy who knew how to do that. He suddenly felt much more at ease. Then the strange way Tom walked—as if there was something out there to be feared—took that feeling away.

Although, maybe it wasn't so much at ease in the first place as it was just simple drowsiness. It was definitely getting worse. His limbs felt heavy. It wasn't like the life was being drained out of him, but as though chunks of his energy left him all at once. He imagined the battery display on his first cellphone. There were four bars. He came into the house with a full display. He had just gone down to three. He crossed from one side of the attic to the other to open the far window. His hands were too numb to even grip it. He was now down to two bars. He caught a glimpse of the statue on his desk. Were Baron Samedi's eyes glowing? He reached for the phone in his pocket as the third bar dropped out of his system, bringing him down to just one. He pulled up the phone app and dial nine, one—

Jack collapsed onto the floor.

Cindy left the grocery store with a backseat filled with bags promising to satiate her overwhelmingly weird appetite for pickles and ice cream. WTIX was playing the oldies, and she used the steering wheel as her drum set, accenting the cymbal crashes to Desmond Dekker's "Israelites" with a quick twitch of her head. Her short ponytail bounced. She removed the Blow-Pop from her mouth and checked her purple tongue in the mirror.

She sang in her deepest voice and shook her head in disapproval but kept singing anyway. No one could hear her, although every time she had that thought a tiny voice in her head reminded her of that Jim Carrey movie, *The Truman Show*.

She pushed everything out of her mind except for her husband, her baby, and pickles and ice cream. She also had the makings for something she'd never wanted, a baked beans and grilled cheese sandwich, but was jonesing for pretty ferociously. The radio continued playing the songs of a time before hers, and the car continued forward.

The city became the suburbs, and those became the heavily wooded road with her hidden driveway. Cindy used the panel to open the gate. She drove through and waited for the gate to close behind her before she pushed forward. It paused, wide-open, longer than she was used to. She watched it in the review mirror. Her eyebrows went up. She took the sucker out of her mouth, and turned around. Just as she was starting to get out of the car, the gate creaked shut.

"Weird," Cindy told no one.

She turned down the radio so she wouldn't forget to before she got out and drove toward the house.

The driveway was as normal as ever. She couldn't be happier with it.

Tom's truck was gone now so Cindy had no problem getting to her spot next to Jack's Xterra. She eased the Kia under the house and took a moment to look out onto the river. The water reflected the afternoon sun.

Maybe we'll get a kayak.

She got out, and without thinking about it, she locked her car. That would be a difficult habit to break, but once she was given reason to suspect the worst, it was hard to let it go. She knew it would come. There would be a finite amount of times to open the security gate until even her subconscious mind took over the duties of that too.

"Jack," Cindy called. She walked up the stairs. "I have a few groceries, could you come get them for me, please." She held out the word "please" like a child begging his parents for another toy at the store.

No one answered. The air was unsettlingly quite as she made her way up to the house. Her footsteps seemed to pound on the wood.

She opened the door. The noise startled her and she panicked as she disarmed the alarm. She pressed one, four, eight, then four. For a moment she forgot what to do next. She searched wildly across the panel for the word DISARM under one of the numbers and pressed it. The chiming noise silenced, and she exhaled. "Baby? Why'd you set the alarm if you're here?"

She walked to their bedroom and continued around the house. Neither Tom nor Jack were anywhere to be seen.

"Tom?"

Cindy decided to check the attic before allowing the panic to take control. She knew how Jack could get with his work. Probably had Tom tied up somewhere just so he would be quiet. She ascended the stairs as a noticeable heat flooded down from the open door. She saw a green light at the end of the stairs. She was sweating before she had the chance to remove her jacket. At first she thought Jack was dead lying on the floor the way he was. But when she saw him breathe, she breathed as well.

Jack stood in a forest somewhere. He knew this wasn't real. There was a point where three trails, carved out of the ground by footfall, came together to make a single line, and it was at that joint where Jack stood. He looked behind. He watched each of the beaten paths reach a dozen or so yards away and taper off into foggy nothingness. There was only one way to go. Hesitantly, Jack stepped forward to the overgrowth lined trail similar to his driveway, only here the trees where so thick Jack couldn't tell for sure if the sun or moon ruled the skies. The trees were so dark they looked black instead of brown. There was no sound. Not a bird, or cricket, or frog made a noise, and the silence was so deafening that Jack let out a low, short hum just to let himself know that he wasn't actually going deaf. The low sound came and left in the same moment.

As he walked, the oddly colored grass—it was almost a blue shade—whispered beneath his footsteps. The trees waved back and forth, but there was no wind. At the end of the overgrowth there was a tiny wooden boat waiting by a short pier. It lay on a narrow stream flanked by more of those dark, waving trees. Jack turned behind him, and much like the other trails, what lay behind him disappeared into black fog.

He stepped onto the boat.

The boat moved forward without a motor or paddles. Jack waited for it to take him wherever it wanted to go. The water was only a black surface over which the boat moved. He saw nothing.

Soon the raft touched land. It was an island about twenty feet far and wide. He stepped onto the blue blades of grass.

He waited.

Jack heard the wind pick up, but not all around him. It was as though the wind was concentrated to only a few feet in from of him. He couldn't even feel it. On the ground a white light, like a Christmas bulb, sparked up and shined for a moment. Jack wanted to move closer, but he couldn't. He couldn't budge. Even his heart rate, which he knew should be drumming, was barely more than his resting beat. All around him children were laughing, but he couldn't see anyone, moving or otherwise.

Color rose from the light. The most vibrant blues, yellows, and reds spiraled up from the ground, swirling into each other making purples, oranges, greens, and browns like Jack had never seen. The whirlwind of color began to fade, and a figure materialized on the island with Jack. The first thing to take a recognizable shape was the top hat with the ribcage dripping blood onto the brim. Next was the sharp, dead face with its sinister, toothy smile and bulging eyes. The tattered and ripped tuxedo came next, followed by the shiny red shoes. Jack had never gotten down to the shoes before. That was a detail that surprised him. He would have to remember to add that.

He stared at Jack, the smile pointed and unwavering.

"What do you want?"

"You came here," the King said. "You must want something."

"I'm asleep."

"Are you?"

Jack, a whisper came to him. It was Cindy's voice. *Wake up, babe.*

"Wake up, Jack," the King said.

"What do you want?"

"I said wake up."

"*Tell me what you want!*"

"I want to burn you and everyone in your life."

Jack, baby, wake up.

"I want to change who you are on the inside." The King's bloodshot eyes locked on Jack.

"Why?" Jack asked.

"Wake up or I'll kill her first."

Jack's heart beat furiously at that. He wanted to charge the King, but before he could move the King was on him, swinging a haymaker in his direction. Before it connected, his fist turned into the black fog. He entered through Jack's mouth. His chest, his stomach, his blood, all burned inside him. Jack choked.

"Wake up, Jack."

Jack's eyes opened.

"Hey, baby," Cindy said. She sat beside him on the floor. Her voice was soft and comforting. "Why are you sleeping on the floor?"

He inhaled deeply and stretched. The dream was already a fading memory. "I guess I just sat down and dozed off."

"Where's Tom?"

Jack honestly couldn't remember. "I forgot. I think he went hunting or something." Something had *made* him forget.

"Here? What's he hoping to catch? A panther?" Cindy grinned.

Jack shook his head and pulled Cindy over on top of him.

"What'd you guys do today?"

"I was having trouble with something so we went into town to find something to help me get over it."

"Did you find it?"

"We did," Jack said. He cleared his throat. "I needed something better for the King's belt. I didn't like how plain it looked. We found a harmonica case. It's pretty cool. Remind me to show it to you."

"Sure thing," Cindy said. "I just need your big, strong muscles to carry in the groceries."

"We have groceries inside the house. Why would we bring in more?"

"We didn't have some stuff." Cindy leaned up from the ground and brushed the loose hair from her face.

"Like what?"

"Baked bean-grilled cheese."

"*Oh*," Jack exclaimed. "Oh, no."

"You don't have to eat it."

"Good." Jack grimaced.

"Unless you make me carry it in by myself."

"I'll be right there."

Cindy stood up. "Oh, no," she said, with genuine dismay. She picked something off the floor. "What happened?"

"What do you mean?" Jack stood from the floor.

"The statue broke," She said, holding out the Baron side of the statue. "What happened?"

"I don't know, babe. I guess I knocked it off the table and forgot I did it."

"That's sad," Cindy added. "It's a pretty clean break though. If nothing else, we have bookends for our paperbacks." She handed Jack the statue. "Come on. I don't want anything to go bad."

Cindy descended the stairs, leaving Jack in the attic. The

stairs creaked and popped as she took them one by one to the bottom floor. The heat suddenly wasn't a problem anymore. She thought she might even want to find her jacket before too long. She crossed the house and walked outside. A wind blew and despite the warm sun, she shivered a little. She scanned the yard in search of Tom. She secretly hoped she would be able to pawn the chore of unloading the car on him. She called his name, but there was no response. *I'll just have to be quick about. Like a Band-Aid, Cin.* She jogged down the stairs keeping her eyes scanning for Tom. That was her problem. If she had just focused on the car, she would have seen something strange about the car and went back inside for Jack.

When she grabbed the handle and pulled, the driver's side door was locked. As she reached into her pocket for her key, she turned to face the car. What she saw through the window was the smiling, dead face of the King of Evil. Those wide eyes pierced her, causing her heart to leap. His huge teeth stretched from ear to ear in a villainous triangle, covered in red blood. She tried to scream, but the terror inside her clogged up her throat. Tears spilled onto her cheeks as whimpers escaped her mouth.

"Scream, child," the King said through the glass.

Cindy heard it as if he whispered it into her ear. She was trying to scream.

The King reached forward. His sharp talon-like fingers tapped on the window, paused, and then slowly melted through the glass like dipping his fingers in water. He grabbed her wrist. He burned her, allowing the screams to escape her throat.

Run, she thought. *Just run, get out of here. Run!*

Her voice ripped through the open air around the house. She snatched her wrist away from him and she fell backward against Jack's car. He laughed at her. He stuck his dripping red tongue out and ran it up the middle of the window.

She shrieked.

She could hear his sinister, clown-like laughter all the way up the steps to the front door. She threw the door open and tripped over the threshold, colliding with Jack. Her head bounced off his chest and the two of them went to the ground.

"Baby, what is it?" He swept the hair out of her face with his hand.

She trembled, letting out short hysterical sounds, but nothing made any sense.

Jack hugged her tight as they sat on the floor between the front door and the couch.

Cindy made a stuttering *k-k-k-k-k* sound. Jack thought she was mimicking a machine gun.

"What is it, Cin? What happened?"

"I saw him," she said, quick and choppy as if the faster she said it, the quicker he would be able to understand what she meant.

"Shh," he soothed his crying wife. "Hey, hey. It's okay. Nothing is going to happen to us. We're fine."

Her crying tapered off. Not because his attempt at abating her terror had worked, but because Cindy slipped into a very powerful sleep.

Jack picked her up and laid her gently on the couch. He dried her cheeks and kissed her. "What happened, Cin?" he whispered to the living room.

Jack went outside with the shotgun from upstairs, scanning the yard for anyone or thing that wasn't supposed to be there.

"Tom," he called out, looking out to the river. He walked down the wooden steps to the ground level. Tom's truck was gone. Jack assumed Tom would at least have let him know if he would be leaving. He checked his phone for a missed called or text message. There were none. Not from Tom. *Maybe I didn't see the note*, he thought.

Jack replied, "Almost finished with the first draft," to Joe's text asking how things were coming along. Then he tried to call Tom.

The phone rang. Rang. Rang.

"This is Tom Dwyer, literary and talent agent. I'm sorry I missed—"

Jack hung up on Tom's voicemail message.

"What happened, Cin?" he said again under his breath.

He stepped up to her car door and cupped his hands around his eyes, peering into the driver's window. He saw nothing out of the ordinary, other than the unlocked door. He opened it and leaned inside. He's first inclination was to smell. Nothing but the feint, lingering scent emanating from the new-car air freshener clipped to her air conditioner vent.

In the back seat sat three bags of groceries. He opened the

back door and gathered the plastic handles around one wrist and closed both doors.

Jack peered around the yard again.

It was just an empty, wide patch of grass interrupting the woods along the river. He climbed the steps, put up the groceries, and waiting on the couch with Cindy's head in his lap until she woke up.

Jen had changed from her work polo and khakis to a modest, and only slightly revealing, black dress. She was more than excited for her first date with Bradley. Normally she'd be nervous, but something about knowing him for the few months he worked at the facility put her mind at ease. She felt like she knew more of him than her past first dates despite never really talking to him.

Jen checked her watch and smoothed out her dress in the tall bathroom mirror. No Doubt's "I'm Just A Girl" blared through her iPhone speakers. Even after all these years her favorite song in junior high was her favorite song in adulthood. She checked her makeup and hair one last time. Satisfied that she was perfectly presentable, she left the bathroom and sat on the dining room chair.

She sat there, because it was the farthest place to sit away from the door in her apartment other than her bedroom. She didn't want to seem too eager or anything, like she was standing at the door watching through the peephole for Bradley to come knocking. That moment would be coming soon. He didn't seem the type to be fashionably late.

She felt warm all of a sudden. Her apartment felt stuffy. Little beads of sweat dappled her forehead. *Oh no*, she thought. *I can't look sweaty for our date. He'll be here any second.* She wanted to stand up, but her legs wouldn't let her. Her energy was falling out of her. She leaned out of the chair, hoping to create enough momentum to lift her to her feet. She made it two steps closer to the front door before she tumbled down onto her living room carpet. She saw shadows in the crack between the ground and the door. Brad was here. *This is so embarrassing. Brad is here, and I can't get off the ground. I'm so embarrassed.*

She dragged herself to the couch, leaving carpet burns on the tops of her legs. She thought she was dying. "Help," she breathed.

A thump on the door. Not a knock but a battering ram-type bang that rattled the door on its hinges. Jen flinched at the sound. She kept dragging herself. She had just enough strength to pull herself onto the couch in a seated position.

The door banged again.

Jen's vision swirled in and out of focus. She felt like she was staring into a fire. The sweat started on her forehead and spread down her spine.

The door banged again. Then there was the sound of a body falling onto the concrete walkway just outside, then the overwhelming sense, not of just being watched, but being joined by someone in the room filled Jen.

Jen didn't see the eerily thin man in the tuxedo standing beside the couch; her eyes wouldn't move in that direction.

She felt him there though.

She didn't scream. She wouldn't have if she had the power to. If there was anything to be learned from the Lifetime Channel, it's that the bad guys always got off on the screams of their victims. If Jen was going to die, she was going to give him as little pleasure from it that she could. Luckily the man's bloody grin didn't register in her peripheral sight. She focused on the wooden coffee table in front of her. Her arms crossed at her stomach.

"Whoever you are, whatever you want, I don't care. I'm not who you're looking for."

She leaned forward without wanting to or thinking about it. Nothing forced her. There was no hand on the back of her neck. She just did it, her body acting on its own.

The vision of the coffee table rushed toward her face. Her head smacked down onto the flat surface of the table and bounced up. The pain was colossal. Tinnitus rang in her ears, blocking out all other sound. Her head went down again and split the table. It hung together with splinters. She didn't feel it that time. The adrenalin blocked the pain. One more swing and the table broke completely. Jen fell to her knees, then to her stomach. The last thing she saw as her vision pinholed to black was the fiery red shoes on her assailant's feet. She reached foreword, grasping for the shoes just as her energy drained completely.

When Cindy came to, her memory of what happened

had jumbled in her mind. She remembered something about Jack's King, but was that just a nightmare? It couldn't have been real. That was just a drawing. But hadn't she seen Papa Legba in the hallways of the facility? She wasn't sure. She remembered a face. The way eyes stared daggers over a bloody smile. But now, she wasn't entirely certain she hadn't just dreamt that. And if she hadn't, what had her so hysterical before? Could've been a snake. She remembered trying to run. That was logical. Although the way Jack described the way she had reacted made the possibility of a snake unlikely, no matter how much she hated them.

Jack sat beside her at the computer. They were sitting in the glow of the monitor. The sun had fallen since she went under. Jack pulled up the NetProperty website and backtracked the few hours of the footage to when Cindy arrived home.

"Okay, this is you driving up." Jack pointed to the screen. The yellow Kia Soul came into view with Cindy still bobbing her head to the music.

"Yeah," Cindy agreed, her head still watery.

"You get out. The lights blink when you lock the car, and you walk upstairs."

Cindy watched as the dome light in the car faded. She followed herself as she walked out of the camera's view. "I don't know what I saw baby, but something must have freaked me out."

"I know," Jack assured her. "Just keep watching with me. I want to figure out what it is so we can get rid of it."

They watched together in silence, neither of them dared

to look away from the screen. Jack slid his hand onto Cindy's thigh and pulled her closer to him. He wanted her to know that he was still on her side, regardless of what they saw. His gesture said exactly that.

The only motion on the screen between Cindy leaving and reentering the screen was a bird flying across the frame. Other than that, Jack and Cindy might as well have been staring at a picture.

"Did you see anything happen?" Jack asked.

"Huh uh," Cindy said, preoccupied.

When Cindy walked by into frame she looked tired. Her ponytail was a mess and her head and shoulders visibly drooped. A bird flew across the screen, but little else happened. She stopped by the car looking into driver's window. She didn't move. She just stood there, balancing on her feet. For a moment Jack thought the bird would come back and peck at her face. At least fly close enough to her to send her running up the—

The screen blinked white and then Cindy on screen started shrieking. She fell back against Jack's car, without it Cindy would have went sprawling onto the concrete. She jerked her hand over her head and sprinted out of the picture.

"I didn't see anything," Jack said. "Did you?"

"No," Cindy said, her voice dripping with sad disbelief.

"Let's just watch it again."

"You don't have to do that."

"Just one more time, I just want to see if I can see what happened."

Jack rewound and rolled the feed again. Neither of them saw anything the second time through, so Jack went back again without asking.

"Baby, it's okay. I just had a moment of senility."

"I don't think that's what it is, Cin."

"*Please*," Cindy said sternly.

Jack flinched. He was immediately thrown back to the days when the best he could hope for was a passing glance across the living room over a week's time. She had done that since the two of them had rebuilt their marriage, but it never registered with him so intensely. Something about it, something was different now. His heart broke. "I... I'm sorry."

"Look, it's fine," Cindy moved closer to him. Hugged him. "I'm just embarrassed. I freaked out over nothing. Maybe it's the baby." She knew it wasn't that, but she was embarrassed. More than she had been in a long time. "Maybe it's just the hormones going crazy, and I just had an episode. Can we just drop it?"

"Yeah, sure."

Cindy kissed him. "I'm sorry, Jack."

"It's cool," he shrugged. "We're all good."

"Come here," Cindy kissed his neck. "I really am sorry. You know that?"

Jack got up in the middle of the night. He was awake. Fully awake. The moon draped a blue glow into their bedroom, giving Cindy's bare back a frozen look. He left the room without making a sound. He reached the first step when the board's groan made the first noise of his ascent to the attic. He froze. He listened for the rustle of bed sheets. Cindy lay, resting in their bed, face down on her pillow.

Jack shook the mouse activating the screen. He took a moment to enter the password and was greeted by the paused display of his wife driving up the driveway. For a moment her face appeared distorted, smeared in a long lopsided smile. He took a closer look and recognized the motion of her bobbing head caught between frames of the camera's shutter for what it was.

He played the recorded feed over and over. He couldn't find a single moment between her arrival and her return to the car that might suggest something was there to generate that reaction. The only abnormality was the quick blink of white that took over the screen just before she started to scream.

That can't be it. It wasn't even a nanosecond.

Jack wound back the footage to just before the flash and slowed it down to a point where only a click of the mouse moved the frames forward.

One frame she stood next to the car's door.

The next the screen was totally white.

The next she was standing by the door again.

Everything was the same before and after.

But wait, Jack told himself. *She's not standing the same way before and after.*

Jack was right. There was a single difference between the frames before and after the white flash. Before the flash, she wasn't wearing her wedding ring, after she was. When she got out of the car, there it was on her right ring finger. When she came back, gone. Then the flash and there it was again. Jack backed the film up again and watched close for any other glitches in the feed.

One pass.

Then another.

Then on the third time through he noticed that the bird flying across the screen was a distraction. Jack had watched it each time it had gone across. He was supposed to. When the bird flew over as she walked to the side of the car, her position in the carport changed ever so slightly. He wondered now if the bird was actually there to begin with. He could only see the shift in her positioning when he kept his eye on her right foot, but it was definitely there. A little jerk from straight ahead to pointed slightly right. It happened as she moved her head from left to right, looking for someone. *Probably Tom*, Jack told himself. It was amazing that he caught it at all. A splice in the film. Someone, *something*, had altered the footage. What the footage didn't show was whatever happened between Cindy stopping at the side of the car, and her falling back on to Jack's car. Whatever the cameras recorded instead, was a fake.

The footage jerked.

A new window popped up over footage of Cindy. It was Tom sneaking around the shed in broad daylight. He carried the shotgun, and suddenly Jack remembered what had happened earlier, the black void that wouldn't let him get to the gun, the dripping traps hanging in the trees, that terrifying hand reaching out of the hole in the ground.

Jack watched as the King attacked Tom and dragged him under the river. The King glared into the camera. Jack heard him speak. Not through the speakers of the computer. The cameras didn't record sound. He heard it as if it were whispered over his shoulder.

"I'm coming for you, boy." *Boy* slid out of his Cajun mouth like *boa*.

The computer screen jerked again. New windows began popping up all over. Chaotic videos of gratuitous violent outburst crowded his monitor. Animals attacked one another. Crazed doctors operated on bones that were not deadened by anesthesia. People shot each other in streets. Teenagers ollied their skateboards, landing wrong, and shattering their legs. Jack wanted to turn away, but something kept him there, facing the carnage.

Then the popups stopped. The screen went black. Jack struggled to catch his breath in the black attic. Then a single image came to the computer. It was a grainy, night-vision shot of the shed behind the house. The King of Evil stood tall and thin, his head like a metronome ticking back and forth. The top hat made him look forever tall. The low light created holes over his eye sockets. His eyes and the jewels mounted on the mallet shined in the night-vision feed.

Jack stood and looked out the window to the shed. The moon cast just enough light on the yard that Jack could see that it was empty. From all around him came a *tisk tisk tisk*. Jack turned back to the screen, convinced that this was only happening in his mind.

"Boy, you outta knowed I wasn't gone be there," the King said.

Jack sat back down at the computer. His heart pounding. "What do you…" he whispered.

"What do I want?" the King finished. "You should know that, boy. I'm evil. That's all I wan' be. I'm mon' kill you, Jack."

"Why," Jack whispered.

"Cause, Jack. I tolt ya. I mon' burn everyone you love. Until all that's lef' is you. And I'ma burn you slowly. Like kindlin'."

The screen went black, leaving him alone in the emptiness of the night.

There was a click in Jack's throat when he swallowed.

He snuck downstairs, and got into bed. He didn't bother closing his eyes. He was awake for the night.

9

The Next Day

Cindy stood on an island, surrounded by the vast sweeping night. There was only a thumbnail version of the moon weakly shining on the open ocean. Sporadic clouds of fog rose up from the water like ghosts. Everything she saw was a pale blue shade. Everything looked cold. But there was no temperature. She didn't feel one anyway.

Before her, on the opposite end of the island too small to show up on any map, something materialized. It took the shape of a person, slender and tall. She could tell by the outline who would be standing there in the end. Even before the details formed around the silhouette, she knew she was dreaming of the King.

She waited. Part of her snatched at the memory of what she actually saw in the car.

"Don't even try it," a thick Cajun voice came to her like a wind over the sea.

"What do you want?" Cindy's voice was unflinchingly strong, almost annoyed.

"I wan' you, girlie," the King told her. The black shadow around the figure ignited, burning away from his face leaving the ashy gray skin. The wet, red smile became a dark black. "That man of yaws, he brung me here. Now I'm gone ruin him."

"You can't do that," Cindy said, verging on boredom. "You're just a painting on our wall. In a month we won't even see you."

"You not gone like what I do to you."

The King charged.

Cindy shied backward, but the ashy fingers wrapped around her throat. She couldn't breathe. It wasn't the lack of air getting to her body that scared Cindy. It was the pressure on her neck. She could actually feel it. Any other dream, she would just wake up at this moment, but now she wriggled in his hands like a dying animal.

The King inhaled Cindy's scent. His tongue dangled out of his head, and he ran it up the side of her face.

Cindy tried to push him away, but her disgust overpowered her strength, and her efforts were useless.

"You see what I wan' you to see, girlie," the King said. He smelled like an aged carcass. "I'll chase you 'round this world and make you forget as soon as you in that man's arms. I make him think you goin' crazy. And when they lock you up, put you in a room, I'ma keep comin' for ya. Yaw brung this on yaw's self."

Cindy felt the tingle of a hand on her back.

"Fuck you," Cindy spat at the King.

"Get outta here. I'm coming for you. You gave me my power. I'ma give it right back."

When Cindy woke, her sleepy eyes met Jack's. The smell of bacon, eggs, and sausage beckoned her into the kitchen.

"Hey, baby," Jack said quietly. He knew not to be too loud when she first woke up. It was a rare day that he was up before her, but that was a lesson he only needed to learn once, and it stayed with him all these years later. "I made you breakfast."

Cindy hummed her delight. "Yay," she said into the pillow. She stretched beneath the sheets. She tried to speak but her throat was cruddy. She cleared it and started over. "What time is it?"

"About forty-five before you have to go."

Cindy groaned childishly. "But I'm pregnant."

"I know, and you're probably going to have to find a new way to sleep, but 'save the old people' and all that, right? This city needs a hero."

"You go."

"I just don't have the touch. Besides, I've got to stay here and finish. I'm almost done."

"Fine," Cindy said. "But I'm wearing sweats to bed tonight."

"Are you?" He looked at her with raised eyebrows.

"No."

"Come on," Jack led her to the kitchen, giving her a long shirt to use at the table. "You got fifteen minutes to eat me under the table. Once you've done that, you can get dressed and go make some money for the baby you're carrying." Jack sat her down in front of a bowl of scrambled eggs big enough to make a normal person cower.

The table was already set. Cindy felt like she was being spoiled. She dumped half of the bowl's contents onto her plate and filled in the little remaining space with bacon, a couple sausage patties, and what was left of the pepper.

"When did you get up?"

"I can't remember, actually," Jack said. He had actually been up since two in the morning. There was no way he'd be able to go back to sleep. He spent the last few hours not sitting still. He hoped Cindy chose to believe him. She probably knew he was lying. She always did. "The sun was up so I thought I'd surprise the mommy-to-be with a little of Big Jim's finest meat."

"I think you're just trying to get in my pants."

"Right you are, madam." Jack set a souvenir cup from a Pelicans game filled to the top with chocolate milk in front of Cindy. "I'm getting a powerful prego vibe from you, and I want to see where it takes me."

"You're being cute."

"All in a day's work."

"Walk me through your day."

"First, I'm going to work on the sketches of *The King of Evil*," Jack said. "I have to add in the new creepy box for his heart."

"Mmm," Cindy said, whether from what he said or the food, Jack couldn't tell. She seemed happy though, and as long as Jack could keep that fire stoked until he put an end to the King, he didn't care what happened.

"Then I'll work for a few more hours until I get to the end. That may be tomorrow now that I'm thinking about how much I have left."

"*Tomorrow?*" Cindy exclaimed. "That's so fast, babe."

"I know," Jack agreed. He was going to continue, but he could tell Cindy was trying to say something once she swallowed the mouthful of eggs in her mouth.

"Do we still have that peach flavored salsa my mom made?"

"I think so."

"Could you get it for me?"

Jack retrieved the jar and handed it to her.

Cindy dumped the remaining quarter of the mason jar on the eggs and mixed it in.

"Can I tell you something?" she asked.

"What's that?"

"I'm not even hungry," Cindy giggled. A small piece of food fell back onto her plate. "I'm only eating all this because I know I should, and because you made it for me."

"Well you're pregnant, so it's good to eat more."

"This isn't exactly healthy baby food."

"It's not cigarettes or caffeine. Aren't those baby kryptonite?"

"I think there's more to it than just those things."

"Nah," Jack said. "This meal won't hurt. I can add 'pick

up a baby food book' to my list today if you'd like."

"There's a Books-A-Million by the gym," Cindy said. "I can stop by. I'm probably still going to be full after work. I'll need to work it off."

"Well there's your plan," Jack said, putting his stamp of approval on it. He was happy to have her busy after work. It gave him extra time to get rid of their problem.

"You want to go out tonight?"

"Sure," Jack said. "I can meet you in town."

"Now that's a plan," she said. "Somewhere cheap though. Like Popeye's or Baskin Robbins."

Jack laughed. She looked up at him with a dab of peach flavored salsa mounted on the tip of her nose. "You think Popeye's and Baskin Robbins will be in the baby food book?"

"It's in my baby food book." Cindy continued eating. She stopped suddenly. "Don't let me become a fat pregnant woman. I don't want to be fat *and* pregnant. Either-or is fine."

"You're not going to get fat. They're going to call you to model maternity swimsuits."

"Promise me."

"I promise."

"I need your help. No more feeding me like I'm Hansel *and* Gretel. I'm going to eat it. I'm pregnant. I can't be held accountable for what goes in here anymore. I'm like a horse. I'll keep eating until something ruptures. What?"

Jack had stopped trying to hold back his laughter.

"What is it?" Cindy said, barely keeping a straight face.

"You make me laugh, Cin," Jack said. "You always have."

"Shut up," she said, grinning over her nearly empty plate of eggs and bacon. The sausage patties were a memory lost in the ether of her drowsy morning. "Did you ever hear from Tom?"

"No," Jack said. He was hoping to skirt this conversation at least until Cindy came home from work. "Weird he didn't say anything before he left."

"Yeah, I know. You don't think he got into an accident, did he?"

"Nah," Jack said. "We'd know about it by now, wouldn't we?"

"Yeah, I guess you're right. Nothing is a secret. Someone would have said something by now."

"I'll make a point to call him," Jack said, hoping that put an end to it. It did.

"I better start getting ready for work. They probably wouldn't appreciate me coming in wearing just a T-shirt."

"I would."

"I hope so," Cindy blew a kiss to him, then tapped him on the butt and left the kitchen for the bedroom to get ready.

Jack began the laborious task of cleaning the plates and cooking utensils. He kept one ear focused on her direction, waiting for a thump or scream or anything that said something had gotten to her. There was nothing but the sound of the shower through the wall. When she was ready for work, Jack walked her to her car and followed her out the driveway.

When he was certain she wouldn't be coming back, he sprinted to his computer.

Cindy Simmons was the happiest woman on the planet. Her hair bobbed up and down to the guitar riff of "Back in Black" jammed out of her speakers from the WTIX studio. Brian Johnson's vocals were too high for her, but she was confident that the station would play a song in her range eventually. She reminded herself to pull her hair back before she clocked in.

The sun was out and following her to work. The traffic was nonexistent. Well, nearly nonexistent. Someone cut her off in order to pass a handicap van, but it barely registered with Cindy. She was so far above complaint that she would even eat a burger with pickles, and there was nothing worse than pickles on a burger for Cindy.

She pulled into the Louisiana Bone and Joint Specialist parking structure, parked, and then walked to the main entrance. She was hoping to see Bradley in the security booth, but it was someone else.

No big deal, she thought. *Jen knows how it went just as well as he does.*

She made her way toward the gym, nearly skipping.

Cindy passed one of the consultation rooms and stopped. She saw the little old man she mistook for a real life version of Jack's Papa Legba. He was talking to a doctor about something and without his yellow plaid shirt and hat, he didn't much resemble Legba. She knew it was the same person, but now she realized she had been silly before. The old man looked around the doctor. Cindy smiled at him, standing just outside the doorway. He winked at her.

She thought something rather strange then, a single word. "Congratulations." It was odd how the thought came to her. Not as a spoken word, but all at once, almost like a sort of delayed reaction to someone just saying the word. She kept her eyes on the old man. He did something peculiar. She knew the gesture wasn't intended for her. It couldn't be. The man rubbed his hand over the lower section of his stomach. The man wasn't looking at her anymore, so how could that be intended for Cindy? It could've been an unconscious motion. He was probably discussing an illness that brought him to the facility.

But if he had an illness he wouldn't be here, would he? We're only orthopedics here.

Cindy shook the thought out of her head and continued toward the gym. She wasn't quite as bouncy, more pensive now, but still in a wonderful mood. She opened the door to the gym, expecting to see Jen. Samantha sat at her desk instead.

"Hey," she said, purposely adding a hint of confusion.

"Yeah, I know," Samantha said. "I'm let down too. Someone said she called in."

"Well, that's crappy."

"I know, but I think we know how it went anyway," Samantha said with a devilish grin.

"What do you mean?"

"He called in sick, too. Or maybe they said he called in *sore*," Samantha joked.

"No," Cindy said. "That's a little too obvious."

"I'm just telling you what I heard."

"That's crazy," Cindy laughed. "They could at least be a little more subtle about it."

"What can you do? They're in love. I'd want a jump on the weekend, too."

"So what are we going to do today instead?"

"There're enough gaps in the appointments today that we can cover it. We may not be able to greet everyone, but we'll make it."

"That's important," Cindy said. "We may not come in first, but we'll make it."

"Tablet?"

"Sure."

"Oh I forgot to tell you." Samantha handed her the table. "Mrs. Rosenburg can't come in Monday, I told her since I'm coming in Saturday anyway I can work her through her exercises."

"That sucks. You're poaching my patients now?" The feeling of betrayal was only partially authentic. She logged into her tablet. "And my favorite one."

"I'll give her back. I promise."

"What the hell is this?" Cindy's face turned down. A cold, sharp thorn of terror dug into her heart. Cindy closed the application, and reopened it. She logged back in. It was still there, unmoving from the screen as if watching her.

"What's what?"

Cindy handed her the tablet. There was a name in place of the blank bar that had plagued her since April twelfth. The bar now read, "New patient added Apr. 12. Simmons, Jack. FRX left tib/leg. Multiple FRX rib."

"Who put his name is here? Jack's fine. I was with him all morning."

"It could be someone else, Cindy."

"Why would they have added it on the twelfth? This is the one we've been having a problem with."

"I don't know, Cin." Samantha said, trying not to work her up. "We can send an email to see if we can find out who it is. May not be back to us until Monday though."

"Let's do that."

"Okay, why don't you call him and make sure he's okay," Samantha suggested.

Cindy was already out the door and pulling up his contact on her phone. She tapped the phone icon and hit call.

Jack's pace had slowed considerably. He found himself adjusting the sketches on his computer and looking out the window for the King. He wasn't afraid. He was coaxing the King out of the water. He knew that's where he'd find him. That's where he came from in the book, a river. A river so deep that half the dig to hell was made by swimming. That's the way Joe described it anyway. That's what he was dealing with now. Not a drawing, but a demon. A demon looking to escort him to the underworld.

The only thing now Jack didn't understand was why he wasn't showing up. Jack had realized what brought the King to them in the first place. *I created him with the drawings. He always comes with the drawings.*

What he didn't know now was why he wasn't coming for him alone. Why did Cindy have to be here? Why couldn't he just come after Jack and leave her out of it.

Because. He's the King of E—

His cell phone rang. Part of him hoped it was Tom. Jack hadn't bothered calling him, not after seeing the footage. He knew the King had him. He expected the King to use Tom against Jack. Bad for the sake of being bad and all. Instead of the dryer picture that popped up on the screen it was a selfie of Cindy in her Pelicans garb sitting in stands.

"Hey babe," he said.

"Okay," Cindy answered. "So you're fine."

"Not as fine as you," Jack said. Feeling creepy, he immediately apologized.

"It's fine," she said, offering him a courtesy laugh. "You're apparently not the only Jack Simmons in the area."

"Nah," he said. "I'm only like two or three on the top-ten list. That's just in the greater New Orleans area."

"Shut up," she laughed.

"So you found another one?"

"Your name popped up as one of my patients."

"Must have freaked you out."

"That's why I called."

"You're sweet." Jack checked the yard through the attic window again.

"Thanks. And thank you for breakfast."

"No problem. You deserve it. Big fancy job that you just got and are about to take maternity leave from almost immediately."

"I know. Employee of the year." Her voice was shaky. Jack bet that she was wiping tears from her eyes.

"You okay?"

"I'm fine. Just scared the shit out of me is all."

"Well, I'm alright. No physical ailments whatsoever."

"I'm glad to hear it. Okay, I'm going to go. I'm sorry I interrupted you."

"You're fine. I love you, Cin."

"I love you too, Jack."

Bethel Rosenburg walked up the three steps from the carport to the kitchen, thanking God and everything that she didn't buy a flood house like everyone else in this area seemed to do. Three steps were almost too much with her faulty hips even if she had gotten used to the laborious maneuvering on replaced parts.

Thank God I left the AC on. I'll take the bill as long as I ain't dead, she thought.

A sweat mustache had gathered across her olive colored skin. She didn't make much money in retirement, but she would gladly give up the chore of cooking breakfast for a day to sit down in a cool house.

"I guessin' winter's gone," she told the quiet house. The

AC breathed in response. "Thank you, darlin'. Thank you."

She took a break at the dinner table until the low throb in her joints subsided to the pain killer she chewed in the car as she drove home from her appointment at the pool. She found that a good swim was the best supplement between two good days of working out with her new therapist, Cindy.

Bethel loved that Cindy girl. She'd be lying if she said that anyone in the state cared more about making her better than Cindy. There was a powerful energy from that girl that made Bethel believe, even though it wasn't likely, that this would be the last hip Bethel would need for the rest of her life. She never thought about her past therapists. Those had come and gone. But Cindy, she stayed with a person, even when she wasn't there.

Bethel would also be lying if she told herself that those *feelins* she'd been getting from her hadn't also been powerful. That's how she thought of them. *Feelins.* Bethel had seen the bruise on her face that day. That was the only thing that kept her from butting into Cindy's life. Maybe that man of hers had tried taking a piece out of her, and if that was the case she'll wake up one morning having killed him.

But there was part of Bethel that knew that wasn't it. The way Cindy talked about that man. Just didn't make sense. No one can bring herself to talk that good about a man if he's tuning up on her. Bethel thought about their conversation, the one about her good luck coin. She wondered what that husband of Cindy's was doing as he blindly tampered with a religion he had no knowledge of. She didn't think that could end well, and that's what made her think that it wouldn't be so bad to step in and tell her to get out of that house until her husband finished his work. But if nothing was wrong in the first place, Bethel would look even crazier than the rest of the people practicing an unpopular religion in the Bible Belt.

Bethel's arms strained, but she lifted herself back to her feet. Her hip was more than just singing now. *Come on, girl*, she told the new joint. *No bellyachin'. Get to the couch, and I'll give you another break.*

She sat down a little faster than she had meant to. After her day she was exhausted, and as long as it didn't hurt when she stood up, she didn't care if the drop onto the cushion was a little too fast. Maybe ten laps around the pool on her rest day was a little too much.

On her way onto the couch, she caught a glance at the gold-plated cross hanging next to the hallway door. Something, maybe it was the heat or exhaustion or just the sight of the crucifix, came upon her then, and she decided to pray. She usually waited until the end of the day when she was in bed, but she was tired and God never cared if you prayed early. He always welcomed a thankful voice. Bethel wouldn't be asking for anything today, so he'd have no reason to let the machine pickup.

"Heavenly father," Bethel began.

Something hit the carpet, and Bethel opened her eyes.

She expected to see the cross on the floor, but instead it was the television remote that she rarely used. She couldn't remember for sure if it was teetering over the edge of the coffee table, but it must have been if she nudged the table enough for it tip over like that.

"And you can stay there, too," Bethel told the remote. She wasn't getting up for anything right now.

She turned her focus back to the cross on the wall and settled back into her rhythm. Then a rustle sounded from above her television. A stack of Patricia Cornwell novels had tipped over in the wind of the overhead AC vent.

Bethel closed her eyes again.

Then the sound of something spinning annoyed her into opening her eyes. It was the cross, circling like a propeller on the screw it hung on. Bethel shuttered backward against the couch.

A voice spoke up in the living room.

"What I gotta do to get your attention, old lady?"

The propeller cross stopped upside down and froze against the wall. It lifted as if picked up. It floated in mid air and lay flat as if on an invisible surface. A flame sparked up just under the tip like a cigarette. The top surface of the cross glowed red. As Baron Samedi inhaled, filling his dead lungs with smoke, his silhouette took form. A face appeared behind the dirty gray haze. The wide eyes watered and Baron Samedi coughed.

"I prefer the filter, really. These are a little too pure for my taste."

"Leave my house."

"Oh, I will, old lady. I just want to talk to yaw." He coughed again. It was a loud hacking cough. "I think we got an eavesdropper."

Baron Samedi sucked on the end of the lit cross. He pulled it away from his lips and attached to the end was the head of a snake. Baron Samedi bit down, severing the snake's head clean. It dropped onto the wooden table and rolled toward Bethel. He pulled the rest out of his mouth like a macabre birthday clown doing a trick with a handkerchief.

Baron Samedi cleared his throat and spat snake blood onto the carpet. "I know what you been thinking about, but you don't wanna help those people. Trust me. That'd be a huge mistake for you. I ain't afraid'a you, woman. You help that woman and her man, I will kill you. I'll take an old woman just like I'll take that baby of theirs."

"Do you always say that to the people you ain't afraid of?"

"I'll make you a deal. You get to remember you seen me, but if I catch you tryin'a help them—"

Bethel Rosenburg's loud laughter cut him off. "You think I'd make a deal with the devil? No. If I wouldn't with him, I show as fuck wouldn't with you."

Baron laughed quietly with her. "I guess I could kill you now."

He threw the cross into her throat.

Bethel rolled backwards against the couch, gasping for air.

She woke up, still sitting at the kitchen table. Her heart was racing. She put her hands against her throat, feeling nothing but her old skin, and she settled. Cicadas droned outside.

"I guess I was out," she told the empty house.

She stood up, weak from the painkillers and her work out. She shambled on a walker to the bedroom where her landline was. Bethel told herself the snake and the blood wouldn't be there, but she couldn't stop herself from looking all around the table to be sure. She never did buy a cellphone, too afraid of brain chiggers or cancer. She didn't know which, but she was certain the cellphone would give her at least one of the two.

She sat on the bed exhausted.

She fell backwards, heaving breath.

Two thoughts came to her mind then. One was hers, and it was that she needed to call Cindy and tell her to leave her house. The other came to her. It said that if she did, her life would end immediately.

Cindy checked her face in the reflection of a bathroom mirror before going back into the gym. Her eyes were a little puffy, but she knew everyone would understand. She composed herself and reentered the gym.

"Everything alright?" Samantha asked.

"Yeah," Cindy said. "I'm sorry I freaked out."

"Don't. I would've done the same exact thing. Come here."

"Thanks," Cindy whispered, then she hugged Samantha.

"Just shake it off and we'll get back on track."

"You're right," Cindy said, pulling up her hair. "Let's go."

"What the hell happened?" Samantha sounded angry.

"What?"

"On your neck?"

"What's on my neck?"

"It looks like someone tried to choke you, Cindy."

"Shut up, that's crazy."

"No look." Samantha took out her cellphone and took a picture. Finger-shaped bruised showed up in the picture.

"Come on, you're messing with me."

"No, I'm not." Samantha was angry. "Does Jack choke you?"

"What?" Cindy's heat elevated. "What the hell do you mean?"

Cindy left the gym for the bathroom again, rubbing her neck. Samantha followed her. Cindy vaguely remembered something about someone choking her. Not in her conscious life though. Just a dream. She snatched flashes in her mind.

Cindy checked her neck in the reflection, pulling the collar of her polo far from her neck until it stretched. "See, nothing there." She was clearly aggravated.

"Let me see." Samantha looked closer, seeing nothing. She physically turned Cindy toward her, and went in for a closer look. "Cindy, I am so sorry."

"Well, you should be. That hurt. You thought Jack choked me? Jack loves me. He's the one who kept us together when I…"

Cindy trailed off, unconsciously putting her hand on her stomach.

"Then what was it?" Samantha asked. "It looked like

someone had hurt you. I was obviously concerned. I'm not trying—"

"I don't know what it was," Cindy tried to push Samantha out of the way.

"Whoa," Samantha said.

"*Stop it.*" Cindy tried to push her out of the way again, but Samantha grabbed her arms. Cindy jerked and struggled to get away, but the softball player deep inside Samantha could still hold her own.

"Look, I'm sorry."

"That was not okay, Samantha. Jack wouldn't hurt me. You should know that."

"I was just trying to look out for my best friend. I don't want anything bad to happen to you. You can't blame me for that. You saw that picture. What was I supposed to think?"

"I don't know," Cindy stared into her eyes. "Jack wouldn't do that. He wouldn't hurt anybody. Maybe the Jack with the fractured ribs and leg, but not my Jack."

"Yeah," Samantha laughed awkwardly. She was thankful that fight had passed quickly. "Weird day at work so far, huh?"

"Damn right."

"Oh, Mrs. Rosenburg wants you to call her by the way. She seemed elevated. I made sure she wasn't hurt, but she said it was very important that you call her when you got off."

Cindy took the scrap of paper Samantha held out to her. There was a number scrawled across it. "Is that a normal thing for a patient to do?"

"It's never happened to me."

"I must be special." Cindy stuffed the paper into her back pocket. As soon as it left her fingertips, the paper was forgotten, just like the dreams, just like the negative feelings, just like the living breathing manifestation of the King of Evil himself. It waited there in her pocket to be remembered when it was too late to do anything about it.

Jack needed to draw the box on the pad before adding it to the computer. Something about the program just wasn't doing it for him. He drew a picture of a heart and tore it off the bottom of the page. He laid it in the harmonica case and examined it the way a jeweler examines a pure, bright diamond. He stood the case up like a tiny skyscraper on his desk. He turned it slightly so he could get a sense of what it looked like at an angle.

"There we go."

He slumped over the pad until his nose nearly touched it. He mashed down on the pencil without realizing it. He drew until he was satisfied. The strokes from the lead were heavy enough to make indentations ten pages deep into the pad. When he finished he tore it from the page—something he absolutely never did, that's how drawings were lost. It was an absent-minded act, but when he held it in place against the picture on the screen he knew the job was done.

"Now why couldn't you do that for me?" he asked the

unmoving computer monitor.

There was no reply.

"The high road, I see."

Jack yawned.

Now that he had something to work off of, getting the picture onto the screen took a matter of minutes.

When he was done, Jack saved his work and dusted imaginary dirt from his hands.

Done deal, he thought. *Almost finished.*

His energy was suddenly gone.

"A quick rest of the eyes won't kill me," he said, lowering his head to the desk.

Thanks, boy, a voice came to him. He didn't react as he slipped further down to the dreams. Down where the King waited for him. *Now I'm whole.*

Bethel Rosenburg was exhausted mentally and physically. She used all her power getting from the bedroom back to the kitchen table. She couldn't remember if the gym closed at seven or eight, but if she hurried, and the traffic was kind to her, she could make it there before either. She needed to get to Cindy.

"Oh, child," she whispered to herself. "I can't help you if I'm just sitting here on my hind end." She rose to her feet with the help of her walker.

She navigated the three steps down to the carport, and after a few minutes of maneuvering around the car she got in, sweating and out of breath.

Navigating through the city would be a long, bothersome task. The drive took nearly an hour in the middle of the day when there was no traffic, but people would be getting off work soon. She asked herself if she could do it. There wasn't any choice. She had to do it. Cindy needed her help, and she wasn't going to stop just because that coward spirit came to her in a dream with his party tricks, trying his best to scare Bethel.

She knew he was making her forget all the terrible things he was doing to her. That's the way he operated. He stockpiled the memories of the heinous things a person sees, not allowing them to remember, until he sees an opportunity to bring that person down. That's when he opens the floodgates.

He allowed Bethel to remember, but she wouldn't let him do that to Cindy. Bethel wondered just how long he had been doing it to her? How long had he been following Cindy and her husband? Bethel guessed it was long before he started messing around with that art of his. Probably before they even came to New Orleans. That's how powerful he can be.

After gathering her strength in the car, she turned the ignition and eased out of the carport, expecting Baron Samedi to be waiting for her. When he wasn't there at the end of the driveway, Bethel didn't know whether to accept that as a good thing or not. Baron Samedi would stop at nothing to get a soul. She knew that better than anyone. She could still remember seeing that man standing in the middle of the nursery. No one else could see him, not the nurses or the doctors, not even her parents as they looked in at Bethel and her sister through the window. They say you can't process memories at that age, but she knew why she remembered him standing over her sister's bed. Because he made her remember.

All these years later, how many had he taken? Or had he taken any? After all this time could it still be her sister this monster was living on, carrying this spirit forward to the next victim. She couldn't accept that. She couldn't make herself believe that her twin was forced to be the battery for an evil entity while Bethel got to run free all the way into senility. That was unacceptable.

The dirt road turned onto a paved road, and from there it was to the interstate, bringing her back to Louisiana Bone & Joint.

Bethel hurried behind the painted yellow and white lines on the road.

The truth was Samantha still felt awkward, partially because of what happened but mostly because she didn't want to be alone with Cindy right now.

Even though she thought differently, Samantha's suspicions about what Jack could be doing to Cindy weren't confirmed or denied, only covered up. She knew that if the two of them were alone in the gym long enough she would break and hound Cindy with questions, sending their friendship spiraling into a fight. She knew the bruises on Cindy's neck were gone when the two of them were in the bathroom, but she had examined the picture on her camera over one hundred times since taking it. She knew a bruise when she saw one. No one could be a physical therapist for thirty minutes on the clock and not know a bruise like an old neighbor.

"Why don't you go ahead and go home, Cin," Samantha said. "All that's left is the appointment change log, and we both don't need to be here for that."

"You sure? I don't mind. It's only a few minutes."

"Yeah, you had a weird day, let me take care of it. Besides, I may want something to do between my noon and two o'clock tomorrow. I might leave a few unimportant things undone."

"Okay," Cindy said, gathering her things. Her face lit up. She walked toward the door, then turned back. She hugged Samantha and apologized for getting as mad as she did.

Samantha apologized too.

The door eased closed behind Cindy, leaving Samantha to the empty, quiet gym.

Samantha meant to remind her to do something before she left. Return an email or stop by Dr. Douglass's office. She couldn't remember. It was right there in her mind, but it was almost as though something blocked her mental hand when it reached for whatever was there. She remembered handing Cindy a note. The note had a number, so it was clearly for a call. She just couldn't remember whom had called.

That's why you write things down. To remind people of what they were thinking about before. She got the note, she'll remember to call them back.

Alone in the gym, Samantha's thoughts ran wild.

Her distrust for Jack grew. She thought she had let it go, but something about the picture and the strange defensive way Cindy snapped wouldn't let her. That wasn't Cindy at all. It was like someone else had taken her over for that brief moment, playing her like a marionette.

Somewhere in the walls, she heard a child giggling. Was that the first time she had heard it today? No. The first time she had heard it, she assumed it was the background noise from one of the songs on the radio. The radio was silent now. She heard it again. That didn't make sense. There were no rooms with shared walls.

Samantha poked her head out of the gym door, scanning up and down the halls for any sign of children. She walked around the corner just beyond the gym doors from the entrance and looked both ways. A doctor engulfed in a form clipped to a notepad walked toward her.

"Hey, Dr. Townsend," she said quietly. He was cold and always made Samantha anxious. He was shorter than Samantha and completely bald. She wondered what it would take for him to smile. Probably just tired she guessed. Every single time she had ever seen him.

"Ms. Breckermeyer," he nodded politely.

"Have you seen a kid roaming around?"

"Hmm. Nope. Not recently." His nose pointed back to the clipboard and he disappeared down the hallway.

Samantha looked around wondering where the laughter

was coming from.

Cindy pulled into the parking lot of both her new gym and the Books-A-Million. She stopped first at Books-A-Million knowing that when she left the gym she wouldn't feel much like walking around a store for half an hour. A rush of cool air poured over her as the glass door opened and she entered the building. The aroma of glossy paper came to her, and without thinking about it she inhaled the scent.

"Hello, ma'am," a very effeminate male voice said. He was very tall, and his bleached hair was thinner than someone's twice his age. Then as if under his breath he said, "Excuse me."

"Hi," Cindy said, ignoring the weird way the kid said that second part.

"Can I help direct you to a specific section today?"

"Actually could you point me in the direction of a maternity health book."

"No problem. Is it for you, ma'am?" he coaxed.

"It is actually." Cindy's inner mom swelled.

"Congratulations, ma'am," he said, perfectly feigning his excitement to a believable degree. "You must be so excited, excuse me."

"No, it's fine. I'm very excited. We just moved here," Cindy explained. "I'm ready to start my new life."

"I'm very happy to hear that, ma'am, excuse me." The

way he said excuse me, Cindy now noticed, was as though it came out without his permission, like a tick. His face scrunched up slightly when it came out like he was trying to stop it. "The maternity books are along that wall and about half way to the back of the store."

Cindy turned and pointed, to the wall behind her. "Just back there?"

"Yes, ma'am, do you know what you're looking for? I can see if we have a specific book in our system, excuse..." he trailed off, able to stop the second part of his catchphrase.

"I actually have no idea," Cindy said after waiting a moment for him to finish. "I'm just trying to find something that can keep me on track with my diet so I don't mess the baby up too soon," she laughed.

"I think you'd be better off in the dietary section. It's on the same side, excuse me, and there are books about maternity in it, too."

"Alright then," Cindy said. "I'll look there first." She stood there, accidentally staring at the kid.

"Well if you need any help, excuse me, just let me know."

Cindy walked to the maternity section utterly confused by whatever just happened.

She heard giggling around one of the rows of books. There were a few voices, but a little girl's was the loudest.

Cindy checked each row, her motherly intuition threatening to take over. She made it to the health section without finding the kids. She perused the shelves until she found one strictly for maternity diets. She thumbed through the pages too quickly to read anything, but there were pictures so that helped. The smell of glossy pages sealed the deal.

Satisfied with her selection, she turned back to the register. At the end of the row, she saw the little old man from the doctor's office. There was no mistaking, or arguing, it was Papa Legba. He wore the yellow plaid shirt, the overalls, and the straw hat. He hunched over his cane with the corncob pipe jutting out from between his lips. He was grinning. It was a sweet smile, happy and full of life. He lifted a finger toward her and laughed. His hand came back down onto the top of the cane and rested there. Cindy didn't move.

"Do I know you?"

He giggled his old man laugh and walked away.

That same strange way it had before, a thought came to her. *Be careful, child.* As if processing what someone had just said all at once, instead of someone saying it in a straight sentence.

Cindy walked to the end of the row, searching for the old man. She didn't find him. When she checked out at the register, the effeminate man hadn't seen him walk in or out. He politely apologized, excused himself, and invited her to have a wonderful rest of the day.

She scanned the parking lot for the little old man as she used the sidewalk to get to the gym. She called Jack to remind him that she would be coming home late tonight. He didn't answer so she left a message when his voicemail greeting ended.

"Hey babe, first of all, remind me to tell you about the

kid at Books-A-Million. Also, I just wanted to remind you that I'll be home in about an hour from the gym. I know you're working at the moment, but if you felt the urge to whip up some of that delish spaghetti soon, I will never leave you for a pool boy. I love you. Bye."

Bethel clipped the curb as she turned a little too hard into the parking garage of the facility and her hip let her know about it. She knew Cindy drove the yellow Kia. This afternoon, the Kia was gone. She did see Samantha walking to her car though. That was almost as good. They had a friendship outside of work, and Bethel didn't have to be clairvoyant to see it.

Bethel stopped the car behind her. The car didn't jerk or skid to a halt for fear that another jolting move would send another lightning bolt of pain up her side. Rather it slowly grinded to stillness behind the dented black BMW. It took all her strength to open the brown Lincoln's hefty door. Once she was certain the door wouldn't swing back on her, she swung her legs out of the car. She peeked her head over the windshield and called out to Samantha. "Hey, darlin'! Please, wait just a minute."

Samantha had already completely stopped what she was doing to watch Bethel fumble around inside her long rumbling car.

Bethel reached between the seat and the side of the car for her walker. Samantha ran around the front of the car.

"Mrs. Rosenburg, are you alright? Don't worry about getting up." She did her best to calm Bethel, but Bethel was more tired than worked up.

"I'm fine. It's not me, child. I'm worried about Cindy."

"What's wrong with her?" She was more cautious than worried. She was trying not to give away her own suspicions before hearing what Bethel had to say.

"Something is after her. A spirit."

"I'm sorry," Samantha scoffed. "A spirit?"

"Yes," Bethel said solemnly, hoping that was enough to convince Samantha. "Did you give her my message?"

Then it clicked in Samantha's mind. The thing she wanted to remind Cindy to do. She had given her a note, but something made her forget what it was. "Ah, that's right. Yes, I gave it to her almost as soon as we hung up."

"He already gettin' to her then."

"Who's getting to her?" Samantha asked. An alarm went off in her mind.

"The spirit, child. That husband of hers done stirred up something bad."

"What do you mean?"

"I mean that job he got. The picture job. The one Cindy always talkin' about. The one about voodoo. He messed around with something very real, and now it's after her."

"What do you mean? He's just drawing a comic book."

"Yeah, but who he drawin' come to life."

"How?"

"Baron Samedi is a spirit that feeds on the life of a person. He goes after the souls of people who are the most powerful. He needs them to come to this world. He feeds off their energy, their passion. And when he finds someone who is powerful enough to bring him to this world, he latches on, and he don't quit till he takes everything."

"This world? Look, I'm sorry Mrs. Rosenburg, but I think you've made a mistake. A drawing can't suck the life out of people."

"No, you're not listening."

"I heard what you said, Mrs. Rosenburg."

From the entrance, security guards walked toward them.

"She needs help, child. Cindy needs help."

"Ma'am, I need you to move along," the security guard said. "We can't have people harassing the employees outside."

"She's fine," Samantha said, waving him back. Not away, just back.

"No, you're not listening, child."

"It's okay, Mrs. Rosenburg," Samantha said. "We'll talk about it tomorrow, when we come back up here. Will that work?"

"Please," Bethel said. "She needs help, Samantha."

"I'll call her," Samantha said. "Will that help? I'll call her and make sure she is not hurt, then tomorrow when we come back here we can talk about it."

"Go to her home, child. Promise me."

Samantha exhaled, ready for this exchange to be ended. "I will. If I can't get her, I will go over to her house."

"Make sure there ain't nothing wrong with her."

"I will, Mrs. Rosenburg. I'll see you tomorrow, okay?"

"Promise me you will."

"I promise. I'll see you tomorrow," Samantha said, closing the door to the Lincoln. She waited for the car to start and drive away before moving away.

"Everything alright?" the security guard who wasn't Bradley asked.

"Yeah, we're fine."

"What'd she want?"

"I have no idea," Samantha said, and suddenly she really didn't.

"Weird. You're the one coming in on Saturday this week?"

"Yeah."

"See you tomorrow then."

Samantha and the security guard walked in their own directions. Both of them had no recollection of the encounter with Mrs. Rosenburg.

As Cindy drove up to the gate, she realized that something had drastically changed her mood. She could feel herself frowning. After a workout she usually felt like a new person, ready for anything. After a shower that was. She felt like it had something to do with that man in the bookstore. What did he mean be careful? Was that a threat? And how was he talking to her that way? She had never experienced that before. It was as though someone had put those thoughts in her mind rather than her ears delivering them.

She opened the gate with the keypad and drove forward enough for the Kia to clear its path. She waited for it to close behind her.

When it didn't move after a long minute, Cindy got out. She eyeballed the place where the gate had receded. She tried pulling on it, but it wouldn't budge. There was nothing she could see that was blocking the gate from closing, but when she used all her weight to pull it free, it didn't move. *Whatever*, she snapped to herself. *I'll just get Jack to look at it.*

She got back into the car and moved it forward.

All of a sudden, something happened. She remembered something. The dream, the one about her and the trashy love triangle from their old life.

She remembered sitting on the sidewalk against the building, her stomach bleeding. She remembered the truck revving up, and the screaming. She remembered it lurching forward toward her.

Jack sprung up from the desktop. The King had swung his mallet again and shook him awake. He was hunched over and lying with his face directly on the desk, which left him stiff and groggy. His computer had gone into sleep mode for some time. He shook the mouse and the screen asked for his password. He entered it into the system and the web browser activated without his efforts. He waited for it to load, wondering if he had actually clicked anything and didn't realize it. The window displayed the cameras' views across the yard and around the house. Just then Cindy pulled into the carport under the house. He lifted a little, happy to see her, until he realized once she parked the car that she was crying. Not just crying but crying the way she used to before things got better. Jack ran downstairs, nearly falling.

He opened the door to go outside and he noticed a black circle about five feet wide on the moving surface of the river. The circle rippled and waved with the river but the circle itself never moved. Jack ignored it and ran to Cindy. She opened her door and nearly fell into his arms.

"What is it, Cin? What happened?"

She was crying too hard to answer.

"Cin, talk to me," he said. He knew that she wouldn't be able to talk until she got some of this out so he waited for her to speak. She put her hand on the back of his neck and squeezed as she soaked the front of his shirt.

"The dreams, Jack. Have you had them?"

"What dreams?"

"Of your drawing. Of what happened. I keep having to relive it. It all came to me just now. All at once. Why are they coming back?"

"They're just dreams."

"Then why did I forget them until now? Why did I forget all of them?"

Jack pulled her closer. "Come on, let's go inside."

He turned her, looking down to make sure she didn't trip over anything. There was nothing to trip over. He didn't see the King rise out of the river from the black circle. He didn't see the water dripping off the King in dark, smoking drops like burning blood. He didn't see the red shoes at they separated from the water a few inches, then a foot, then two. He didn't see the wide eyes and sharp, menacing smile.

When the King lifted his staff, a green light emanated from the center of the triskele at the end. Jack saw the green light, but it was too late to do anything about it. Cindy already belonged to the King.

Jack felt her step away. He watched her step ahead of him, thinking she was going into the house. When she avoided the steps and walked toward the pier, Jack grabbed her arm.

"What are you doing, babe?"

Cindy pulled her arm away from him so hard that Jack nearly stumbled to the ground.

"Cindy, *stop*."

They were half way to the dock then. Cindy rounded on him, pushing him back. The force was so strong, so inhuman, that Jack left his feet. Cindy glared at him, but something about her was different. Her eyes were the same color as the light from the staff.

Jack watched the King drop into the river. Then a gray hand reached around Cindy and lay on her belly. Black smoke rose and formed the rest of the King, even the dripping top hat. "You can have her back, Jack," he said. "Soon as I get what I want from her."

Jack scrambled to his feet.

Cindy and the King disappeared in a black cloud.

Jack screamed in fury.

The two reappeared over the black circle above the river. Jack could see Cindy's unnatural eyes glowing. They stopped shining, and Cindy shrieked. The King dropped her into the river. "You can have this one back. I don't need it no more."

Tom was hurled out of the water and landed on the ground in front of Jack. He lay there. His dead eyes stared blankly like the plastic ones in the animals on his office wall. His face was covered in burn marks, and the way his scorched arms were angled told Jack that an ambulance would've been necessary if Tom was breathing.

"This too," the King said.

Behind Jack, Tom's truck dropped down onto the driveway.

Jack flinched away from the sound and when he turned back to the water, the King was gone.

Jack panicked. He ran toward the pier, nearly tripping over Tom. Before he reached the pier the King materialized in front of him, swinging the mallet.

Jack went down. His vision pinholed, and as he lay on the ground, slipping into the blackness of unconscious, all he heard was the sound of children laughing.

10

The Next Morning

Samantha's boyfriend knocking on the bathroom wall woke her. "Babe, *stop*." If anyone should know that Samantha didn't like banging noises in the morning, it definitely should've been him. "What the fuck are you doing?" Samantha threw the comforter off her and stomped to the bathroom. She flung the door open, "What the—"

Her boyfriend was beating his own head into the wall. When he turned to her, a tooth clung to his bloody face. He dropped to the floor.

Samantha didn't know what to say, so she tried to scream.

The King appeared through a puff of black and grabbed her by the throat, choking her scream off before it could be more than a groan. He pulled her in until there was no more than an inch of space between them. His mouth yawned open.

The buzz of cicadas took over the apartment.

Samantha struggled to get away when she saw the bugs crawling out of him. She closed her mouth, but he squeezed her neck. Her mouth opened, giving the cicadas a place to enter. When it was over, he dropped her to the floor. She could feel them wriggling down her throat.

"Stay away from that voodoo woman, or I kill both of you. It's your friend I'm here for, but I don't mind giving you a piece of what I got."

As quickly as he appeared, the King vanished.

Samantha fumbled to her feet, hoisting herself up with the side of the bed.

She checked to make sure her boyfriend was alive, and called for help.

Stay away from that woman, a voice said. Children were laughing all around her.

Jack brushed the dirt and grass off his face. It was morning now. He had been out through the night.

"Tom, Tom, are you okay?"

He shook his agent and friend whose eyes stared blankly toward the sky. Tears stung his eyes as realization spread through him.

"Where'd he take you?" Jack reached for his cellphone. He dialed out but the phone displayed a message.

Call could not be made.

Jack tried again with the same result. He made an effort

for a third time but the tears wouldn't allow him to see the phone's screen.

"I'm so sorry, Tom."

It doesn't want you, Jack. It's Cindy. He's after her.

The words came to him all at once. Like a thought instead of a spoken sentence. Jack wiped his eyes and scanned the yard. He saw nothing, and when the aged hand slid onto his shoulder he knew that Papa Legba stood behind him. The smell of tobacco drifted up into Jack's nostrils.

"Why does he want her? I'm the one who drew him."

You only copied something that was already there. Baron Samedi already existed before you started this project. It was your passion for your work that influenced what he looked like, but it was Cindy who had the power to bring him here. It's her life force, her experience that made her a stronger person. That's what he latched onto. He sucked it from her and used it to materialize here. He felt her love for you and your paintings and latched onto it. The passion you two share, that's what brought him here.

Jack remembered the figure in their back yard before they moved. Could this have gone that far back? Even before he knew about the King? And if it went back that far, did it stop there or go even further? How long had Jack and his wife been followed by this…this spirit? "Why did he take Tom?"

Because he's evil, Jack. Bad for bad's sake, I believe is how your wife put it. He plays mind tricks, whatever it takes to get what he wants. And he doesn't want her. He wants the baby. He needs it to live. He takes the life it has left, and adds it to his own. He knows the child will be the best of both of you. You must stop him, Jack. If he gets the baby, this will end your wife.

Jack watched the old hand pointing to his dead friend. "What do I do?"

It's the drawings. That's what brings him here. Your passion for them is an energy he can't resist. He feeds off it like a vampire. I'll take care of your friend. I'll bring him with me. You've got to save your family now, Jack. Go.

When Jack turned, no one was behind him. He left his friend on the ground and limped up the stairs to the house. When he got inside, he tried to call for help on the control panel for the security system. It had no power. He tried to set the alarm and set it off. Nothing happened.

No one gonna help you, boy, Jack heard. It wasn't the voice of Papa Legba this time.

He walked to the medicine cabinet in the bathroom. He filled the dropper of the melatonin bottle and squirted the contents into his mouth. He repeated.

He walked up stairs and sketched the King on his yellow pad. He dropped the pen and went back to the bedroom. Before lying down, he filled the dropper one more time, and emptied it into his mouth.

He heard children laughing through the walls.

Samantha told the truth about what had happened with her boyfriend in her apartment, even though she knew what it probably meant for him. She woke up to him slamming his head into the bathroom wall. She did however leave out the part with the man in the hat. She had no problem remembering the conversation she and Mrs. Rosenburg had in the parking structure after work. She figured the "spirit" in her apartment was responsible for her forgetting.

The doctors took her boyfriend back for x-rays, and she didn't have to be told to stay in the waiting area. She was afraid she had made a mistake in telling the truth. He would no doubt go through a psychiatric evaluation, and Samantha had no idea what that would determine. That wasn't a prime concern. He had no history of mental illness, so she expected for him to come into her professional care, and need to be closely watched. The incident as a whole didn't allow him an easy story to tell when his boss inevitably asked.

The hospital was less than a mile from Louisiana Bone and Joint. In her experience she estimated an hour's time before the x-rays were taken and a conclusion would be met. She could run there and back before she was able to see him again. She left her cellphone number with the nurse on duty and nearly ran out of the building.

Samantha got into her car and felt an incredible heat. She could feel those things moving around in her. She pulled onto the road and felt something in her arms trying to drive the car off the road. The radio came on, blaring the sounds of children.

I told you to stay away from that woman, she heard.

The wheel yanked to one side and she used the full weight of herself to steady the car on the path down the road. The facility came into view. The parking structure was nearly completely empty. That was good. Samantha swerved her way up to her floor and jammed the brakes in the closest space to the entrance she could find. There would be only a few doctors in today. She thought she could make it all the way to the gym without being seen.

She opened the door of her car and vomited black gel onto the ground. The cicadas buzzed inside her.

Samantha ran inside. She tripped over the door and landed spread-eagle on the welcome mat. Children laughed at her from all around. She got to her feet and stumbled down the corridor to the gym. She used her card key to unlock the door.

She logged in on the first tablet she found and opened her appointment log. At first it refused to log in, not accepting her password and shut down. Two tablets later, she got in, found Mrs. Rosenburg's information, and called her number just before the tablet went dead.

The phone rang twice. Then the headset blared the sound of children laughing. There was a click somewhere behind it all. The noise died down and Mrs. Rosenburg spoke up.

"He got to you didn't he, child?"

"We need to help her. Can you come to the emergency room?"

"The one by your facility?"

"Yes," Samantha said.

"I'm coming, darlin'."

Samantha hung up and called her earlier appointment to cancel.

The children stopped laughing, and the bugs inside her stopped moving around.

Bethel hung up the phone. It was a call she had been expecting. She was dressed and had her walker ready to go. She stood up with no pain at all. On the way out she grabbed her bag and hung it over the side of the walker. Inside the bag she had packed her Bible, a pair of scissors, a bag of salt, and a piece of paper. The paper had instructions for contacting Papa Legba. This day would end with her needing all the help she could get. She made the sign of the cross over her chest, saying a prayer for Cindy. A voice stopped her at the garage door.

You don't listen for nothin', woman.

"Leave that girl alone."

I should'a taken you, too. You are nothing like your sister could've been.

"Yaw less than the devil. I'ma get her back."

You'll die, woman.

"If I have to."

Bethel crossed herself again and left the house.

She would need two more things when the time came, a lock of hair from a relative who had been taken, and the blood of an infected. Both would be available to her, but she hoped she wouldn't need it.

Jack stood waist deep in the river. He could feel the hands under the water, pulling him down. The King stood over him holding Cindy like a cat by the skin on the back of her neck. Her stomach radiated greenish light from under her clothes. Jack was up to his neck. He reached his arms up but skeletal hands grabbed him. They were much stronger than before. They couldn't be broken apart like his past dream. "I'm going to kill you," he told the King. He was only given a laugh in response. Children joined in with him from all around the riverside.

"You ain't got nothin', boy. You gone burn like the rest of'm."

The King rested the mallet on Jack's head and pushed him further under the water. Jack opened his eyes. Skeletons charged him. They bit at him and clawed at his skin. Jack could feel the blood rushing out of him. He was dying. He still felt them beating him and tearing away at his body. The life was slowly draining out of him.

Samantha explained to the doctors one more time her relationship with her live-in boyfriend. She hadn't had breakfast or lunch yet and the orange shade of the sunlight told her dinner was next on the list of meals she didn't have today. The doctors allowed her to see him even though she wasn't immediate family. He had requested someone named Sam, but she didn't even think of herself as Sam. He was the only one who got away with calling her that.

She pushed through to the room, her heart dropping at the sight of him. His skull was fractured and his face was swollen like a boxer. The heart rate monitor beeped, breaking the heavy silence of the room.

"Baby, are you alright?" she asked.

He groaned. His tired eyes met hers. They slowly blinked.

"You hurting?"

He groaned again. He slowly closed his eyes. The beeping slowed and stabilized. He was asleep.

She stood up to visit the hospital's cafeteria down the hall. It was garbage, but she was hungry enough to eat literal garbage at this point. She felt a tickle in her stomach. It had been nearly two hours since she was able to leave the hospital to call Mrs. Rosenburg. She was beginning to worry if something happened to her. Something with her steering wheel or maybe the man Samantha saw in her apartment gave Mrs. Rosenburg a visit also.

There was a line of three people ahead of her at the cafeteria. She read the menu and nothing in particular struck a chord. She ordered a sandwich and made her way back to the room. On the way back she heard Mrs. Rosenburg's voice saying that she couldn't remember the last name just that her name was Samantha and it was urgent.

"Mrs. Rosenburg," Samantha called out.

"It's Bethel, child," Mrs. Rosenburg corrected. "Yaw look like shit."

Samantha hadn't seen herself in the mirror since leaving the apartment. She hadn't so much as went to the bathroom. Her milky skin sagged, and the rings around her eyes looked like bruises. Her hair looked like she had just spent a sweaty night in bed, and her hands were stained red from her boyfriend's blood.

"Come on, child. We in a hurry. Get yaw car and meet me at the entrance."

Samantha hurried to her car while Mrs. Rosenburg waddled on her walker to the entrance.

She checked herself in the mirror and flinched. Her eyes were bloodshot and yellowing. Her lips were cracked and red. She looked like a zombie. She shook it off and backed the car out of the spot. She parked at the door and walked Mrs. Rosenburg the rest of the way to the car. They were on the road toward Cindy and Jack's house just as the sun dipped down below the tree line. Her arms felt weak. Her eyes blurred and she ran over onto the shoulder of the road.

"Eyes up, darlin'," Mrs. Rosenburg said. "He gone keep messin' with us until we stop. He don' wan' us there. Not you, specially not me."

"Who is *he*?"

"He a spirit, child. Older than everythin'. He feeds off emotion and life. In the beginning people would come to him as a rite of passage. He could read your body, your mind. He had a permanent place in the world. Somewhere along the line he was set free. It was bittersweet because he could go anywhere he want, but his life drained dramatically. He had to start finding people to take. People with a lot of life and powerful personality. That's why Cindy and her man are in trouble, their baby is in trouble. He took my sister. My parents loved the two of us so hard, so passionately. The doctor say she was barren. But they proved them wrong. They had me and my sister, but we was so strong that he only needed one. Two wouldn'ta done him no good anyway. He couldn't save one for until the other run out.

"When he find his prey, he takes everything from them. Their friends, their family, anyone in their lives who can help. That's why he come to you. That's why he come to me, and anyone else he can to make their lives miserable. He is evil."

"He's the King of evil," Samantha said, pulling the car back onto the road again.

"You fine to drive, child?"

"I feel sick." Samantha slid off the road again and the tire exploded. "Fuck," she whispered.

"You know how to change one of those, right?"

"I do. I need to throw up first, though." Samantha leaned out the car and spilled more black phlegm onto the ground. A cicada crawled out of her mouth with it.

"He did get to you," Mrs. Rosenburg remarked. "That may not be such a bad thing." She looked at the paper she would need to call on Papa Legba, more to ensure that it was still in her bag than anything else.

"Better hurry," Samantha said, wiping her mouth. She popped the trunk and started on the tire.

Jack woke. He was no longer on his bed but face down on the floor next to it. The light filtering through the window was gone. The melatonin had worked too well. He took a deep breath and looked out the window. The King stood in the open yard between the house and shed. His hat was cocked to the side, his grin lit up in the moonlight. Jack could smell the smoke from his suit.

"Come on down here, boy."

Jack didn't move.

"Okay," the King said. He knocked his mallet on the ground. Cindy rose through the ground, crouched like a dog. The King snapped and a flame burned from his fingers to the back of Cindy's neck. Where the flame burned a leash was created. "Come get this bitch."

Jack sprinted to the door.

He left the house and could hear his wife.

Cindy growled and grunted in fury. At the sight of him, she leapt up. Running at him, her neck snapped back against the leash.

"There's my boy," the King said, watching him on the steps. He let her go.

Cindy ran barefoot across the yard, screaming and swinging her arms.

The sound of her feet pounding the ground came to him before her small fist struck his cheek and knocked him backward. His head connected with a step, cutting open the side of his face. She pounded him. Her fists met his torso and face. Jack tried to stop her, but when he grabbed her arm she ripped it away from him and continued her assault. Blood rushed down his face, into his eyes and mouth.

Cindy stopped long enough to shriek in his face. She resumed her attack.

"*Baby, stop!*" Jack cried, hoping his voice would break through the trance she was in.

"Baby, stop," she growled. It was a gravel-lined voice, almost male. "Baby, *stop! Baby, stop! Baby, stop!*" Cindy cackled.

Jack's stomach turned to stone. His wife was turning on him again. Only this time she was literally beating him to death. Children laughed as if mocking him further. The immense pain in his heart slowed him down dramatically, and something caught in his throat as he fought off his wife's blows. He knew deep down that this wasn't his wife, but his exhausted mind, victim to lingering effects of the melatonin, wouldn't allow Jack to accept the truth.

Jack leapt up and wrapped around Cindy. He slowly dragged her to the ground, being careful of her stomach. He held her on the ground, looking around the yard for something to restrain her.

"Thanks for watching out for the goods, Jack," the King said. He marched across the yard and kicked Jack in the abdomen. Jack's breath evacuated, leaving him gasping. Cindy leapt on his back, screaming.

"Does it feel familiar, Jack?" the King yelled, following them around the carport. "Your wife ready to break your neck at a snap of my finger? Are you nostalgic? How does it *feel*, Jack, to know that you got yourself out of the worst phase of your entire life by moving across state lines, and now you're here, and you're right back in it? Only now you don't have to worry if your wife still loves you."

Jack was flailing around with Cindy on his back, trying

to grab ahold of her dirty clothes to pull her off of him. The King kicked Jack's legs out from under him. A sharp pain rose up his shin. It throbbed and dulled. The pain caused him to wretch. He knew the bone was injured.

The King tapped the ground with his mallet. "Come join the party, my brothers."

Beneath him, arms made of the ground from his yard sprung up, scraping and punching at Jack. Cindy pounded his face onto the ground twice, then crawled away. The arms latched onto him, pinning him to the ground.

"She only loves who I tell her to love. I wouldn't give y'that. I wouldn't give yaw nothin'. Ain't nothing in life free, Jack. Not even yaw death. Oh, I'll let y'have it awright. But yaw gon' earn it first, boy."

When the King raised the mallet over his head, his coat opened and Jack could see the ribcage box dangling from his belt loop. The mallet crashed down onto his chest. There was a muffled crunch as two of his ribs fractured. A dirty light rose from the direction of the gate. The King turned away from Jack. "You," he commanded Cindy. "Finish up."

Cindy jumped on Jack and continued pounding.

The King walked toward the light. He lit a cigar and puffed as he waited.

"We get outta the car," Mrs. Rosenburg explained. "Come straight to the front. We have to hurry. I only hope the spirit hasn't started in on them just yet."

"How's your hip?" Samantha asked.

"My hip is fine, child."

"What are you going to do?"

"I am going to call on Papa Legba."

"So like a curse or a hex or whatever?"

"No," Mrs. Rosenburg said. "This isn't like that. It's real."

"What do *I* need to do?"

"I just need yaw to be there, child."

"That's it?"

"That's all. Just be there and hand me what I tell yaw to hand me."

The car ran off on the side of the road again, but even in her greatly weakened state, Samantha was able to steer it back on track.

"Here it is," Samantha said.

"Gate's not doing no good being open."

"It's automatic. It shouldn't be open like that. The police should be here or at least the security people."

"We're not dealing with something police can help anymore, child. Let's keep going."

The first cicada dropped onto the windshield. It buzzed. The noise was piercing.

The wipers slapped it away. Samantha continued forward the best she could with shaking hands controlling the wheel.

Blood dropped onto the glass.

"What is that?"

"It's from those," Bethel said. She pointed to the blood soaked string dolls hanging from the trees as if from nooses. Dozens of them dripped onto the car. The smell of burning sulfur entered the car. "He's here."

A string doll dropped and splattered onto the windshield.

Samantha let out a scream.

Bethel went into her bag and unfolded the paper. She had every letter memorized down to the imperfections of the writing style, but she checked just to make sure one last time.

"What is the laughter from? Do you hear it? The children laughing?"

"It's the souls of the children he takes. They don't get to grow up. They're that age forever. He uses their life, not their souls."

The car was silent.

"Remember to get out and go straight to the front of the car." Bethel readied her walker.

The car rounded a curve and the scene came into view. Cindy was beating on Jack, but between them, the root of it all stood, confidently smoking a pipe and grinning like a fool.

"Floor it," Bethel said.

"What? *No.* What if I hit them?"

"I said floor it."

Bethel leaned over and put all her wait on Samantha's leg. The BMW revved loudly in the open yard.

❖ ❖ ❖

There are some things that take even the spirits off guard. When the black car suddenly accelerated forward in the driveway, Baron Samedi wasn't expecting it. The bitch woman came. That's when the grille of the car rammed into his abdomen and sent him rolling across the yard. The bitch woman whose sister's life he was still living on had actually come to save them. Baron Samedi waited too long to collect a new life. He was weak, and the bitch woman's presence was making him weaker. He would have moved, but he expected the car to stop. He should've known, but the bitch woman somehow prevented him from leaving. It was the twin. Her soul kept him here. He could feel her inside him reaching for the other one. Hoping to get out.

The car rammed the King so hard that he was launched over Cindy and Jack. As soon as the car struck the King, his possession over Cindy was broken. The arms released Jack from their grip, and crumbled to dirt. The green shine in her eyes faded nearly to black in the moonlight. She had realized what she had been doing. She looked down at her husband's bloody face with his hair in her hands.

"Oh my God, baby, I'm so sorry." She began to cry.

Cicadas roared as the King thrashed on the ground from the shock and pain.

"Jack, I'm so sorry."

"*Cindy!*" Samantha shouted. She ran to the front of the car and waited. "Are you all right?"

"It's Jack. I think I hurt him."

Jack groaned beneath her.

Bethel had made her way to the car. "Take the salt out of the bag," she told Samantha. "Draw a circle around us."

"With the salt?"

"*Yes*, child," Bethel was clearly in no mood for stupidity.

Samantha poured the salt in a circle around the half-grass and half-dirt patch where they stood. "Okay, I did it."

"Scissors in the bag," Bethel opened her palm, waiting for the scissors. Samantha handed them over, and Bethel immediately cut a lock of her old, gray hair. "I need to see yaw hand."

"What?"

"Give me yaw fuckin' hand, child."

Samantha showed Bethel her hand.

"I'm sorry," Bethel said, raking the blade across Samantha's palm.

Samantha shrieked.

Bethel squeezed her hand, dripping black blood on to the grass.

"Cindy," Bethel said. "Y'gotta get off that man now. I need yaw help."

Cindy reluctantly left Jack on the ground writhing in pain. "What do you need?"

"I need you to find the thing that brought him here, the thing that gave him power. Find something you were both passionate about."

"I don't know what that is," Cindy said.

"Well, yaw gone have to, darlin'. We ain't got time. He's

getting back on his feet."

"The painting," Jack's voice wafted up to her.

"What is it, baby?" Cindy kneeled down to him.

"The paintings in the office. You gotta destroy them."

"I can't do that."

"They're nothing, Cin. You have to."

Cindy looked down at him.

"Run, Cin." Jack pushed her away from him. He rolled away, moaning in pain as the King's hammer crushed the ground between them. Cindy ran into the house.

"Papa Legba, hear my voice," Bethel said.

"Don't you *dare* say that name, woman," the King's voice buzzed out of his throat. He rose the mallet over his head, threatening to swing it down onto that bitch woman. Behind him on the ground, Jack's voice screamed.

"Papa Legba, hear my voice!"

The King looked back to him, not lowering his weapon. He dropped his mallet onto Jack's leg. That familiar crunch sounded beneath its weight. The sound that erupted from Jack's mouth was concentrated agony. He felt his bone splinter.

"Papa Legba, hear my voice," Bethel repeated. "I pray thee, banish this spirit to the depth from where he came. Cast him down to the fiery underworld where he belongs."

The King spun, fury in his eyes. The cicada buzz roared through the yard. Fire ignited all around them. A wide circle of flames rose in the air.

A light appeared just before Bethel and Samantha. It brightened and they could see a white silhouette forming from it. Even the cane and corncob pipe took shape.

"*Move*, old man," the King screamed.

The old man simply shook his head and grinned.

"They're mine," the King slapped Papa Legba. He fell to the ground, his pipe and cane rolling away from him.

The King turned his attention to the bitch woman. He lifted the mallet over his head, his scrawny body shaking. Just as he meant to swing it down on Bethel, the mallet dropped to the ground, a flame burst open his chest. The cicadas bellowed from his mouth. The children's laughter spurred louder. His body jerked so violently that the hat tipped off of his head.

Behind him, Cindy dangled the corner of the Homerun Killer into the flames. She dropped it on the ground where the fire burned up the sand. She added the King's own painting. Flames exploded from the King's mouth.

Jack crawled toward the hat on the ground.

The place where the King's heart should have been burst outward. He weakly shambled toward Cindy.

She dropped *Bone Dry* and *Cursed Devils* on top of the pile. The King was a smoking wreck when Cindy dusted her hands clean.

With each burning painting, the King buzzed louder and jerked more violently. He collapsed on the ground.

Jack picked up the hat and broke off the already fractured rib.

The fire around them died. The canvas paintings were little more than burned matchsticks. Cindy leaned over and kissed her husband. They heard Samantha vomiting by the car. Bethel was rubbing her back.

"Getting it out of her system," Bethel told Cindy. "She'll be fine."

"Is he gone, Jack?" Cindy asked quietly.

"No," he answered.

A jagged green light flashed across the open yard. The King released a buzzing scream and swarmed down on them. "I told yaw I'd kill ya!" he shrieked.

Jack leaned up and stabbed the rib into the box dangling from the King's belt. Dark liquid poured out of the crack in the box.

The King fell to his back, screaming, burning, and gasping for air. He tore at his throat hoping to relieve the pain. From a hole in his chest, he began to burn outward until his limbs and face were nothing more than ashes.

Behind them, Bethel lay on the ground, dying. The bolt of green light had struck her in the heart and burnt a hole through her. She heaved blood.

All around them children giggled. The sound slowly faded away, until there was one solitary voice left. It was a baby, no more than an infant. No one would have been able to give that baby a face, but Bethel knew exactly what that baby looked like.

"That's you, Virginia." Bethel sobbed with the last of her fading life.

There were no more words, no communication at all. She only listened to her baby sister as the last of her life faded into the black night. A tear rode the arch of her cheek. No one knew when Bethel no longer saw the starry night that she stared up into. But she died with a smile on her face. That was important to all of them.

Samantha joined Jack and Cindy at the place in the yard.

"How are you feeling?" Jack asked.

"I'm fine," Samantha said. She was crying. "I think Mrs. Rosenburg is dead. How are you? How's the..." She motioned toward Cindy's stomach.

There was a rustling sound in the grass near the car. Out of the shadows came the old man walking on his cane. The corncob pipe had been found and replaced between his lips. Cindy stood from the dirty ground.

He took her by the hand and smiled his old man grin.

That was all she needed from him, and when the thought came a second later in that strange way the thoughts always seemed to, she didn't need it. *Your family is safe.*

"Is he gone?" Cindy asked.

He's never gone. You just won't see him again.

"Is Bethel going to be alright?"

Yes. She's with her sister now. I'll take care of them.

When the night was over, Samantha slept on the couch. Jack and Cindy slept in each other's arms.

None of them dreamed.

11

Two months later

"Jack," Joe's voice was exuberant and loud coming through the cellphone speaker. "Just got finished with your colors."

"And?" Jack asked, he silently hoped the noise from the kids in the back of the bike shop wasn't being picked up in the receiver. "What do you think?"

"Goddamn it, Jack. They're brilliant." Joe was unable to contain his laughter. "I love the way the story unfolds. I love your vivid attention to detail, and the gradual real-life picture-to-drawing you talked about. This guy, he is a bad bloke. I love it all, especially the scene where Robert Taylor becomes victorious in the end. It's all magic. Really"

"Great man," Jack said. "Hang on just a sec."

"Sure, sure."

Jack pulled the phone away from his ear. "Babe, I'm going to go ahead and bring these out to the car."

"So, I gotta pay for your shit now?" She grinned a goofy, loving smile.

"I'll be outside." Jack repositioned the phone between his face and shoulder. He had held a bike in each hand and was thankful the door was automatic. When it opened, the bright sunlight caused him to squint. "Sorry about that, Joe. Cindy and I are at the bike shop."

"Ready for a bike?"

"Yep, I'm finally around enough to test out the bike trail across the river from the house."

"Well, good on ya, Jack. How's the wife?"

"She amazing. She's starting to show, but when you see her next week, you can't tell. I think the hormones are doing their thing. She cried at that commercial with the cats and the sexy people throwing them treats in slow motion."

"Oh no," Joe said. "What's sad about that?"

"I have no idea." Jack dropped the kickstand on the bikes and waited for Cindy to unlock the car. "I'm assuming you have notes on the book?"

"Not as many as I thought I would. You seemed to have nailed it all down. It's like you were there, ya know? You see everything, even things I didn't know where there. I really feel that from the drawings. That's a great sign."

"Great, make a list though. Be nitpicky. Nothing is too unimportant."

The Kia beeped then unlocked. Jack opened the back door.

"I agree one hundred percent. I'll make a list and we'll discuss it when I come to town next week. In the mean time, be thinking about how we bring him back."

"Wait, bring who back? Taylor doesn't die."

"No, the King. It's a serial about the King, not Robert Taylor. Yeah he is killed in the end, but he's a spirit, he can't really die. He just goes back down into the flames until he's powerful enough to come back, ya know? Are you there? Jack? I can't hear you anymore, mate. Hello? Jack?"

About the Author

Josh Stricklin is an American author and musician with degrees in English literature and advertising from the University of Southern Mississippi. *The King of Evil* is his first terrifying novel with Silver Leaf Books. He's currently hard at work continuing his first series.

CPSIA information can be obtained
at www.ICGtesting.com
Printed in the USA
FFOW04n1558090816
26498FF